ARRIVAL

First in the "Miandi" series

A.P. Lynn

Order this book online at www.trafford.com
or email orders@trafford.com

Most Trafford titles are also available at major online book retailers.

Printed in the United States of America.

ISBN: 978-1-4669-3867-0 (sc)
ISBN: 978-1-4669-3866-3 (e)

Trafford rev. 09/10/2012

 www.trafford.com

North America & international
toll-free: 1 888 232 4444 (USA & Canada)
phone: 250 383 6864 ◆ fax: 812 355 4082

For Mom, with love and thanks

I

The crash of a full dish tub snapped Mark Daniels from his reverie. He blinked his brown eyes hard, and then turned in the direction of the sound. A woman he judged to be just out of high school gave him a sheepish shrug, gathered up the tub, and disappeared toward the kitchen. "So much for manners," he muttered, mimicking his partner's voice and cynicism toward this younger generation.

He ran a hand through his freshly cut, dark brown hair and diverted his attention to the front windows. There, the citizens of Mason City, Washington carried on with their lives. It was an odd sight. He glanced about the mom-and-pop restaurant. He should be out there. What was he doing here? He smiled at the woman approaching him. "Excuse me? Did I order something?"

"Chicken salad on wheat with chips, and a bottle of water," she replied, setting the bottle and glass of ice down on the table. "Did you wish to change it?"

"Oh. No, I don't. Thank you."

She studied his face. A look of concern came to hers. "Sir? Are you all right?"

"Fine," Mark replied, a little too quickly. "I'm fine."

She nodded and walked away. Mark stared at his drink. He didn't remember coming in, or anything else he had done since rising that morning. Then again, he didn't recall much of what occurred these past five months. Since that horrific day in November, it had been a series of nights filled with horrid nightmares, and unnerving days of unchecked grief. Now it was near the end of March, and today seemed to be a continuation of it. Would it ever end?

"Detective Daniels, fancy meeting you here," a deep baritone voice chimed.

Mark looked up at the tall frame and round face of J. Jacob Embry. His balding gray head was neatly trimmed and he stared at Mark through lively green eyes. His lips formed a wide smile under his gray-white moustache. This was the first time Mark could remember seeing him without his black robe. Today, the judge wore a charcoal gray business suit and royal blue shirt. His tie was a perfect match and complemented his hair and moustache. Mark went to stand, but Judge Embry waved him off. "May I join you?"

Mark hesitated, and then he gestured to the chair across from him. Judge Embry undid his jacket and sat down. He gazed about the tiny restaurant. Mark's server returned. The judge ordered a bowl of chili, hoping it was as good as he remembered it to be. When she left, he turned his attention back toward Mark. "How are you, Detective?"

"Fine sir and you?"

"I'm busy dispensing justice, as usual." The judge unfolded his napkin and tucked it into his shirt collar. "Your presence hasn't graced my chambers lately. I was beginning to wonder if you were still on the planet."

"I just took some time off, sir. I'll be back at work soon."

"You don't need to give me an explanation, son. I'm well aware of what's happened with you and Nelson Chambers."

Mark swallowed. Nelson Chambers was the subject of one of his nightmares. "It was a mistake, sir. I reacted instead of acted."

"Not to worry, my boy. I don't know if I would've reacted the same way, were I in your shoes. I'm glad that the chief realized that he shouldn't fire you because of it."

Mark didn't know how to respond. Their server returned with their meals. Mark found it hard to look into the man's face, even though he had known him since childhood. Judge Embry's signature had graced many search and arrest warrants he requested these past seven years. Mark kept glancing about, hoping that no one he knew would see them. He also forced himself to eat his sandwich, although it tasted more like sawdust on paper than chicken salad on wheat. Finally, Judge Embry spoke again: "I have to admit, Detective, you've been on my mind a bit these last few hours."

"Why's that, sir?"

The judge sighed and set his spoon down. The light glittered off his law school ring, as he gazed over his hands at Mark. "Maybe it's because I hadn't seen you or your partner. Is he all right?"

"Yes."

Judge Embry took another bite of his chili. "There were other reasons why I thought about you," he continued. "Perhaps it's because the quality of the warrants being presented hasn't been up to snuff. I know that being a cop wasn't what your father wanted of you, but he taught you to be thorough, I must say."

"Thank you, sir."

"Yesterday was when I realized that I hadn't seen you in a while. I signed some papers that had your name on them." Judge Embry reached for his glass and took a sip of water. "Your eviction papers, I believe."

Mark paled. He thought only his best friend knew how desperate things had become. "Your Honor . . ."

"Don't worry, Mark. What's happening in your personal life is your business, although if there's anything that I can do to help?"

"No. I'm going to the bank to see what can be done."

Judge Embry leaned forward. "Mark, if they've requested eviction, there's little that can be done. I've seen this happen to many times in my line of work. Unless you can come up with the money quickly, there's nothing anyone can do."

Mark set his sandwich down, his appetite now gone. He sat in silence and watched Judge Embry polish off the last of his chili. It was almost as good as the judge remembered it. He pulled his napkin from his shirt, retrieved a $20.00 bill from his wallet, and laid it on top of the bill the server had left. "Lunch is on me, today, Detective." He stood, pulled a card from his monogrammed card case, and handed it to Mark. "If the bank won't listen, call my friends here. They might be able to help."

Mark wasn't sure what to do. He took the card, his hands shaking. The name of the company, Lemont-Bay Industries, barely registered in his head. "Thank you, Your Honor. I'll keep it in mind."

"You're welcome, son. I hope to see you back in my courtroom soon, dealing with issues regarding your job, and not your life."

Judge Embry gave him a pat on the back, turned and strolled out of the restaurant. Mark watched him go. Then he turned his attention back to the business card. The telephone number on it was a local number. He ran his fingers over the raised print. The judge's offer seemed sincere enough. Should he accept? His face hardened and tears stung his eyes. Silently, he slipped the card into his jacket pocket, picked up his change, and walked out of the restaurant.

He drove around town in an attempt to kill time. Still, he reached the bank well ahead of his 3:00 p.m. appointment. He parked his truck and sat there, staring at the brick structure. With all that had happened, it was hard to believe that in a few minutes, the rest of his life would be decided. Would he be able to live with the inevitable outcome? What would he do? Where would he go? He got out and walked with determined steps toward the front door. He greeted the secretary: "My name's Mark Daniels. I'm here to see Mr. Smith, the bank president."

"Yes, Mr. Daniels, he's expecting you."

She picked up the telephone receiver and punched in a few numbers. Mark made his way to a chair. A few moments later, Mr. Smith walked out of his office. His gray suit was wrinkled, but the knot in his black tie was right against his Adam's apple. "Come in Mr. Daniels," he said, motioning to his office.

He gestured to a chair, and Mark sat down. He glanced around. He truly was in a glass box, he noted. Mr. Smith's office offered a full view of the goings on in the bank. He saw two women at the counter, gently bantering with each other. Off in another corner, a young couple waited as another bank official laid out some papers in front of them. He adjusted the fit of his jeans and watched Mr. Smith read Mark's file. Mark saw that his dark hair was beginning to thin on the top. Unconsciously, Mark ran a hair through his hair. Despite everything, no bald spots had materialized on his head and he smiled at the thought.

Mr. Smith cleared his throat, breaking Mark's concentration. "Things are not looking very good for you, Mr. Daniels. According to the records, you're already more than six months behind with the mortgage. We are aware that the loss of your wife's income and your extended leave of absence. I'm certain they understand the financial and emotional strain that you're going through."

Understand my ass. They've done nothing but harass me. Mark cleared the lump from his throat. "I was just wondering if there was any way to delay the final sale. I have a buyer for the last of Jessie's work, and I should have some rent money coming in shortly. That income should help to offset some of the back payments."

"I'm afraid not. You need to have the account paid in full before close of business tomorrow, or the bank will take it." Mr. Smith's expression turned grave. "You've probably already done this, but is there anyone you can contact for help?"

Judge Embry's business card seemed to burn against his chest. Mark took a steadying breath. "No, there isn't."

"Then I'm sorry. I wish I could do more for you." Mr. Smith stood up and offered a hand. "I'll make a note of this conversation for the file. If things change, please let me know."

Mark stood and took Mr. Smith's hand. He looked into Mr. Smith's eyes. Was the concern in his face real, or was it the face of a well-accomplished actor, used to delivering news like this on a daily basis? Mark let go quickly, and made his way out of the bank, his eyes fixed on the floor. He waited until he reached the parking lot and his vehicle before slamming his fists into the hood of the truck. There was a deep boom, as he heard and felt the vibration move though the hood. He pressed his knuckles into his eyes. "Jessie, if you can hear me, help me! Please!"

He fought back the tears and clambered into the truck. As he drove, he tried to remain focused on the future, not that it looked any better than today did.

Monday, he was due back to work after three months of administrative leave. His boss had informed him of the conditions for his return. Given all he was going through, was it worth the effort to return? Perhaps it was time to employ the other final solution to all his miseries.

He turned onto his tree-lined street and swung the truck into the driveway. Mark was so distracted, he didn't notice the vehicle in it. He slammed on the brakes just in time. He backed up, swung his truck to the right of the vehicle, and shut off the engine. He studied the strange car in his driveway. It was a new Ford Escape Hybrid. Its dark blue paint and chrome bumpers gleamed in the afternoon sunlight. He admired its fully loaded dashboard and black leather interior. Once his curiosity was satisfied, he made his way to his front door. He was halfway there when he stopped. A young, well-built black woman sat on the top step of his front porch, writing something in her notebook. Her hair was short and straight, nicely cut with a slight wave to it. She was dressed in a dark denim jacket, white T-shirt, black boot-cut jeans, and low-heeled black boots. She started chewing on the end of her pen as if pondering a thought, and didn't notice Mark as he walked up to the porch. He stopped just a few feet away from her, eyeing her. "Excuse me? Can I help you?"

She looked up, startled. Then her expression softened. Behind the black angular glasses, her deep brown eyes showed warmth and friendliness. "I hope so. Are you the owner?"

She pointed at a sign in the garage's second floor front window. Mark looked to where she was pointing, and then back at her. "Yes."

"Oh, good. I thought I might've missed you."

She stood and stepped down off the porch. As she reached his level, Mark realized that she was almost as tall as he was. She placed her pen and tablet in the black messenger bag that leaned against the front step. Mark spotted a newspaper tucked inside its dark folds. She picked up the bag, threw the strap across her left shoulder, and held out her right hand for him to shake. "Juliana Warren," she said, smiling. "It's nice to meet you, Mister . . ."

"Daniels, Mark Daniels."

They shook hands. Juliana sighed and redirected her attention to the windows above the garage. "Mr. Daniels, I know it's late, and you must have other obligations, but I read your ad and I saw the sign. I was hoping I might be able to get a glimpse of the place. I've spent weeks hunting for a place to live and you're my last hope."

Mark's attention returned to the window, where the "For Rent" sign stood in prominent view. A few months ago, he sought to rent out an apartment above his garage to help fight the foreclosure of his home. More than two dozen eager applicants appeared at his doorstep. They all disappeared the moment they discovered his occupation. He figured she wouldn't be any different. "Sure. No problem."

He turned on a heel. She rushed to follow him. As he reached the stairs alongside his garage, he remembered the paper he had seen inside her bag. "I could've sworn I took my advertisement out of the paper," he commented, as he began his ascent.

"You did? Well, the paper I have is from a couple of weeks ago. It's just taken me this long to get to this side of town."

"Why's that?" Mark asked, pausing halfway up the stairs.

She gave him sheepish smile. "My job. I have to travel a lot. I hope your statement doesn't mean that you've found someone to rent it."

Mark took his time finding the right key. Did he dare tell her that the property would be going to the bank in a few days? He had no doubts that the bank would appreciate finding someone living there who believed she had a legal right to be there.

He reached the landing, fitted the key into the lock, and pushed open the door. The bottom hinge squealed and he cringed. Then he breathed the stale air. His thoughts flew back to Jessie and her paintings. He could see them leaning against the wall, her last canvas unfinished on its easel, and the tubes of color and multitude of brushes scattered along her worktable. He moved aside so that she could have a full view. She stepped into the doorway. A peculiar odor caught her attention. "That smell? It smells like oil paint, like the type they use on pictures."

"It is. This is my wife's studio."

"Your wife's an artist? Wow!"

"She used to be." Mark paused. "She's dead."

"Oh. I'm sorry, I . . ."

"It's all right."

He stood in the doorway with his arms crossed. Her bag rustled against her hip as she walked cautiously around the place. Her footsteps echoed through the empty structure. Jessie had made sure that her studio was a functional place to live as well as work, since sometimes her projects could take days or weeks to complete. It felt wrong that someone else would just live here, oblivious to the artistry created within it.

Juliana paused to look out the kitchen window, which offered a view of the giant maple that grew between Mark's house and the garage. Its leaves were beginning to flower, and its wing-nut seeds littered the ground. When it was through, it would block the view of everything but the driveway. The front room had two smaller windows. One faced Mark's dusty green house, the other the yellow house across the street. She reached for the kitchen faucet and watched the water flow from it. Then she took a few steps into the larger open area. Mark followed her around the corner, watching as she dipped her head first inside the small bathroom to her left, then the bedroom, whose window also faced the yellow house. She walked out back into the living room. She turned in a circle, took a deep breath, and closed her eyes, feeling Mark's steady gaze upon her. Then she opened them. "It's a little smaller than I hoped," she murmured, "and yet . . ." She took another glance out the kitchen window. Then she smiled and turned her attention back to Mark. "I'll take it," she announced.

"What?"

"I'll take it. Now, how much did you say a month?"

His arms dropped to his sides. "You want it?"

"Yes. That is, if you're still renting it?"

Mark eyed her. "Are you sure?"

"Yes, I am. Shouldn't I be?"

"But . . . you haven't pestered me with questions, like the other applicants have."

Her brow furrowed and she rubbed her chin. "What questions should I be asking you, outside of how much rent is, and when it's due?"

"Aren't you curious as to what I do for a living?"

"Okay. What's your occupation?"

"I'm a detective with the Mason City Police Department."

She looked at him quizzically. "And why should that have anything to do with me renting this place?"

"It doesn't . . . it shouldn't . . . I mean . . ." Mark caught his breath and considered his words: "My other applicants weren't too keen on having a cop as a landlord, and since most blacks have an instant dislike of cops, I . . ."

He paused when he saw the flash of anger in her eyes. "Sorry. I'm not trying to be racist or anything. I just thought you should know up front who you'll be dealing with when the first of the month comes."

"Your occupation doesn't matter to me, Officer Daniels."

"Detective," Mark corrected her.

She nodded. "Detective Daniels, my race has nothing to do with whether I like police officers. My goal today was to find a suitable place to live. If anything, your occupation works to your benefit. Seeing as I've agreed to take you up on your offer, all I want is for you to maintain your end of the agreement." She pulled out her notebook and pen again. "Now, how much is the rent again?"

"Julie? May I call you Julie?"

"Yes, if I can call you Mark."

"Julie, you should know that I may not be the owner of the property for much longer." Mark wavered, unsure if she should say anything more. "I'm having some issues with the bank."

"Oh? Nothing serious I hope."

"Yes. No." Mark shook his head, hoping the action would help him say what he meant. Why hide it? It made no sense, since it would be of public record Monday. Then again, maybe this would be a short-term thing. At least he could get enough money from her to make up a couple of mortgage payments, and maybe stay the procedure altogether. "I'm just giving you fair warning that they may not be happy that you're here."

"Well, we'll deal with that when the time comes. In the meantime . . ." Julie eyed him carefully, pen in hand. When he continued to stare at her in disbelief, she raised an eyebrow. "The rent?"

Mark scratched his head and racked his brain, trying to remember the terms he had generated: "The rent's $625 a month, plus half of the heat, water, and electricity usage. I'll need last month's rent as a security deposit, and no pets."

Julie scribbled the information down. "Okay. I'll have a check for you by Monday. Great! Now I'll have to call the movers. They won't be too happy with me giving them such short notice, and I'll need to get in touch with

Jennifer to let her know I've finally found a place, and have her set up the appointments for the tech people to come in. Oh, and I'll need to make arrangements with you to sign the lease and pick up the keys. Perhaps I can delay that trip to Somalia a day or two, and I should call Simon so he'll stop worrying, not that he ever stops worrying, and I need to get to the bank to get you your money, and call the warehouse where they're storing my things, and . . ."

She seem to say all of this in one breath, as she stuffed the notebook back into her bag and made her way past him. Mark watched her in stunned silence, and then followed. She was already halfway to her car and still muttering to herself when Mark caught up to her. He grabbed her left arm. "Wait, just wait a minute!"

Julie turned. She looked confused. "Is something wrong?"

"Yeah. Are you sure about this? I mean, you barely looked at the place, you may not be able to live here very long, and I've already pissed you off. What gives?"

Julie placed a hand over his. Her touch was warm, gentle, and reassuring. He met her gaze. To him, it seemed like she was looking deep into his mind, his heart, and his soul. For a moment, he thought he saw something flicker in them. He blinked and it was gone. She smiled. "Mark, I have few needs," she assured him. "As I told you, I travel a lot, so I won't be much of a bother to you, or anyone for that matter." She released a deep sigh and she cast an eye back up at the structure. "Besides, I do like it. It has a warm, comfortable feeling to it, like someone was meant to live there."

Mark took this information in and let go of her arm. Julie opened the driver's door and climbed inside. After she started her vehicle, she rolled down her window and handed him a business card. "I need to return to San Francisco for the weekend," she informed him. "I'll stop by Monday morning with your check and to pick up the keys. What time do you normally leave for work?"

Mark took the card, still struggling to accept everything that just happened. "Around 8:00 a.m.," he heard himself say.

"Then I'll see you then."

Julie winked at him and backed out of the driveway. Still a little bewildered, Mark walked down to the edge of it and watched her drive away. He looked down at the card. She was a consultant for some company out of San Francisco called The Foundation. "Building a stronger universe one life at a time," he murmured, reading the slogan underneath its logo. "Lofty goal."

He waited until he saw her vehicle disappear around the corner before returning to his truck to retrieve his dry cleaning. He tossed it over his left shoulder and headed to the front door. A nagging feeling gnawed at his subconscious. There was something wrong about what just transpired. *Ignore it*, his heart told him. *So many doors have closed around you. This is your first window. Granted, it's a small window. Still, climb through it, and enjoy the view.* He turned and took one last look at Jessie's studio, and then opened the door and went inside.

Julie drove to the end of his street, and pulled to the side. When she was certain no one was watching, she reached into her bag. She retrieved the gun from within. She stared at it with disdain. "A final solution," she whispered. "He's right, but there's always another way, Mark." She looked up at the roof of her vehicle. "NIK?"

Yes, Ambassador?

"Rerun that profile on Mark Anthony Daniels, please, especially his finances. I need to understand what's going on."

Accessing.

A tingling sensation surfaced at the base of her neck. It was her indication that NIK was hard at work on her request. When that was completed, Julie sat back in her seat. "Well, that confirms what I learned from him."

What would you like me to do, Ambassador?

Julie set the gun down in the passenger seat. Then she waved a hand over it. It vanished into nothingness. Her path was clear, but she decided not to follow it. "Contact Elise. Make sure that she has a check ready for me. Have the others prepared for reference checks if he asks for them. I also want Elise to help you take care of Mr. Daniels' finances, especially his mortgage. Discreetly, please."

You do not trust my abilities, Ambassador?

Julie smiled as she headed her back to the highway. If she didn't know NIK was a computer, she would have thought it was pouting. "Not your abilities. It's just this human's incessant curiosity. I don't want him finding out more than he needs to know."

As you wish, Ambassador.

Julie glanced out the rearview mirror. The Mason City skyline grew smaller against the red-orange haze that signaled the beginning of the evening sunset. She settled back into her seat and breathed a long sigh. After much arguing and debate, Halbrina finally arrived back on Earth. The human part of her was thrilled. The immortal wondered how long she would be able to stay.

II

Mark's father's law firm was a ten-story building that took up the corner of Fifth Avenue in downtown Seattle. He was there now, in the lobby of his father's top-floor suite, waiting for him to finish up a phone call. He stared at the abstract painting that hung in the lobby. Mark loathed abstract art. Jessie once offered to donate one of her scenery paintings for the lobby, but his father declined. *Why, Dad? Would it put you too close to the son that you've been fighting all your life to push away?*

He moved his eyes to the table. An array of magazines lay before him. He picked one up and started paging through it. Mary Cunningham, his dad's long-time secretary watched him thoughtfully over her reading glasses. "How are things, Mark?"

"All right."

"If there's anything that I can do . . ."

Mark fought not to cringe. Mary came to the funeral and helped deal with the guests when they stopped by to pay their final respects. Lately, he had had it with all the sympathetic words and the lack of meaning behind them. He tried to maintain a sincere look on his face. "There's nothing, but thank you," he said.

The intercom buzzed and Mary picked up the receiver. "Yes?" There was a pause, and then she said, "Yes, Mr. Daniels." She replaced the receiver and looked at Mark. "Your father will see you now."

"Thanks."

Mark stood and walked determinedly toward the office door. As he reached for the brass doorknob, he paused. What was he doing here? Why had he come? Because Jessie would've wanted this. She tried their entire marriage to get the two men to reconcile. In the end, not even her death had been able to do it. Taking a deep breath, he turned the knob and opened the door.

He stood in the doorway to his father's office. Two walls were nothing but views of the Seattle skyline, with the dull, gray-colored sky, and the Space Needle shimmering in the background. The other two walls were cherry bookcases filled with curios, knickknacks, and many photographs. Mark noticed that the wedding picture Jessie sent him was not among them. There were also no pictures of Mark or his mother anywhere. Like always, it was as if that part of his father's life didn't exist.

Mark forced his gaze away from the bookcases and toward his father. Robert Sebastian Daniels stood, but otherwise made no move to greet his only child. He looked impeccable as always, in his tailored dark navy suit, his solid yellow tie knotted perfectly. Except for the eyes, Mark had inherited his dad's looks. He also had none of his personality. Mark thanked his paternal grandmother for that. They stood there, staring as if they had never seen each other before. "Well, sit down," Robert ordered him, gesturing to a chair in front of his desk.

Mark found himself unable to move. He had no reason to be intimidated by him, yet he could feel his knees knocking. It was like he were seven years old again, explaining how he broke old man Wilson's kitchen window. With a great effort, he crossed the room and slid into the chair his father had offered him. He stared at the immaculate desktop that reflected the scene outside the window. He heard his father take his seat. Then he finally brought his eyes to meet his father's gaze. There was more silence. "It's been a while," Robert Daniels commented.

"Yeah."

A few more moments passed in silence. Robert picked up his gold-plated letter opener. "I take it this isn't a social call."

Mark shook his head. Robert twirled the letter opener in his hands. "Well?"

Just ask the question, idiot. The sooner you do, the sooner you can get the hell out of here. Mark took a deep breath: "Dad, I need a favor of you."

Robert put the letter opener down and sat back in his high-back leather chair, rocking it back and forth. "A favor."

"Yes." Mark looked down at his hands. "A loan," he mumbled.

Robert rested his elbows on the chair arms. His green eyes bore down on his son. It was his "Convince me," look. Mark was intimately familiar with it. He hated with a passion. "I'm . . . having problems with the mortgage," Mark explained. "Jessie's illness took everything that we had. The bank's going to take it Monday. I have to come up with the money before the end of the day today, or I'm going to lose it."

His father's gaze didn't waver. Mark fought back the wave of sadness that threatened him. "Dad, I'm trying to save my home, the one little piece of Jessie that I want to hang onto . . ."

"And you want my help," his father finished.

Mark cursed at himself. He should've known this was a waste of time and gas. Judge Embry's offer dangled in his brain like a carrot on a stick. However, coming to his dad wasn't much different. His dad hadn't approved of Jessie the one time that she had met him. He didn't come to the wedding, nor set foot in their house. When Jessie became ill, his father hadn't lifted a finger to help them. He didn't even come to her funeral, not that Mark had expected him to. He watched in brooding silence while Robert reached down and picked up the letter opener again. "And what guarantees do I have that this money will be repaid?"

"Sir, I will pay you back. I'll find a way."

Robert put the letter opener back down on the desk. Then he stood and walked over to the window. He stared out at the expanse before him. "Not unless you quit that job of yours, or are you still on that 'justice for all' bit?"

"Dad, I like my job. I'm not going to quit it to come here and be another overpaid pencil pusher."

"Even if would provide you with the financial stability that you so desperately need right now?"

Mark stared again at his father's desktop. His father had the look on his face again. He could see it in the reflection. A wave of fury replaced the sadness inside of him. "You're doing it again."

Robert turned from the window. "Doing what, Mark?"

Mark waited a beat before speaking again: "Blaming me."

"Blaming you? For what?"

"For everything. For Jessie, for Mom, as if Mom's death was my fault."

Robert's facial expression hardened. "I don't think that, son. I've never thought that."

"No. You just imply it every single time you look at me." Mark shook as he stood up, but he didn't notice. "You know, ever since Mom died, nothing I've ever done has pleased you, not when I made the all-state baseball team in high school, not when I graduated from junior college and the academy, all of my promotions, my awards, when I married Jessie. None of it!"

"Mark, that's not true."

"Yes, it is! No matter how successful I am at something, no matter what I do, you ignore it. Whenever I needed something, I always have to explain why, and it's never enough. You always have to put some sort of condition on everything just to get a simple recognition of love from you!"

"No, I haven't, and you know it."

"Yes, you have!"

Robert crossed his arms. "So, do you want the loan or not?"

Mark looked around the office. "No. I changed my mind. I don't like the penalties if I default."

Mark stormed out of his dad's office before his father could reply. He slammed the door behind him. He didn't bother to say goodbye to Mary. He reached the elevator banks and punched the "Down" key. It seemed to take an immeasurable long time to get to his floor and when it reached his floor, it was mercifully empty. He marched toward his truck and left the parking lot in a squeal of tires. He headed back toward Mason City automatically, scarcely aware of the tears that blurred his vision. When he finalized realized that he was weaving all over the road, he pulled over. Seconds later, he broke down. He wanted it to end; his guilt, his grief, his self-doubt, and his life. He stared at Jessie's wedding band, now on his right pinky finger. "I'm so sorry, Jess!" he sobbed. "I tried. I really tried! I just don't know where else to turn. I don't know what else to do!"

* * *

From San Francisco, Julie drove toward the northern portion of Washington State. As she drove the miles of crowded highway, she stared in dismay. All she encountered were sprawling communities, with a sprinkling of what NIK called shopping centers and strip malls. "Strip mall is right," Julie concluded, as she thought about the hundreds of thousands of trees that had paid with their lives so that the human population had a place to set up their homes and businesses. This is not how she remembered this planet at all. How much it had changed! Once she crossed into Washington, the cities disappeared and more trees and open land appeared. The traffic that she had been driving in began to thin as well, and the highway dropped to two lanes. By the time she reached the other side of Okanogan, there was no one else on the road. Two miles from her destination, a sign informed her that she approached Amendu tribal land. About five minutes later, she saw a familiar grove of trees, and then a dirt road. She turned onto it and paused at the gate. She smiled. There were thousands of more trees here, but otherwise, it still looked the same.

Her attention returned to the gate. It triggered unpleasant thoughts about the latest attempts to buy and develop it. Several times during their negotiations, they trespassed on it. Now Julie saw why. "NIK? Are the generators and projectors in place?"

Yes, Ambassador, and they are fully functional.

"Could you give me some variations of some impassable roads, please? I need to discourage anyone else from venturing into here."

While Julie watched, the road surface in front of her seemed to ripple, and then changed in appearance. It changed several times before Julie found one that she liked. "Make sure to integrate the image into the computer banks so that it can be constantly maintained. A couple of real bumps and some fallen trees wouldn't hurt, either. Also, remind me to talk to the Caretaker about replacing these gates. I don't want anyone getting access to this land again so easily."

As you wish, Ambassador.

Julie made the gate dissolve into nothingness, while the pothole-filled dirt road NIK had created seemed to glimmer and then turn smooth. She dropped the car into gear and drove up the road. Deeper in, the forest thickened into hundred-year-old hardwoods coming into leaf. The shadows grew longer and deeper. After about five minutes, she saw a silver roof. She slowed down and turned into a clearing that opened up near a lakeshore. A huge red barn was off to the left and a crumbling farmhouse was to her right. Lush evergreens framed both sides of the deep blue lake, hiding the remains of the setting sun. She shut off the engine and climbed out. She stood in the middle of the yard, breathed in the pine-scented air, and surveyed her surroundings. There was a bite to the air here that she hadn't noticed in Mason City yesterday. It felt wonderful. The tension she had felt the last few days began to lift, but not the gentle throb inside her head. She closed her eyes and willed the cause of it away. It wouldn't last long, she knew. The Eldar were undaunted and unyielding. They would be back at it in a few hours.

She sensed someone approaching and turned her attention to the farmhouse. An older black man emerged from the structure, and cautiously climbed down the broken, creaky steps. He wore a filthy, faded pair of denim blue bib overalls and a tobacco-stained red plaid shirt, and carried a cane-fishing pole in his huge right hand. His worn worker's boots and the bottom third of his overalls were soaking wet. He lumbered toward her, running his fingers through his salt-and-pepper hair with his free hand. She smiled. "Hello, Caretaker."

The man did not slow his approach. He stopped in front of her and bowed slightly. Then before her eyes, his form changed. The older man in overalls vanished. A tall, elegant figure stood in his place. His whole body glowed white except for the spot where his watery brown eyes had been. They were now large black ovals that glistened with moisture. *Greetings,* miandi. *It is good to see you,* her mind heard him say in a language no human had ever heard, and many throughout the universe thought was gone forever. It was Illani.

Julie approached the white form and paused. Then she held out her right hand, touching it against the spot where his human temple had been. *And you too, Caretaker,* she responded in his native tongue, tears coming to her eyes.

He repeated the gesture to her. *How was your trip?*

As well as can be expected. How are things here?

Quiet, except for the nursery, of course.

And the humans?

Their interest in this place has diminished, thanks to you, and the company's new director.

He gestured toward the red barn and they began walking toward it. The large door on the left slid open on its own and they stepped inside. She smelled the fresh hay stored in the lofts. Outside of a few tools scattered about and the bales of hay, there was nothing inside.

The two of them walked toward the far wall and another door opened, revealing a glowing white chamber. As they approached she paused. Already, she could sense the new lives ready to come into being. There were so many that she couldn't quite count them all. She looked at the Caretaker quizzically. "How many?" she asked aloud.

"It's the largest brood we've had since our arrival here."

They stepped into the elevator. The doors closed behind them and they descended rapidly through the earth. Julie swallowed a few times, wishing as always that she could change her humanoid form to accommodate for the ear popping she was experiencing now. The car stopped, and the doors opened to a brightly lit courtyard. The air was heavy with moisture. She stood in awe when the scene before her revealed itself. Off in the distance, a thin, angular tower glowed green and blue against the bright white sky. Dozens of smaller buildings in haunting shades of yellow and lavender surrounded it. To the left of the shortest tower was an orange-domed structure, sheltered by the water gardens that housed plant life from across the universe. Before her, thousands of white forms walked silently along unmarked paths. Except for the slight hum of the machines that took in the energy produced by the planet's core and converted it for their own use, there was no sound.

As soon as Julie stepped from the elevator, the white forms stopped moving and turned. An overwhelming sense of joy washed over her, as the white forms bowed and communicated their greetings. Many of them approached, attempting to touch any part of her. Julie welcomed the warmth and love they offered. However, she felt undeserving. She was the reason for the Illani being here on Earth, rebuilding a civilization that once lived in peace and seclusion.

After a bit, the Caretaker led her out of the crowd to a square building off in the corner. Unlike the outside, the air here was cool and refreshing. The atmosphere buzzed with excitement. She followed the Caretaker down to the end of the long hallway and to another door. She sensed the new lives now more than ever. She breathed it in. There were so many, she realized, but how many? She scanned the Caretaker's thoughts, but he blocked them. She frowned. He knew that she could force her way in, but she resisted the urge. Apparently, he wanted to surprise her.

The door at the end of the hallway opened silently. There was nothing but darkness at first, but when she stepped into the room, she gasped. She stared toward the floor. All she saw was row upon row of white spheres. They pulsed simultaneously to the rhythm of the machines keeping them cool. The glow of the spheres reflected off her face and her eyes. She pushed her glasses into her hair, gripped the railing, and held her breath. She was afraid to do anything that would disturb this perfect sense of harmony around her. "How many?" she whispered.

The Caretaker took a position beside her. "Three hundred eighty seven," he replied, a note of pride in his voice. "According to the latest tests, there are three progenitors among them."

She whirled. "Three!"

"Yes."

Julie turned back to the glowing spheres. "Alexandra's experiments worked."

The Caretaker closed his black eyes and nodded. "Apparently, *miandi*. They all have their Illani names. Our problem has been cataloging and correlating Earth names for them."

"Don't worry. I think I can find you a book of human baby names. I saw one in a bookstore that I stopped in on my way here."

They stood there silently for a few moments longer. Then the Caretaker took her hand again. He led her to a ramp and they descended to the ground level. They walked about a third of the way through them before the Caretaker paused. She watched as he squatted down to pick up one of the spheres. He cradled it in his arms, and then offered it to Julie. She backed away. "No! I couldn't!"

"Yes, *miandi*, you can."

He handed her the sphere. Still scared, Julie held it away from her. She stared at the casing. She sensed life within it, but nothing else. "Is it a boy or a girl?"

"A girl."

Julie looked at the sphere and then at the Caretaker. "How can you tell?"

"We just can."

Julie's gaze fell back on the sphere. She felt the child's strength growing with every pulse. She brought it closer to her chest, holding it as if she had held a human child. Instantly, the sphere's pulse rate changed, speeding up to match the rhythm of her heartbeat. She stole a glimpse back at the Caretaker, who watched her, his black eyes unblinking. If he still looked human, she would swear he had a broad smile on his face. "Am . . . am I doing all right?"

"You're doing fine, *miandi*."

She stroked the outside of the sphere, imagining what the child inside it would look like if she were to become humanoid. An Earth name that she had heard many years ago came to her head. "Angela . . . this one should be called Angela."

"Then Angela it shall be," the Caretaker agreed.

She rocked Angela gently and then looked out at the remaining spheres. The sob she had fought back rose in her throat again, and tears streamed down her cheeks. Despite how far they had come, how well they had adapted and survived, it didn't stop her from feeling the anguish of what she had done. She stared back down at the sphere. "I'm so sorry, Angela," she whispered to it. "I'm sorry that you can never see your true home world, to feel its sun on your face. I'm sorry for everything I did to your ancestors, and to you."

"Don't, *miandi*."

Julie looked up. The Caretaker had resumed his human form. His watery brown eyes had a quiet, reflective quality to them. "Why do you continue to blame yourself when you know you were not at fault for what happened to us."

Julie sniffled. "Maybe not for all of it, Caretaker, but enough of it."

"What happened occurred two million Earth years ago. We have accepted what happened, and have treasured each day of the new life that you have granted us. You continue as if it all happened yesterday. Isn't it time for you to begin to forgive yourself?"

"I wish I could, Caretaker." She handed the sphere back to the Caretaker, who carefully tucked it back into place with the others. "Your lives are long, but they do end. Mine will go on, with no end in sight, and no relief from the guilt or the remorse. Everywhere I go, I live with the morbid fear that I can take away any life with just a thought. How can you still trust me after all I did to your people, and your home world?"

"Because we know you, *miandi*. We know your heart. We know what happened then will never happen again, so long as you exist. Our existence makes that plain to all that would see it." He reached up to touch her shoulder, a comforting, human gesture. "If it would help, do not concentrate on that day," he encouraged her. "Think instead of the days that you have given us here, in this life. That is what matters to us, and to those who will follow. That is what we wish to celebrate with you today, and always."

Julie took a deep breath, and then took one more gaze at the new lives waiting to experience the wonders of this planet, and the universe beyond it. There was so much for them to see and she wanted to be the one to show them. She held her head up, took the Caretaker's outstretched hand and nodded. "Yes. We do have much to celebrate, don't we?"

III

Mark spent the entire weekend trying not to think about Monday. Saturday, he drove his best friend Tyler Martin to the airport. Tyler worked in the squad's technical evidence department. Today, he was heading to Los Angeles to assist in expanding a regional computer database that tracked illegal immigrants imported by the Russian mafia. "Two weeks of sun, sand, and tan women in bikinis," Tyler said with pleasure, reclining his seat as far back as it would go and resting his cowboy-booted feet on Mark's dash. "What could be better?"

Mark snorted. "Only the coffee shops you'll visit, and the online war games you'll be playing instead."

"True. I'll have to make time for those."

"You mean make time for the other things. I've known you for more than 10 years, and in all that time, you've never come close to approaching sand and ocean."

On Sunday morning, Mark gave the studio one final cleaning and inspection, still wondering how and why

Julie had said "yes" to it. He hadn't heard from her since that day, which bothered him a little bit. His last task was to oil the studio door's bottom hinge until it moved without a sound. As he made to shut it, he sighed. There would be no way for Julie to understand the many days of happiness the couple shared within it, nor would he ever be able to explain it to her. He was certain of that.

That afternoon, he met Jessie's parents at the cemetery. Mrs. Barnes walked between the two most important men in her daughter's life. As they approached, they discovered that the headstone had arrived. Mr. Barnes slowly knelt at beside Jessie's grave. His blonde hair had turned snow white in the months since his only daughter's death. He laid a bouquet of yellow tulips on top of the headstone, and reached out to brush aside the leaves gathered on top of the grave. Then his shoulders began to tremble. Mrs. Barnes knelt next to him, cradling his sobbing form in her arms. Her tears fell silently into her husband's hair. Mark managed to hold back his until he got home.

That night, he barely slept. He stared at the ceiling, wondering if he could delay his return just one more day. He could delay his return permanently. The choice was his. Instead, he forced himself out of bed. He took an extra-long jog through the neighborhood. When he returned, he showered and shaved, and put on his lucky black slacks, polo shirt and boots. He entered the kitchen and busied himself by scrambling some eggs with ham and cheese, and toast. While he poured his coffee, he glanced up at the nearby wall calendar. He had circled the target date of his return many weeks ago in red marker. It was only now that he actually looked what day it was—April 1. *April Fools' Day, and I'm the fool,* he thought with a sardonic note.

He had almost finished eating when he heard a muffler backfiring. That meant the morning newspaper had arrived. Still munching on a piece of toast, he made to retrieve it. The delivery person missed his target, as usual. Mark paused in the driveway to begin reading. Two articles caught his attention. One was about alleged pollution caused by the hydroelectric plant a few miles outside of town. The other dealt with a fire in downtown Mason City, the second in two months. Arson was suspected. Mark shook his head, took another bite of his toast, and looked at the front door. He tilted his head. Taped to it was an envelope. He looked out and the street, and then pulled the envelope off the door. There was a piece of paper tucked inside. When he tugged at it, another piece of paper fluttered out and sailed to the porch floor. He regarded it, and then unfolded the paper and began to read:

Dear Mark,

I wanted to present this to you in person, but I had to return to San Francisco. I'll pick up the keys from you when I return.

Thanks again,
Julie

Mark retrieved the second piece of paper. He looked at it, and then did a double take. It was an official check in the amount of $10,000.00. Mark stared at it in wonder and reread the note. He ran the numbers in his head. The amount would more than cover the security deposit, as well as the utilities and her rent for the entire year! Why would she pay for the full year in advance? He thought that he should call her to let her know, but he had no phone number for her. Then he remembered.

He walked to the hall table, where he had left her business card. There were two numbers listed on the front; one for Stockholm, Sweden, and one for San Francisco. He dialed the number to the San Francisco office. To his surprise, a female voice answered the other end: "Thank you for calling the Foundation, how can I help you?"

"Hi. I apologize for calling so early, but I'm trying to reach Julie Warren, please."

"I'm sorry, sir. She's out of the country, and is unreachable at this time. May I take a message?"

Mark thought for a moment. Who was he to question why she paid the rent for the whole year? He should just take the money and be grateful. After all, she did say that she traveled a lot.

"Sir? Are you still there?" asked the voice on the other end of the line.

Mark snapped out of his reverie. "No, no message. Thank you."

Frowning, he took the check to his office and placed it and her note inside the folder with the unsigned lease. He shrugged. The mystery of her intent would have to wait for a day or two. He went to retrieve his weapon and paused. He kept in a safe hidden by a painting. Jessie was painting it the day they met. He stared at the scene before it. So many days they had recreated that moment. Now, those opportunities were gone. He bit back the tears as he retrieved his service weapon. He checked it carefully, then locked the front door, and climbed into his truck. While he drove, he stole a glance at the dashboard clock. He was still early. He chewed on the inside of his right cheek, thinking. His gun dug into his side and an idea came to him.

He took the next exit ramp and made two right turns in the direction toward the firing range. He parked his truck near its entrance. He inhaled the smell of spent gunpowder. The range reverberated with the sound of gunfire. It made his forearm hairs tingle. How long had it been since he had been here? He spotted a familiar face here and there, as he walked toward the counter. Mark warmly greeted Randall, the range officer. Randall was a dead-ringer for the driver Dale Earnhardt, only with a slight potbelly. He smiled heartedly at Mark and handed him his targets, goggles and headphones. "It's been a long time, Detective," he told him. "It's nice to see you back at work."

"Thanks, Randall. How have things been?"

"Not bad, although some of these youngsters around here could use a little training from the master."

He cocked his right thumb and index finger, pointing them at Mark. Mark grinned. "And give away my secrets?"

He made his way toward one of the open booths and attached a target to the railing. He sent the target out about five yards, picked up the headphones and goggles and slipped them on. Then he placed a clip in his weapon, took a cleansing breath, aimed at the target, and fired. He felt the familiar kickback as it discharged, and didn't even flinch at the flash of light that signaled his bullet was on its way toward its destination. A satisfying smile came across his face. He fired off a few more rounds and felt himself begin to relax. He retrieved his target, refreshed it with a new one, and sent it back out. He repeated this action several times, increasing the range at five-yard intervals, and emptying five clips in the process. When he finished, he laid the targets out to review. He removed his goggles and shook his head. He wasn't happy with himself. Granted, they showed mostly tens, but a few nines and an eight had slipped in. That wasn't good.

"Not bad," a female voice said behind him.

Mark turned. A sandy blonde-haired woman was scrutinizing his targets. She wore a sleeveless green mock turtleneck shirt, dark navy twill pants, and brown shoes. Her fair skin glowed with perspiration from firing, and her blue-green eyes twinkled mischievously. "Thanks," he replied.

The woman studied the targets again. She shrugged. "Nope, not bad at all, but I bet I could do better."

"Excuse me?"

"You know something. I *know* I can do better."

"You think so?"

She grinned. "Care for a contest? Best person wins fifty bucks."

Mark laid down the target in his hand. Mark appraised her and then looked over at Randall, who gave him a baffled look. Apparently, Randall had never seen her here before, either. She must work in another department or have a special permit to practice here. A shot of adrenaline hit him. He straightened. "You're on, Miss . . ."

"Cassie Edwards." She offered a hand and Mark shook it. "But I have to warn you, I'm not someone to mess with when it comes to this."

Mark raised his eyebrows and glanced back down at her used targets. Maybe this was just what his ego needed. He signaled to Randall. "Randall, can you give us two new targets, please?"

Randall gave him a mock salute and went to pull two fresh sheets. He returned and handed one to each of them. Mark gestured to his booth. "Ladies first."

"Thank you." She turned to Randall. "Ten rounds at twenty five yards," she told Randall. Cassie turned back to Mark. "Fair enough?"

"It's your money."

Randall placed Cassie's target in the holder and sent it out onto the range. Cassie picked up her headphones and goggles, adjusting them slowly. She reached down for her gun and installed a new clip. Then she planted her feet, squared her shoulders, lifted the gun up, and began firing. Mark watched from a few yards away, studying her technique. She was left handed. She also had a tendency to dip her supporting arm a bit after firing a round. She would have to work on that. It would help to improve her accuracy. Meanwhile, Randall had informed the rest of the shooters about the contest, and a few of them had gathered around to watch. Even through the headphones, Mark heard them muttering in the background.

When Cassie finished firing, Randall hit the retrieval button and brought the target back in to her. "Seven tens, three nines," he called out when the target moved into range.

There was a chorus of "Oohs." Cassie removed the empty clip and reloaded her gun. She holstered it on her right side, a confident smile on her face. "Beat that," she taunted Mark.

Mark gave her a wide smile. "All right, if you insist." He turned to the Randall. "But move the target out to fifty yards, if you would, please?" He turned back to face Cassie. "You can't give me too much of an advantage."

Cassie just smiled. There was no way he was going to beat her from that range. He would have to be an exceptional shooter if he did. A couple of the men behind them elbowed each other. Randall's moustache twitched, as he loaded up Mark's target and sent it out onto the range. It took a good minute for the target to move into position. Mark inserted another clip into his gun, adjusted his goggles and headphones, and walked up to the stand. He took careful aim and fired. This time, he fired smoothly and effortlessly. Cassie stood off a ways, watching.

When Mark finished, he stepped away. He waited quietly while Randall recalled the target. When the target was within sight, he looked over at Cassie. The supreme smile she wore disappeared. Mark had hit the bulls-eye with every shot. There was a hole at least two inches wide in the paper target. Randall unclipped it and handed it to Mark, a broad grin on his mustached face. Mark in turn gave it to Cassie. He savored the crestfallen look on hers. "Did I mention that I'm one of the top marksmen in the state?" Mark asked.

"No. You didn't."

Cassie reluctantly took the target. Then she reached into her pocket and pulled out two twenties and a ten-dollar bill. She stared at them as if they were a beloved companion, and then handed the money to him. Mark took the money from her. "Thanks. It was nice chatting with you. Maybe next time?"

He held out his hand. She tucked the reminder of their contest under her arm and shook it. He winked at her, picked up his jacket, and waved goodbye to the group of people who had been watching.

About five minutes before 9:00 a.m., he drove past the visitor's parking structure and pulled into the lot reserved for the Mason City Police Department. His favorite parking space was open, as if it expected him. He parked his truck and stared up at the tower. He sat there, reflecting. Was he doing the right thing? Was he ready to go back to this? Could he come back? Did he want to? He exited his truck, and headed for the entrance. A few people who worked in the building greeted him. He smiled and waved back. He took the elevator up to the seventh floor, where the Serious Crimes Unit made its home. As he approached the open double doors, he wiped his sweaty palms on his pants and took a deep breath. *Well, time for the moment of reckoning.*

He pushed open the door. He didn't know why he had worried. The minute he walked through the doors, he knew he was home. By the coffee maker, he saw Detectives Ed Peabody and Harry Carson, two veterans of the Serious Crimes unit, engaged in their morning ritual of who gets the last cinnamon raisin bagel. They turned at the same time. Broad grins spread across their faces when they saw Mark.

"Hey Detective, where've ya been?" a voice called out.

Mark turned. Davenport Dan, a petty pickpocket that Mark sometimes used as an informant, sat on a chair next to an empty desk. His black hair was matted down against his head, his clothes were tattered and torn, and in some places, falling off him, and he looked like he hadn't bathed in at least a week. However, Dan's smile was as bright as ever. "Dan!" Mark called, not daring to go any closer. "What's going on?"

Dan held up his cuffed hands. "Well, you know," he replied, his words slightly slurred. "Same stuff, different day. I'm hoping it's an April Fools' joke."

Mark chuckled. He had seen Dan arrested so often, he believed that Dan committed some of his crimes just so that he could get himself a good night's sleep and a decent meal. He caught a whiff of Dan and said a silent prayer of thanks that he was not the officer who writing up this report. After greeting and chatting with some of his coworkers, he walked up to the lieutenant's door. Through the blinded window, he could see his boss, her deep auburn hair hanging in her face, a black telephone receiver glued to her left ear, writing something down on a piece of paper. Mark tapped on the door, pushed it open, and poked his head through the opening. "Lieutenant?"

Lieutenant Allison Michaels looked up from her note taking. A smile touched her lips and the corners of her deep gray eyes. She waved him into her office and gestured for him to sit down. He shut the door and grabbed the blinds to prevent them from rattling. He slid into one of the chairs in front of her desk and waited quietly while she finished her call. He noted a few new pictures of her eleven-year-old son, Alex. He was looking more like his father every day. The picture of her husband, Rick, in full Marine dress was still in its place on the windowsill behind her head.

After a few more seconds, she wrapped up her phone call, hung up the receiver, and sighed. "The district attorney's office," she told him. "They're having problems reading some of our reports. They want me to remind you to either print, or type them up on the computer." She shook her head. "One of the highest closing rates in the state, and they're worried about illegible handwriting."

She pushed her shoulder-length hair out of her face, and leaned back in her chair, appraising her returning officer. She was in a pair of gray-cuffed slacks, a light blue oxford shirt, and white walking sneakers. Her badge and gun were clipped to a thin black belt on her left side. She sipped her coffee from her husband's Marines mug. Mark saw her relax and knew instantly that she truly was happy to see him. "How are you?"

"Fine."

"You look great."

"Thanks, Lieutenant."

"I talked to Dr. Jarvis. He says that you're ready to come back to work. What do you think?"

"Anything's better than sitting at home."

"I know that feeling, but you don't have to rush this. If you need more time . . ."

"I don't, Lieutenant. I want to get back to work. I think it'll help." He took a deep breath, preparing himself to say the one thing on his mind: "I also thought about what you told me about breaking in a new partner. I'm not sure if I'm ready for that. Maybe I should go it alone for a little bit? You know, just to see what it's like?"

"We did. Remember how that worked out?"

Mark squirmed in his chair. "Can't we chalk that up to an isolated incident?"

"No. I don't want to lose you again. We have seven open files right now, including two homicides. You're the best I have, and I need you." She sat up in her chair and her hair fell forward in her face. She reached up to brush it away. "Besides, I think your new partner would benefit from your patience and experience. She's a little anxious to please."

"She?"

There was another rap on the door. "Come in," Lieutenant Michaels called.

The door opened and Mark turned to see who had entered. His jaw dropped. It was Cassie. She had thrown a white denim jacket over her green shirt. She smiled broadly when she saw Mark's stunned face. Lieutenant Michaels looked from Cassie to Mark. "I see you two have met," she commented.

"Down at the range." Cassie sat down next to Mark. "It's nice to see you again."

Blood rushed to Mark's face. "And you," he stammered.

"Well, enough of the niceties." Lieutenant Michaels set down her mug and pushed a file toward him. Mark picked it up and opened it. Cassie leaned over to read what was in it with him. "A woman was found unconscious early this morning in Veterans Memorial Park," Lieutenant Michaels began. "She'd been beaten up pretty good. She's in the ICU at Mason City General."

"Is she going to make it?" Cassie asked, as Mark turned a page in the file.

"They're not certain. She's suffered some blunt force trauma to her head. According to the last reports, the doctors were still trying to stabilize her for surgery."

"You think this was drug related?" Mark asked, continuing to read.

"That's what you're going to find out. I need you two to get over to the hospital and see what's going on."

"Yes, ma'am," they chorused.

The detectives got up and headed out toward the main workroom. As Mark reached the door, the lieutenant called out to him: "Mark?"

He turned back. She got up and approached him. Her eyes held a motherly, yet stern look. "You realize what strings I had to pull to get you back?"

"Yes, ma'am."

"Not too many of us get second chances. Make the most of it."

"I will. Thank you."

She nodded and headed back to her paperwork. Mark headed toward his desk, now barren from its five months of non-use. He positioned his feet on its immaculate surface, retrieved the file and began to read: *Jane Doe, age estimated in her mid-twenties. No ID, no distinguishing marks, possible concussion, broken left cheekbone, broken jaw . . .*

"Hey."

Cassie bent over his desk. Her hair fell into the police report. Mark glanced up from his reading. "Patience, Cassie. I need to get a feel for what this case is about."

"It's a mugging, Mark. What more do you need to know?"

"Who the victim is, where they were found, who investigated the case, and what they saw for starters."

"So you're going to read a third-hand report? That's doesn't sound like you."

Mark's gaze dropped back to his reading. "Oh? And what have you heard about me?"

"That you tend to act on intuition more than with facts. That you can tell when the evidence is lying to you and when a suspect is lying, too. That you leave no stone unturned, no piece of information untouched without going over it with a fine tooth comb. You're good." She sat back up and crossed her arms, grinning. "You're very good."

"Just how good do you think I am?"

"I know that you and your last partner had the highest case closure rate in the state, three years running."

"Yes, and we wouldn't have closed half of them if Charlie failed to remind me not to jump to conclusions and to exercise a little patience."

"True, but the trail's already getting cold. The sooner we can get back on it, the sooner we can find who did this to her." Cassie glanced over toward the blinded windows and frowned. "Besides, I really need to get out of here."

Mark looked up and noticed that Cassie's hands trembled slightly. She also looked a little pale. He smiled at her and handed her the file. "Fine. Let's go."

They took his truck, and headed toward Mason City General Hospital. The ICU bustled with activity. Mark had to pull Cassie out of the way when a gurney with a gunshot victim whizzed by them with no intent on stopping. The officer following it stopped to shake Mark's hand. "Good to see you back, Detective," he said, a broad smile on his face.

"Thanks, Ted," Mark replied.

Mark walked up to the counter. "Detectives Mark Daniels and Cassie Edwards on the Jane Doe," he said, as the two of them showed their badges to the attending nurse. "We're looking for Dr. McFadden, please."

They heard Dr. McFadden's name over the loudspeaker. It was a little while before an Asian woman about Cassie's height rounded the corner and approached them. She wore her white lab coat over green surgical scrubs, and her straight black hair was pulled back in a ponytail. "Dr. Evelyn McFadden?" Mark asked.

She nodded, holding out her hand. "You're here for a follow-up on the Jane Doe?"

"How is she, Doc?"

Dr. McFadden reached to rub a spot between her shoulders. "She's just come out of surgery. We're keeping an eye on the brain swelling. Barring any complications, she should make it."

"Can we talk to her?" Cassie inquired.

"No. She's still unconscious."

Cassie retrieved a long spiral notebook. "Are you any closer to finding out who she is?"

A woman's shrill voice screaming at the top of her lungs caught their attention. The trio walked back to the end of the hallway. They heard the voice again, and another voice trying to calm the woman down: "Ma'am, I don't know if you friend is . . ."

"The news reported that a woman was beaten last night. I haven't been able to get a hold of Madison at all today. I think it's her and I want to know if she's here!"

The detectives walked up to the woman arguing with the attending nurse. Mark placed a restraining hand on the woman's shoulders. She turned. She was much shorter than he was, with brown eyes and a work-weathered face. She wore a brown tweed coat that looked twenty years out of style, over sagging pale pantyhose and a shapeless blue suit. "Ma'am? What seems to be the problem?" he asked.

"I heard on the morning news." The woman blew hard into an already ragged tissue. "They said a woman had been attacked in the park last night and brought here. Something told me that it might be Madison."

"What makes you think it was your friend Madison, Mrs . . . ."

"Livingston, Barbara Livingston." She saw their badges displayed on their jackets and realized what she had done. "I'm sorry. I shouldn't yell. This is a hospital, after all."

"It's all right. Doctor, do you think . . ."

Dr. McFadden nodded. "You can't go in, but you can look from the window."

She led the group toward a set of swinging doors in the middle of the hall. Dr. McFadden stepped through the door and took a chart from a nurse waiting by it. Mark and Cassie stood while Mrs. Livingston approached the door. Even standing on her tiptoes, she could barely see through the window. She strained her neck to stare inside. Inside, a few people hovered around a bed where a woman lay unconscious. One of them moved and Mrs. Livingston gasped. She brought her hand to her mouth and her tears started anew. "It's her! It's Madison!"

"It's all right, Mrs. Livingston," Mark assured her. "Please, may we have a word?"

Mark gestured to the small waiting area at the end of the hallway. Mrs. Livingston nodded. Cassie gave her an understanding smile, as she led the three of them to a table with a few chairs around them. Mrs. Livingston sat down, still clutching the ragged tissue. "Is she going to be all right?" she asked in an anxious tone.

"The doctors won't be certain for a little while," Cassie explained.

Mrs. Livingston sniffled. "When she didn't come to work, I began to wonder."

"Where do you work, Mrs. Livingston?"

"Botsworth Real Estate, at the downtown office." Mrs. Livingston reached into her bag and pulled out a battered business card. She handed it to Cassie. "She's only been working there a few months, handling some of Mr. Carnegie's more tricky files."

"Do you know if she was meeting anyone last night, like a boyfriend or a classmate?" Cassie asked."

"No. She just broke up with her boyfriend a few weeks ago, and as far as I know, she wasn't seeing anyone new."

"Did she make mention of her plans for the weekend?"

"Nothing special. She was stopping at Mr. Kim's to pick up some groceries on Friday, take her cat to the veterinarian, visit some friends, and study. She's a sophomore at the university. She has a test coming up on Wednesday, she told me." Mrs. Livingston fished inside her deep handbag for another tissue. "She never goes out after dark, especially alone. She's too smart to do that."

"You said earlier that you knew it was her. How?"

Mrs. Livingston shrugged. "She's been anxious the last few days she's worked. Our boss, Mr. Carnegie gave this file to research last week; a parcel of land in the northeastern part of the state. When the information on it came back, she looked so confused. It was as if she found something incriminating. Mr. Carnegie took it from her the instant she was done, and she wouldn't tell me what it was about."

"What was so unusual about that?"

Mrs. Livingston looked up at the officers. "A couple of days ago, Mr. Carnegie called her into his office. When she came out, she looked close to tears. Then that same day, a man came up to Madison when she was returning from lunch. I think he threatened her."

Cassie and Mark exchanged glances. "Threatened her?" Cassie pressed.

Mrs. Livingston nodded. She managed to find another tissue and dabbed at her eyes. They could see her mascara running down her face. "I don't know for certain. I know that I never saw him around before."

"Can you describe him?"

Mrs. Livingston looked at Mark. She blushed as she stared into his eyes. They reminded her of a man she had a crush on in her youth. She thought for a moment. "Not as tall as you, from what I could tell. He had greasy blonde hair. He looked up at the window, and I could see that his face was all pockmarked, like he had been ill at some point, and he had a tattoo—a red snake or something, right here," Mrs. Livingston added, pointing to her left forearm.

"Where did this confrontation you witnessed it take place?"

"On Thursday afternoon, just outside of our office. I saw it from the window. I didn't hear what he said, but it was obvious to me that it was some sort of threat." Mrs. Livingston bit her bottom lip to prevent herself from crying. "When Madison came back into the office, she was shaking."

There was a moment of silence while the detectives made their notations. "Mrs. Livingston? Do you know if Maggie knew anyone who would deal with illicit drugs or anything?" Cassie asked.

Mrs. Livingston looked at Cassie as if she came from another planet. "No, never! Why?"

Mark placed a consoling hand on hers. "Mrs. Livingston, this may be hard for you to hear, but a preliminary report shows that they found traces of ecstasy in her blood."

"No! I haven't worked with her long, but drugs are the reason she broke up with her boyfriend," she stated flatly. "She wouldn't!"

Mark sat back in his chair and glanced at Cassie. She too had raised an eyebrow. He stood up. "Stay here for a minute, Cassie," he instructed her. "I'll be back."

He walked back to the ICU doors and motioned to Dr. McFadden, who was standing inside. She handed the chart back to the intern she had been speaking with and walked back outside. "Yes, Detective?"

"Doc, could there have been a mistake made when they did the blood work on Madison?"

"It's possible. I'll have the lab run the test again, just to be certain." She glanced at her watch. "I need to go. I have more rounds to complete. If her condition changes, I'll notify you."

Dr. McFadden turned and walked down the hallway. He heard footsteps and turned as Cassie approached. "Mrs. Livingston went to contact Madison's parents.

They live in Oklahoma." She crossed her arms and tapped her pen against her lips. She tried to make out the look on her new partner's face. To her, it seemed to be one of intense concentration and doubt. "You think there's any merit to what she just told us?"

"It's hard to say." Mark stared at the doors to the ICU. He also thought back to what Mrs. Livingston had said, especially about the man who had accosted Madison. Something told him that there might be a connection. "Let's see if Mrs. Livingston can give a description of the man she saw to the sketch artists, and have her go through the mug books. Maybe we already have the guy on file."

"Anything else?"

"Yeah. Call the lieutenant and have her post a guard here. Also, we should send a uniform over to her place, just to make sure that nothing gets touched."

"Just because of what Mrs. Livingston told us? Granted Mark, I know that you're thorough, but you really don't believe her, do you? This looks like a robbery gone badly."

"No, but I'm not ready to take any chances, either." He checked the wall clock. By the time they finished their errands here and back at the station, it would be lunchtime. He considered the places where they could eat, and smiled. "Hungry?"

"Starving."

"Great! I'll treat you to lunch."

"Yes, with my fifty bucks." She grinned. "Where at? Not here, I hope."

"I know of a place, but first, I need to make a stop upstairs." He reached for his keys and tossed them to her. "No joyriding in it, okay? "I'll be back in a few."

She stuck her tongue out at him, before retrieving her cell phone and walking toward the exit. He waited until she had disappeared through the sliding doors, and then headed to the elevator. He rode it to the fourth floor. Unlike downstairs, it was more than quiet. He greeted the nurse at the duty station, who shyly smiled back. He headed for Room 413, knocked on the door, and pushed. A squat woman sat next to the only bed, reading a Charles Dickens book out loud to its occupant. She looked up as the door opened. Her eyes turned misty. "Mark," she whispered, setting the book down on a nearby table.

"Hello, Mrs. Danvers."

She walked over to him and gave him a bear hug. Her blue and silver-haired head barely reached his chest. He bent down and she reached out to pat his cheeks. Her brown eyes studied his face. She wasn't pleased with what she saw. She clicked her tongue. "You haven't been eating. You look so thin!"

"I'm fine, too."

He grasped her hands and they turned to the bed, where another woman lay. Her thin form barely made a dent on the sheets. Monitors beeped periodically, as a breathing machine slowly moved up and down. Her left arm had an IV needle taped to it. Her wavy dark hair cascaded against the pillow. She hadn't moved the whole time Mark and Mrs. Danvers greeted each other.

He stared at Mrs. Danvers. She nodded and he sat down in the chair Mrs. Danvers had just vacated. He brought the comatose woman's hand to his mouth and kissed it. "Hi, Meghan," he greeted the unconscious woman. "Sorry it's been a while. I've had other things on my mind."

IV

"How's your new home, *miandi*?"

Julie and the Caretaker made their way down the hallway leading away from the nursery toward the courtyard. Julie had talked the Caretaker into allowing her to spend the night inside it. When she awoke, she realized that he had tucked the Angela sphere she held the day prior into her arms. As she lay there, holding a member of the newest generation, a part of her began to wonder what her life would have been like had they not met. "Perhaps less stressful, but much lonelier," she concluded, as she placed the sphere back with her brood brothers and sisters. She turned back to look at the nursery doors sliding shut behind her. Julie didn't want to go. There was so much new life growing and thriving inside that room, and she wanted to be there to experience a little of it. However, other duties called. Julie sighed. "Empty, Caretaker. I need to find some furniture for it."

"I'm certain that it can be arranged. You only need to forward us the request."

"I will. I have a few more errands to take care of on Senal, and I want to go with the others to see the Amendu. Then we'll sit down and plan out my newest home."

"I meant to ask. How was Calif's wedding?"

"It was everything the way King Rigald wanted. Well, almost everything."

"He isn't pleased with Serbata?"

"Yes, but you know he wanted me to marry his son."

The Caretaker stared at the doors. "They still do not know, do they?" he finally asked.

"No, and Simon's determined they never do, not for another couple hundred years. Even so, I made a point of dropping off my rent before I went. Hopefully, Mark has it."

The Caretaker was astonished. "He didn't see you?"

"Caretaker, I've been popping in and out of places long before these so-called high-tech security measures existed. You've lived in complete isolation from them for more than 2 million years. Even if had seen me, he probably wouldn't have believed it."

"You give him too much credit. Did you not read our biography on him?"

"I did, and it was only this one time."

"So you say."

Julie turned to him as the elevator came to a stop. "You know, you're getting to be as bad as the Eldar."

"I shall take that as a compliment," he replied with a nod.

They emerged from the elevator to the main floor of the barn, and the Caretaker resumed his human form. Outside of the occasional Amendu teenager seeking to prove his bravery to a young woman, and the land speculators from a few years prior, no one had come on the land in more than 75 years. Julie's power provided the sunlight that gave them life, and off-world technology kept the planet blind to the city that existed ten miles below the Earth's surface. However, none of that could anticipate a human spotting an all-white form walking the ground above it. They headed toward her vehicle, parked near the farmhouse. "When shall you need our assistance to move in?" the Caretaker inquired.

"That's going to depend upon the Eldar." She rubbed her head. "Hopefully they won't keep fighting my decision to live here."

The Caretaker's solemn gaze left her face and went to the barn floor. "Like us, they only seek to protect you, *miandi*. They . . . worry about the repercussions your decision may cause."

"I know, Caretaker. It's not like I didn't think about that as well, but how am I going to live like a real human if I reside here on the farm away from them? How long again until the children emerge?"

"According to Alexandra's calculations, about three more Earth months."

"Will all of our contacts be back by then?"

"Yes. Jennifer should be on her maternity leave at that time. Elise will be able to order the remaining materials without arousing her suspicions. All of our contacts have been notified, and have made arrangements with their employers to be on vacation."

"Good. Remind me to get with Alexandra, and . . ."

An unexpected sound overhead caught their attention. They looked up. It wasn't unusual for planes to fly above the land, as there was a private airport just over the Canadian side of the border, but something approached them from the south, heading directly toward them. She glanced over at her vehicle, parked in the yard. It disappeared in front of them. Then she took the Caretaker's hand. He felt a flutter of warmth from her hand as she transported them back into the barn. A few seconds later, a black, unmarked helicopter flew over the open land. A man leaned out of the side door, a camera in his hands, snapping photographs at a breakneck pace. The helicopter made five circular passes over the property before it turned south and flew away. When the last of its engine had died away, they reappeared outside. A hard look crossed Julie's face. She thought of the photographer and how disappointed he would be when he found out that his prints and the data backup were destroyed. "How long has this been going on?"

"For at least six of this planet's weeks. They have come at various times, taking photographs of everything here. We have noted their appearances for you."

"Has anyone tried to physically enter the property?"

"No, *miandi*. If they try, I believe the new gate and road will keep them away."

Ambassador?

Julie stared straight ahead. "What is it, NIK?"

Antoinette has just informed me that a new query has been placed with the Okanogan County Recorder's office.

"Who placed it?"

A real estate firm in Mason City. They are looking into the ownership of this land.

"Which firm?"

All information is to be forwarded to a Terrance Carnegie at Botsworth Real Estate, in Mason City. There is something else. According to the Mason City newspaper, Botsworth Real Estate is the name of the company that employed a woman who was found beaten in the park on Sunday night. It is also referenced in a police report filed by the officers investigating the case.

"What are the names of those police officers?"

Detectives Cassie Edwards and Mark Daniels.

Julie bit her bottom lip. Mark had come in contact with Julie's other worlds sooner than she had planned. She turned to the Caretaker, and shared with him what NIK had told her. "Keep me apprised of what's happening here," she instructed him. "If anyone tries to enter, inform me immediately. Don't try to stop them on your own. Be firm, but polite. Call the sheriff if you feel the need."

"What about the human? What if he's one of them?"

"I'll have to convince him otherwise." She checked the time. "In the meantime, I must go run my next errand."

"Are you sure that is wise?"

"If I'm to truly understand what's going on, I need to do this. It should prove enlightening, and what Mark and his father doesn't know, won't hurt them."

*   *   *

Robert Daniels looked forward to his next appointment. A few days ago, the director of a San Francisco-based company had called. They were looking for a firm in Seattle to handle some securities issues, and his firm was on the short list. They were conducting their evaluations, and wanted to stop by to talk to him and his firm personally. He rescheduled a meeting with one of his best clients, canceled a luncheon appointment with the mayor, and made sure that his best paralegals pulled all the information they could on how best to sway this important and incredibly wealthy client. He expected an entourage of people. When Mary announced that only one person had come, he was perturbed. He walked out to greet the tall, black woman dressed in the black-pinstripe designer suit ready to dismiss her, until she introduced herself as Julie Warren, the daughter of the CEO. She was the last person he had expected to come. He recalled the research on the family members who had founded the corporation. On her biography, she listed herself as a consultant. "I really don't have much to do with the day-to-day operations," she explained. "I really hate being cooped up in an office all day. However, my guardian apologizes for not being able to come himself, and he insisted that I go in his stead."

"Why?" Robert asked, hoping that his non-presence did not mean the worst for his firm, or the chance of landing such a lucrative contract.

"He broke his leg while skiing in the Alps a few months ago, during our annual outing for our European offices. He's not recovering as well as the doctors were expecting."

Robert had read the biography on Simon Birmingham III, twelfth lord of Calles-Saffire, and president and CEO of a multi-billion dollar non-profit group called the Foundation. "Skiing? I thought he was in his mid-sixties. He sounds like a pretty daring man to be skiing at his age."

"He doesn't, actually. He was standing too close to one of the trails and one our Stockholm employees accidentally ran into him."

After chatting for a few minutes, Robert had a senior associate and one of the junior partners accompany Julie for a tour of their offices. She walked every floor, and talked to nearly everyone there, including the security guards, the janitors, the court runners, the copier repairman, the water delivery person, and even the office supply deliverer, who seemed baffled when Julie quizzed her about how often he came here, and the type of supplies ordered. Afterward, she joined the senior partners for lunch at the Space Needle restaurant. However, she spent more time enjoying the view than on the conversation. After lunch, Robert ushered Julie back to his office. Julie sat in the same chair Mark sat in just a few days prior. She took in the view from Robert's expansive windows. The clouds were a combination of cotton-candy puffs and paper-thin layers, allowing them a chance to see the rare blue sky and sunshine. She waited patiently while Robert settled behind his desk and leaned back in his chair. "I'm glad to be speaking with you today, Ms. Warren, although I am a little perplexed," he admitted.

"How is that, sir?"

"I'm certain that your guardian meant well, I'm surprised he would only send you to conduct such an important evaluation. When a corporation is planning a move like yours, they tend to bring in the heavy hitters."

"The heavy hitters?"

Robert blinked slowly, his green eyes meeting her gaze. "I usually speak with the attorneys, the accountants, and at least one board member. It's not that I'm complaining. I'm just used to dealing with more people, that's all."

"I assure you, that my report to the board will be most thorough. Our company has studied many qualified firms. The fact that I'm even here shows that we've given your firm a very good look and so far, you've met our requirements. However, it's the personal inspection that we base most of our decision upon."

He leaned forward, staring intently. "Pardon me from prying, but you are an Oxford graduate, correct?"

"Yes. I also have my MBA, and I'm a licensed attorney."

"Yet you seem awfully green. For someone raised within the business, your reactions today were more of a ten year old entering the big city for the first time, rather than a seasoned business woman."

"Oh, that's me normally. For me, everything is new, so there's always surprise, not disappointment at the end of the day."

"As you wish. I read the newsletters that you sent us," he commented. "I understand that the board plans to elect a new CEO. If we're offered the job, when will I meet him or her?"

Julie smiled. "In time."

"That doesn't sound promising."

"The election just took place and the ballots were still sealed until this morning. I'm expecting a phone call from the board anytime, directing me back to San Francisco to meet with them, so I apologize in advance if I'm rude when I take the call."

Robert picked up his letter opener and began twirling it in his hand in a manner similar to what he did when Mark was there. "Doesn't your guardian want you to take his position?"

"He does. However, I'm not one for paperwork. I enjoy traveling too much. I know it seems odd that there isn't an entourage of people with me, but over the years, my guardian has discovered that too many observers muddy the waters."

"So he sent you?"

"He wants me to become more involved and he figures that this is a good way to do it. I think it's his way of telling me that he wants to make sure that the family business stays within the family."

"He's preparing you to take over someday. After all, you're his only child."

"That's true sir. However, I'm adopted."

"Nevertheless, you are his family." Robert laid the letter opener back down on his desk, leaned back in his chair again, and began rocking it back and forth. "If I'm not intruding, what happened to your parents? How did you come to be with Lord Birmingham?"

"My parents died in some sort of accident when I was an infant. My father worked for him at the time. He heard about the accident, learned that I had no living relatives to care for me, and took me in."

"But with all the responsibilities he had, you must not have seen each other much, so who raised you?"

"He did mostly. There were a few others, nannies and such. They've all formed a part of the whole that is my life, and I treasure everything they have taught me, and pass it on to those that I love and care for." She straightened. "Now, about your 'whole,' sir."

"I beg your pardon?"

She gestured to his left hand. "Are you married?"

Robert looked down. Like Mark, he still wore his wedding band, even though it had been nearly thirty years since his wife had passed. "Widowed."

"Do you have any children?"

"A son. He lives in Mason City." He paused. "Our lives don't give us much opportunity to see each other."

Julie glanced around his office, taking note of the many pictures that stood on his bookshelves. Most of them were of prominent business and political leaders from the state and across the country. NIK informed her of such as she stared at the photos. "Do you have any photos of him or his family?"

He smiled wanly. "I have a few. I keep them at home. I don't like to mix my work life with my home life."

"Oh."

His eyes narrowed. "You seem disappointed."

Julie looked at him. "I am, sir."

He squinted at her and scratched at a spot behind his head. "I'm sorry?"

She smiled at his confused expression. "Although this is a preliminary search Mr. Daniels, much of our decision is determined at this time," she explained. "As you are well aware, a company is more than just its production and business statistics. Information is fabricated and figures altered so that they do not reveal the entire truth. That's why our company's personal observations are given the most weight."

"Oh? How so?"

"The evaluator observes and carefully notes how everyone in the workplace is treated, from the men and women who empty the trash cans, to the people who make the ultimate decisions. We speak to and listen to everyone. It's why I spent so much of my time talking to as many people as I could, and not as much on the work that you do. You are aware of our slogan?"

Robert quickly glanced at the notes to his left. He had read it, but he didn't get it. "Your point, Miss Warren?"

"You must understand that if we are to build a stronger universe, we must recognize that each of us is part of that greater whole. How that 'whole' develops depends on how we treat each other. How we treat each other is determined by how our loved ones treat us, and how we treat those we love, work with, and do business with."

Robert's face took on a steely gaze, and his green eyes flashed. "And the fact that I have no photographs of my family tells you that I don't care about my family, or the people under my employment?" he challenged her.

"No, but it makes me wonder what you're trying to hide."

Robert stood, fighting to contain his anger. "Are you trying to tell me that I'm not a good provider, Miss Warren?"

"No, sir, I'm not. I'm just curious as to why he's not among the men and women in the photos here?" She gestured to the bookcase full of pictures. "I wonder why he and his family are not considered a part of the 'whole' you've established for your life? I'm asking why, to my eyes, you've shut out the person who is, and has always been, the most important to you?"

Robert Daniels was incensed. How dare this child come here and tell him how he should treat his family! Who was she to be ordering him about! She was less than half his age, and came from a privileged life. She had no idea the sacrifices that he had made to make his son's life better than it ever could have been, only to watch him throw it away to become a cop, and marry an artist, of all things. "Is there anything else that you wish to criticize about me or my firm, Miss Warren?" he asked through clenched teeth.

A phone rang. They looked at his desk phone. The phone rang again, and they both realized that it was her phone ringing. She pulled it out and studied the number it displayed. She gave him an apologetic smile. "Excuse me, sir. I really need to take this. It's my office calling."

She made her way to the corner of the office, and placed the phone to her ear. "Yes?" After a few moments, she turned to look at him, who still seethed with barely contained rage. He couldn't read the expression on her face, but the sooner she left, the better he would feel about it. She nodded. "Thanks, Jennifer. I'm almost done here. Tell them I'll be there within a few hours." She hung up the phone. "I apologize, but I have to go, Mr. Daniels," she said to him. "Some of the board members want to meet with the new CEO, and they want me to give them my report on your company when they do."

He crossed his arms and gave her his most intense gaze, the one he reserved for the courtroom and his most uncooperative witnesses. "And when you do, I'd suggest that you tell them to take our company out of the running. I also plan on writing a letter to your guardian, as well as the new CEO, to let them know how unprofessional their representative was."

Julie stowed her phone back into her purse and retrieved her briefcase. She didn't seem bothered by what Robert had said. She walked to the door and reached for the shiny brass doorknob. "You can if you want, sir. I certainly won't mind. My guardian's well aware of my philosophy. After all, he shares it, and as for your letter? I doubt that the new CEO will read it."

"How can you be so certain?"

"You've already talked to her."

She walked through the door and closed it behind her before Robert realized what she had said. He racked his brain, and then reached for the research that his paralegals had provided. He remembered what Julie had told him about the elections. The ballots were still sealed. That had been total bull. She was the daughter of the CEO, and he was willing to bet that she had been the CEO when she walked into the building. What she said about controlling information worked both ways. Her office supplied the information in the first place! Who better to evaluate a company, negotiate a multi-million dollar transaction, or get two sides to come to an accord, than to send someone who gave off the impression that she couldn't do any of those things? He dropped the paralegal's research and bolted out of his office. Mary gave him a quizzical look as he rushed past her, through the glass door, and the elevator lobby. Julie stood in front of the elevator banks, her briefcase clutched in front of her, staring at the indicators, rocking gently back and forth. "Miss Warren!"

Julie turned to face him just as the elevator arrived. He ran up to her, panting. "About what I said in there," he began.

"There's no need to apologize, Mr. Daniels. I understood perfectly." Julie stepped inside the waiting elevator. She reached over to press the down button. Then she turned her gaze back toward him. Her brown eyes stared him down, her face stoic. "I'll inform them of your request, and give my recommendations to the board. You'll have our decision within a few weeks. Have a good day."

The elevator doors closed before he could utter another word. He pressed his hands against them, trying to will the elevator back to his floor. Then he took a step back, and sighed in frustration. He trudged back toward his office, his head down. She wouldn't be back, and he knew it. That account was gone. She didn't just beat him at his own game. She trounced him.

Julie rode the elevator down to the ground floor. She so much wanted to tell someone about what she had done, especially Mark, but she knew that she couldn't. She waved good-bye to the security clerks and headed toward her vehicle. She climbed behind the wheel, placed her briefcase on the passenger seat, and snapped on her seat belt. As she reached over to insert the key in the ignition, NIK spoke: *Ambassador?*

"Yes, NIK?"

Did you find what you were looking for?

Her expression grew thoughtful, as she analyzed everything she had learned about Mark's father, not only from her handshake, but also from the conversation in his office. She reached for the gear shift. "Yes, NIK. I understand now what I felt from Mark when I touched him, and I understand some of Jessie's frustration as well. No wonder she couldn't get them to reconcile."

She placed her hand on the gearshift, and moved it into position. As she did so, NIK spoke again: *Ambassador?*

Julie sighed. "Yes, NIK?"

Your . . . what is the human term that I have discovered . . . 'put down' of Mr. Daniels.

Julie waited for NIK to continue. "Yes?"

May I conclude that you enjoyed that?

Julie settled back into her seat. A surge of pride and satisfaction swelled inside of her. "Yes, NIK. I did."

V

Louie's Delicatessen was a small, always occupied sandwich shop on Fuller Street. It was nowhere near the precinct, yet everyone who worked within the building knew of it, as did anyone who liked a damned good corned beef sandwich. It wasn't unusual for Mark to see some of his fellow law enforcement officers there during lunchtime. More than once, Mark solved more than their share of cases while munching on one of Louie's world-class dill pickles.

Mark found an empty parking space across the street and he and Cassie dashed across the busy thoroughfare. Mark held the door open and ushered Cassie into the vibrant red-and-white-checkerboard restaurant. She inhaled the sharp smell of kosher salt and fresh-baked bread. Rows of meat hung above the shiny white serving counter. Couples and trios of business people occupied a few of the table while a biker, his bright yellow helmet on the chair across from him, sat in a corner munching on a Reuben. The look on his face was one of a man who had died and gone to deli heaven.

As Mark and Cassie approached the counter, Louie the owner came out from the back kitchen. He had on a yellow-stained white T-shirt and apron over black pants and his large belly protruded out from in front of him. His handlebar moustache was peppered with gray, unlike his hair, which was still thick and black. He beamed at Mark, his black eyes alight with happiness, and he patted his belly. Cassie waited for him to let loose a big belly laugh. *Rosy cheeks and all*, Cassie thought. *All you need to do is dress him in a red suit and a white beard, and he was a dead ringer for Santa Claus. Something tells me he does just that at Christmastime, too.*

"Mark!" Louis exclaimed, his voice echoing through the half-full deli. "*Bon journo*! Where've you been?"

"Resting, like you told me to. How's business?"

"Business is business. How's Charlie?"

"Fine. Still recovering, but fine."

Louie turned to look at Cassie. Cassie swore his cheeks turned even rosier. "Ah! A new face, I see."

"Louie, this is Detective Cassie Edwards, my new partner. Cassie, Louie Brubaker, deli man extraordinaire."

Louie gave Cassie an exaggerated bow. "A pleasure, madam, and since the detective only dines here when he has succeeded at something, I take it that you were on the losing end of a very lopsided contest."

He winked at Mark, who shrugged in reply. Cassie's ears burned red hot. "What did you do, call ahead or something?"

"Not me, I assure you." He turned back to Louie. "My usual, Louie, and whatever Cassie here is having."

"Roast beef on Jewish rye, horseradish, lettuce, tomato, three pickles, bottled water, coming up," Louie rattled off. "And for you, Madame Edwards?"

"Turkey on wheat, light on the mayo, extra pickles, and a diet pop."

Louie prepared their meals and brought them out to their table, complete with two bags of potato chips. Mark went to pay him but Louie refused it. "On the house, today, Mark." He slapped him hard on the back and Mark winced. Louie's eyes turned misty for a moment. "It's good to see you back, Detective," he told him.

"Thanks, Louie."

They waited for Louie to go back behind the counter before picking up their sandwiches. After one bite, Cassie had to admit that it was the best sandwich she had ever eaten. She pretended to study the décor of the place, wondering how best to broach the subject she wanted to discuss. Finally, she decided that the best way was to be up front. "So?" she said, her mouth full of turkey, "are you going to tell me?"

"Tell you what?"

"Why you were gone for so long." Cassie picked up a potato chip. Her eyes met his and she flung her ponytail off her shoulder. "What have you been doing all of this time?"

Mark felt a stinging sensation on his upper lip. He reached for a napkin to wipe away the horseradish sauce. "I thought you knew."

"I know what I've heard. I want to hear it from you."

"What do you want to hear?"

She took a sip of her drink. "First off, what happened to Charlie? How did he get shot?"

Mark set down his sandwich. At first he didn't speak. Cassie waited. "Jessie, my wife, had been dead a little more than a month," he finally said. "It was my third day back on the job. We had chased this murder suspect into a warehouse. Somehow in the darkness, we became separated. I turned down a hallway, and heard a shot. Then Charlie screamed my name. When I made it back to him, he was lying there, bleeding." Mark felt a lump rise in his throat. "He barely made it to the hospital."

"Did you find the guy who did it?"

"The next day, dead of a self-inflicted gunshot wound."

"Where's Charlie now?"

"He lives in Arizona now, with his wife and kids." Mark picked up water bottle and took a drink. "Happily retired, I might add."

"That's good to hear." Cassie picked up the second half of her sandwich. "So, what happened afterward?"

"Afterward?"

"With Nelson Chambers? The child rape suspect you almost killed?"

Mark went quiet. Sometimes in his dreams, he could still Nelson's eyes staring up at him, his young face pale and sweaty, pleading for his life, while the muzzle of Mark's gun pressed against his forehead. "What about it?"

"What stopped you?"

Mark shrugged. "Tyler, for one thing."

"No, it was more than that. At least, that's what I think."

Mark laid down the remainder of his sandwich and clasped his hands, resting his chin on them. He wasn't certain what had stopped him. During his break, Tyler came to stay with him for a few weeks. Tyler admitted to Mark he had been suspicious of Mark's odd behavior during this case, and out of concern, followed Mark to the suspect's house. He found Mark, ready to kill the man, his eyes filled with the obsessed look he got whenever he thought about the Meghan Danvers' case. He remembered the coolness of Tyler's shaking hand coming over his, and turning his gun away. He also remembered hearing Jessie's voice in her head and seeing the look of disappointment on her face. "I think Jessie stopped me," Mark answered. "I thought I heard her talking to me as I readied myself to blow this guy's face off, and not caring about what happened to me. She told me to come home to rest, and grieve. That's what I did. End of story. So, now that I've told you my life story, let's hear yours."

"Mine?"

He stared her down. Cassie tried not to become too entranced. It was as if he had her in the interrogation room, and he wasn't going to let her leave until he heard what he wanted to hear. Now she understood why he was so good at getting information from even the most reluctant of people. The men probably felt intimidated by his stare; the females fell in love. "What about you?" he asked. "You told me on the way here that you moved here from Seattle. Why pull up stakes?"

Cassie picked up her pickle spear. "My fiancé. He didn't like me being a cop, and I decided that I needed a change. I felt stymied in Seattle. There was little opportunity there for growth." She caught the questioning look on Mark's face. "Don't get me wrong. I was born and raised there. My parents still live there and my brother lives an hour outside the city. I love the town, but I needed to come out and see what life was like outside the big city, and find out who and what I am. He wasn't ready for such a big change."

She bit into her pickle. Her eyes opened wide with delight. He relished the look of surprise on his face. "Oh my God! These are really good!"

Mark smiled. "Louie's specialty. He makes them himself. He takes a month off every summer to make enough to last him at least a year, if he's lucky."

"These are better than any pickle I've ever had!" She devoured the first one and started in on the second. "He should market these!" she managed to say between bites. "He'd make a fortune!"

"Nah. He likes it here. He's happy." Mark toyed with a spear. It suddenly dawned on him that Louie's pickles were the last thing that Jessie had requested. Mark had gone to get them. When he returned, walked into the room, and held up the jar, she gave him a weak smile and whispered, "You're so good to me." Then she fell unconscious. Two days later, she died. She never got to eat them. The jar still sat in his refrigerator, unopened.

Mark pushed the rest of his lunch away. He cursed himself. He had to get a grip on things and on himself. He was back at work now. He had a case to work and a new partner to bring up to speed. Crying over uneaten pickles was not what he should be doing.

He sat back in his chair, forcing his thoughts back to what Cassie told him about herself. Instinct told him that what Cassie said didn't quite ring true. When he got back to the precinct, he intended to do a little research on his new partner. In the meantime, work called. "Enough about us. We should be talking about the case." He gave Cassie a thoughtful stare. "So partner, what do you see?"

Cassie reached for his uneaten spears and tilted her head. "Pardon?"

"It's a thing that Charlie used to do at the beginning of an investigation. We'd sit down and think about what we've learned so far, and theorize. Then we would go gather more information, sit down and theorize again." Mark gave her a mischievous smile. "So I'm asking you . . . what do you see?"

Cassie shrugged. Everyone had his or her way. At least Mark was giving her the opportunity to contribute. Her former partner never did. *She has the brains, but not the courage to stomach it*, he told her last boss in front of the squad. *If she doesn't toughen up, she'll never make it*. Those words sat in her file and rang in her head every night as she laid awake, staring at the ceiling. With Mark, she thought she saw an opportunity to finally prove herself. She wasn't going to waste it. She too, sat back in her char. Her brow furrowed, as she recalled everything she had heard, read, and saw so far. "We have a college student that's been beaten and left for dead in the park," she answered. "And, we have someone who allegedly threatened her." She looked at him. "Why? What do you see?"

Mark picked up the last spear and bit into it. "Same thing, except why this woman? What makes her so special?"

"Maybe she was in the wrong place at the wrong time. I still think this is a robbery gone wrong."

Mark crumpled up his used napkin and stared out at the street. "It could be."

"They did find drugs in her system. Maybe she isn't the angel that Mrs. Livingston wants to believe she is. Maybe she went partying that weekend and got a little more than she bargained for."

"What about the boyfriend? Mrs. Livingston said they broke up because of drugs. Was it his use of them or hers? We need to find him, and get his side of the story."

Cassie wiped her hands. "Okay. So where do you want to go from here?"

He glanced up at the clock. It was closing in on noon. Already, three marked cars had pulled up outside, and the few parking spots that were empty when they arrived were filled. Louie was going to have another busy day. "We check in with the lieutenant, and let her know what we've got so far. Then we reread the incident report, talk to the man and woman who found her, and go the scene of the attack. Then we'll go over to her place. If there's time, let's try to track down her boss and talk to him."

"And then?"

Mark stood. More of the lunch crowd was filtering in. If they didn't leave now, they would never get out of here. "We go from there."

They waved goodbye to Louie over the increasing masses and wiggled out the door, heading for his truck. As they reached it, Mark grabbed her arm. "One more thing—what was today about?"

"Today?"

"At the range? Your little stunt today?"

Cassie blushed. She had gone to the range to get rid of some of her anxiety, not just with meeting her new partner, but also her childhood phobia. "I heard you were good," she admitted. "After all, your marksmanship is known by police forces throughout the state. I heard that S.W.A.T. teams throughout the region have been trying to recruit you for years."

"Yes, they have." Mark enjoyed seeing the color flowing into her face. He thought she had planned her little rendezvous with him, but apparently, she hadn't. "So why the challenge?"

Cassie shrugged. "I wanted to see for myself. Honestly, I didn't expect you to show up there my first day on the job, but when I recognized you from the photos, I just couldn't pass up the opportunity."

"And now that you've seen?"

Her eyes met his. "I plan on winning my money back, sir," she told him in a serious tone.

Mark smiled. *Keep better control of your support arm and you might have a shot.*

* * *

Madison Evans' apartment was about five blocks from the university, where she attended class part time. Madison lived in an area not known for crime, and the news of her assault made more than a few people nervous. The uniformed officer watching her door informed the detectives that no one tried to enter her apartment. However, Mark and Cassie's search yielded little. Mark was slightly disappointed. He had hoped that she had left a journal behind, but Madison wasn't the type who wrote down her problems or feelings. The detectives had Madison's computer taken back to the tech room to see if anything pertinent came up on it. While searching her desk, Cassie found an address book and some correspondence from her former boyfriend. They also found his phone number. When she called it, his roommate told her that he had gone home to Sea Tac Saturday night, and hadn't returned to campus yet. They left instructions for him to call them the moment he returned. The two detectives visited the attack site, but knew that they would find little. It had rained the night of her attack, making evidence gathering difficult. They also interviewed the man and woman who had found Madison while jogging earlier that morning, and talked to them about what they saw. Finally, they spoke to her boss, Terrance Carnegie, and made an appointment to speak with him the following morning.

It was well past six in the evening before Mark dropped Cassie back off at the precinct to retrieve her car. He was exhausted after his first day back on the job, but as soon as the door shut behind Cassie, his thoughts turned to making the drive to the home he no longer owned. On the way, he stopped at the market to pick up some groceries and the evening paper. While he waited to check out, he perused the real estate section, especially the portion that dealt with sheriff's sales. There was no listing for his house, which pleased and puzzled him. Judge Embry had told him that he had signed it. Mr. Smith had told him that they would be publishing the notice today. Perhaps it had just been a scare tactic to get Mark to pay up, but why not follow up on it?

Finally, he headed home, taking the tree-lined backstreets as opposed to the highway. He slowed his approach as he recognized more and more of the streets, and the houses on them. Tears came to his eyes. Why was he bothering? Tyler had offered his place to Mark as a temporary sanctuary while he was in Los Angeles. Why wasn't he heading there? *Because Jessie's not at Tyler's. She's* there. *The woman I loved and everything about her is there. I won't leave her behind and no one's going to make me.*

He let loose a heavy sigh and turned onto his street. He pulled into the driveway without glancing at the front door. He made to climb out and spotted something in his rearview mirror. Ruth Johnson, his neighbor who lived in the yellow house across the street was just walking by the end of it, her black and white Pekingese dog, Nipper, in her arms. He knew that he should talk to her, but really didn't want to. She probably watched them put the eviction notice on his door. He put on a brave face and exited the truck. "Hello, Mrs. Johnson!" he called.

She turned at the sound of his voice. Her wrinkled face broke out into a wide smile. "Mark! You're back at work!"

"Yes."

He walked up to her, pushed the thinning salt-and-pepper hair out of her face, and gave her a peck on the cheek. He was certain that she blushed. "How are you?" she asked, reaching up a spotted hand to pat his, her faded blue eyes scrutinizing him in the approaching sunset.

"I'm fine, Mrs. Johnson." He rubbed Nipper's head and received an affectionate lick in return. "How are you?"

"My arthritis is acting up a bit, but I'm still moving." She nodded to the dark windows above the garage. "I see the sign's gone from Jessie's studio. Did you finally find someone to rent it to?"

"Yes. Unfortunately, she can't move in for a few days."

Mrs. Johnson's eyes lit up. "The young black woman who was waiting on your porch the other day?"

"Yes."

Mrs. Johnson's smile grew broader. "Such a lovely girl. While she was waiting for you, she stopped over to say hello to me. She admired my tulips."

They turned to look across the street at Mrs. Johnson's immaculate yard, already filled with a variety of spring flowers that her daughter and granddaughters had planted. He turned to look back at his yard. Jessie had been the gardener. Along the porch, he could see stems beginning to emerge. He probably was going to have to hire someone to maintain the yard, and plant flowers in it this summer; that is, if he could find a way to save it. He brought his attention back to Mrs. Johnson. "Did you have a chance to talk?"

"A little. She was afraid that she might like it, only to realize that she wouldn't be able to spend much time in it."

"She mentioned that she traveled a lot."

"Yes. It's such a shame. She's so young to be working as hard as she does." She looked down at the mass of black-and-white fur in her arms. "Nipper wasn't too keen on her at first, but he seemed to warm up to her. For a while there, she couldn't keep him out of her lap. It was surprising. Nipper doesn't usually take to strangers so quickly."

"Maybe he sensed her warm heart."

"True." Mrs. Johnson's expression grew distant. "Although it was odd."

"What was odd, Mrs. Johnson?"

"I offered her some tea. When I came back with the tray, I caught her staring at your wife's painting, the one she did of me and Edward. She seemed fascinated by it. Then she said the strangest thing, but I don't think she even realized it."

"Oh? What did she say?"

"She said that Edward told her to tell me that he loved me very much, and that Edward broke the plate that my great-grandmother brought back from China when she was fifteen." She chuckled. "For years, I blamed my youngest son, Robert. He used to love to touch it."

"What was so odd about that?"

"I never mentioned my husband's name to her, and that incident? It happened almost fifty years ago." She blinked the tears away. "Odd, isn't it? How could she have known?"

Mark frowned. It was odd. How would Julie know about an innocuous event that took place in Mrs. Johnson's life half a century ago? Julie hadn't even been born yet and neither had her parents for that matter. Mrs. Johnson shook the thought from her head and patted him on his arm. "I should let you be. You're probably exhausted after your first day back."

"I'm fine, Mrs. Johnson." He gave her a kiss on her forehead. "If you need something, please let me know."

"I will. Thank you."

He waited to make sure that she had made it up the stairs of her porch and into her front door, before grabbing the shopping bag and newspaper. Steeling himself, he turned to enter his home. He looked at the front door, expecting to see more paper taped to it. There was nothing there. He walked up to it and checked all around and inside the doorframe. He made to unlock the front door. His key still worked. Stunned, he took a tentative step inside. Everything was where it belonged. He scratched his head. He had been there once when the sheriff's deputy served a couple with eviction papers, as he and Charlie were arriving to arrest their daughter. This isn't how it's supposed to be.

He hung up his keys just inside the front doorway and walked into his office. He stripped off his holster and moved Jessie's painting, gently caressing the frame. He punched in the safe's combination and placed his gun, badge and holster inside, closed it, and replaced the painting. As he left the office, he glanced over at the desk. The folder where he placed the lease lay on the desk. He went to pick it up, and accidentally knocked it off the desk. Julie's check and note fell out. He picked up the check, making sure he had read the amount on it right. Then he reread her note. It hadn't dawned on him to ask the woman who had answered the phone at Julie's workplace where Julie had gone. Then again, it really wasn't any of his business.

He went to the kitchen, made himself a grilled cheese sandwich, and poured himself a glass of flavored water. He ate without really tasting anything. "What happened to my eviction notice?" he mumbled. "Surely Mr. Smith hadn't forgotten to file the sheriff's deed. Something must've happened to change his mind. Had the judge talked to him and asked him to delay it for a day or two? Could he do that?" Mark shook his head. Tomorrow, he'd check with the county recorder's office and find out what had happened. It was only a couple of floors up from his precinct.

The next morning dawned gray and overcast. Madison Evans' case competed with his thoughts about the phantom eviction while he pummeled the punching bags hanging in the basement. While he dressed, he checked with the hospital to see how she was doing. She had made it through the night, Dr. McFadden told him. It was a good sign, but she was still unconscious. He called Cassie next. She was already at the precinct. *Eager to please*, he thought again, a smile touching his lips. He suggested going to Madison's workplace to talk to her boss and the rest of the staff first thing. "Sure," she replied, "as soon as I get our reports typed in the computer, seeing as you didn't do it, like you promised."

Mark cringed. He didn't mind filing reports, but computers weren't his thing and in the wake of the district attorney's office insistence on having computerized reports, he was one of the few remaining die-hards who used the paper ones. Charlie had taken to the machine like a duck to water. He used to type up their incident reports, and still kidded with Mark that he needed to learn how to use e-mail. "Makes things go much faster," Charlie told him.

He arrived at the complex early and parked in his usual spot. Instead of heading to the precinct, he went up to the fifteenth floor to the Recorder's office. He walked through the double doors, and looked around for an unoccupied clerk. At one window, a lady stood there, asking the clerk to spell some words for her, while she completed a deed to add her daughter to title. At another, a man in a tan trench coat angrily shook a handful of papers at a baffled clerk. Way at the end, he saw a familiar curly-haired topped face, tapping away at her keyboard. He walked up to her window. "Hey, Sandy," Mark greeted her.

Her hazel eyes lit up when she saw who had addressed her. "Mark!" Sandy reached out to hug Mark over the large counter. He felt the genuine warmth in it. "What brings you up to deed land?"

"Personal business. I'm here to check to see if a judicial foreclosure has been filed."

"Sure. What's the name?"

Mark tried to smile. "Daniels, Mark and Jessica."

Sandy gulped. "Oh. Well then, let's see."

Sandy tucked some stray hair behind her ears, adjusted her glasses, and clicked on a few keys. The display came up on her computer, and the smile returned to her face. "Nope."

"No?"

"No other recordings against your or your property since you last refinanced it. I've run every possible spelling." She pivoted her monitor around so that Mark could see. "Look for yourself."

Mark stared at the screen. Sure enough, there was nothing new. He took a step back from the counter. "How soon after a judicial foreclosure is filed before you get notice of it?" he asked aloud.

"It's usually that day. They don't waste time with those." She stared at the screen, and then at Mark. "When was it supposed to be filed?"

"Yesterday, from what the bank told me."

Sandy shrugged. "Then you should've had something on your door when you got home last night. You might want to check with the bank. They may have dropped the ball."

"Thanks." He straightened. "And if you could . . ."

Sandy pressed a finger to her lips. "I don't know anything."

Just before 9:00 a.m., he met Cassie down at the precinct door. He noticed that she avoided looking out the window as they made their way to the elevator, even though he had commented that the sun had pushed through the cloud cover, giving the illusion that it was going to be a beautiful day. They traveled down Main Street toward Botsworth Real Estate's downtown office, where Madison Evans worked. Their route took them by Mark's bank. Mark hesitated, and then swung his car into a parking spot in front of it. "What's going on?" Cassie asked, as Mark reached for the glove compartment, and pulled out an envelope.

"I have a quick errand to run in here. Care to come in?"

"No. I need some coffee." She pointed at the coffee shop next door. "Want a cup?"

"Sure. Regular, black, with two sugars."

"What? Not a latté man?"

Mark smiled and handed her a five-dollar bill. "No."

Mark walked into the bank and greeted Mr. Smith's secretary again. "Is Mr. Smith in?"

"Yes, sir."

She paged Mr. Smith, who came out of his office. "Mr. Daniels! What can I do for you?"

"I wanted to give you this." Mark pulled the cashier's check out of his breast pocket, and looked around Mr. Smith's desk for a pen. "I know that it won't cover all the money that's due, but I was hoping it would keep the foreclosure proceedings at bay until I can get situated."

"That won't be necessary, Mark. It's all been taken care of."

Mark stopped signing and looked at him, puzzled. "I beg your pardon?"

"Your mortgage? It's paid in full."

"What?"

Now it was Mr. Smith's turn to be surprised. "You didn't know? The wire came in before noon on Friday."

"Friday?"

"Yes. The authorization for the transfer came from you."

Mr. Smith led Mark into his office. He walked to his desk and extracted Mark's file out from the bottom of the pile. He opened it up, pulled out a sheet of paper, and handed it to Mark. Mark took it with shaky hands. He stared at the gibberish of numbers and letters. Sure enough, a wire had come into the bank for the full amount due. "I thought you said you had no one who could help you," Mr. Smith said.

"I didn't," Mark whispered, staring hard at the paper. He was afraid to blink, certain that if he did so, he would open his eyes, and realize it was some sort of bad dream. However, the sheet of paper still showed the balance was zero, and his name showed as the authority. Could his dad have actually been a decent human being for once in his life? Or perhaps Judge Embry just went ahead and paid it? He looked up from his reading. "Do you know where it came from?"

"The wire originated from a bank in San Francisco, I believe." Mr. Smith looked at him thoughtfully. "You're sure you didn't know about this?"

"No."

"Well apparently, you have someone out there who cares about you, or they had the wrong account number, although if that were the case, we would've heard something by now."

"Yeah." *The wire originated in San Francisco. Dad's firm has an office in San Francisco. What about Judge Embry? Did he have an account there?* He handed the paper back to Mr. Smith. "What does this mean for me?" he asked, not certain if he wanted to hear the answer.

"It means that we won't be bothering you for payments." Mr. Smith's face broke out into a wide smile. "Congratulations Mark. I'm happy for you."

"Yes . . . thanks." Mark pointed to the paper. "Can I get a copy of that?"

"Sure. I'll go make you one."

Mr. Smith left the office and returned in a few minutes with Mark's copy. Mark folded it and placed it and the cashier's check into his wallet, shook Mr. Smith's hand, and somehow, found his way out of the bank. Cassie was there waiting, leaning against the front of the truck, holding two cups of coffee. She went to hand one to him, and noted the blank look on his face. A look of concern crossed hers. "You okay?"

Mark's didn't answer. He paused, his hand on the door handle. Who paid off his mortgage? He thought about his father again, but immediately dismissed it. His father wouldn't have done it, not without it carrying some major price tag, and reminding him about it every hour of every day. It also couldn't have been Judge Embry. He had never said "yes" to the man. There were too many other repercussions to taking up that offer, and Mark didn't want anything to do with them. Then again, Julie's company had an office there. Did she do it? If she had, then why? Even more important, how did Julie figure it out? Granted, he had made a casual comment regarding the note. What else did she know about him? Was it more than coincidence that brought her to his doorstep?

"Mark?"

Cassie nudged his arm, and he started. He looked at her, realizing where he was. "Yeah," he replied. "Give me a minute, will you?"

She watched as he reached into his jeans pocket and retrieved Julie's business card from his wallet. Something told him to take it with him today. He flipped it over and fished his cell phone from his belt clip. He dialed the number written on the back. Julie's voice answered immediately, an obvious recording: "Hi, this is Julie. Leave a message at the tone, and I'll get back to you."

The phone beeped, but Mark didn't speak. What was he going to say? *Hi, thanks for paying my mortgage off. I'm forever in your debt.* That sounded stupid, even to him. Besides, he didn't even know for sure if she had paid it off, and he couldn't jump to conclusions. He pocketed his phone and the card. "Where are we off to?" he asked, walking back to the truck.

Cassie regarded him. "To Madison's workplace, remember?"

"Yeah. Right."

He took the cup she offered and sipped. The mystery of the paid-off note would have to wait. Work was calling. Cassie frowned at him. "You sure you're up to this?"

He opened his door. "Yeah. Let's go."

VI

Outside of the wooden-log meetinghouse of the Amendu tribe, Kinshan Waterwalker grunted and adjusted the legs of his jeans. The feel of them against his skin did not change. It was if someone had shrunk them a size, and they were cutting into him in all the wrong spots. He rose from his stiff-backed chair, carefully leaned his rifle against the building, and reached his long arms toward the porch roof, hoping to stretch them back into position. He stared upward at his deep red fingers. If he stood on his toes, his middle fingers could graze the roof of the porch above him.

He heard a giggle and turned sharply. Two teenage Amendu women were walking past the porch, their brown eyes fixed on him in a look that was half admiration, half temptation. If things were not so grim, he would have enjoyed the attention. He glared at them through the long bangs that covered his eyes. They dropped their gaze and quickened their pace away from the structure. Smiling, he lowered his arms, pushed his black braided hair out of the way, and rubbed at a spot just behind his left shoulder blade. As he did so, he caught a glimpse at his watch. He frowned and squinted at the gray sky above, trying to make the hand position on the dial work with that of the disguised sun. It had been some time since he had moved from his post, but he had no intent on abandoning it. The leader of his tribe was inside, meditating. No one would disturb him. No one dared to try while Kinshan was on watch.

The sound of a car's tires on the sand-colored gravel greeted his ears. He turned toward the street. A look of contempt came to his face. "Them again," he muttered. The vehicle's design was different. It was the more common form of the limousine, not the stretch kind that had come before and fascinated the younger children. He retrieved his rifle and continued to scrutinize the vehicle. It was white, not black like the last ones, and its windows were deeply tinted. It pulled up to the one-floor structure and stopped. The driver's side door opened. A crisply dressed, black male chauffer stepped out and went to the rear right-side passenger door. Kinshan sized him up. The driver looked strong, but Kinshan believed that he could give him a run for his money. Kinshan's grip on his rifle tightened while the driver opened the door, held out his hand, and helped a tall, black woman exit. She turned back to the interior. "Wait here," she instructed the people who remained inside.

Kinshan approached the two of them, his rifle at the ready. She greeted him with a smile, and pulled out a business card from her case. He gazed at it, but made no attempt to take it. Instead, he focused his attention on the woman trying to present it to him. He saw no fear in her eyes. Kinshan glanced at her driver, and then turned to head back to the meetinghouse, while the couple waited by the limousine. A few minutes later, he returned. The look of mistrust had not left his face. He gave a curt nod to the woman. "You may approach, Miss Warren," he told her in a stern voice.

Julie smiled at him, and then turned and gave the driver a reassuring pat on the arm. He nodded in reply and climbed back into the limousine. Julie followed Kinshan up the steps to the porch. As they reached the doorway, a much older man at least a foot shorter than Kinshan slowly approached. His rich black hair hung loose around his face. He gave her a slight bow. "Miss Warren?" he asked.

"Keanu?" she replied.

The older man held out a hand and she slipped her right hand inside of it. Keanu's wrinkled face broke into a broad, gaping smile the moment it made contact. He remembered holding her hand when she was a girl. It seemed like it held an electric charge that rejuvenated rather than drained. He took a step back to study her appearance now. Then, she was a gangly child who had darted in and around everything, asked what seemed to be a million questions, and never seemed satisfied with the answers. "It *is* you," he whispered, looking into her youthful face and the clear and focused brown eyes now hidden behind glasses. "You've grown quite a bit since I last saw you."

"So my guardian keeps telling me," Julie joked.

He chuckled in reply. Then he gave Kinshan a reassuring pat on the shoulder. "It's all right. She is who she claims to be."

Kinshan stared hard at Julie, his eyes wide. He knew of those who ran the large company that assisted them in protecting their land. They always left them to lead their lives. Some of their representatives came to their ceremonies, but never stayed for long. Now, the CEO's daughter was here. Had the sky children told her to come? He realized how disrespectful he had been toward her, and he stepped away and bowed deeply. Julie reached out her other hand to cup his chin. "It's nice to meet you, Kinshan," she told him.

His eyes met hers. For a moment, he thought he saw the stars that watched over their land at night reflecting in her eyes. She blinked and the effect was gone. A smile came to his face. "Welcome to our homeland, Miss Warren," he greeted her.

"Thank you." She turned her attention back to Keanu. "I could go for cup of *chinti*, please; that is if you still make it."

Keanu turned and gave some instructions to Kinshan in Amendu. He bowed and quickly disappeared around the corner, while Julie followed Keanu into the meetinghouse. Julie glanced around. Covering the log walls were dozens of bear, beaver, raccoon and deerskins, intermixed with wall hangings of the Amendu tribe's history and rich culture. Her eyes wandered the room, examining each one. Near the stone fireplace was one that caught her attention. She went to study it. The tapestry showed a dark blue background and bare trees.

In a clearing, some of the Amendu met with six white figures with black eyes. In the background, another figure stood, observing. Its skin was not red or white, but brown like hers.

Keanu touched her arm and motioned to a huge black bearskin rug in front of the roaring stone fireplace, which provided the only heat and light for the room. She went toward it, knelt down, and turned her attention to the man across from her. In his red, wrinkled face and deep brown eyes, she saw the kindness and ageless wisdom of his ancestors, people who had walked the land for more than 10,000 Earth years. Her tailored suit stood in stark contrast to his well-worn blue jeans and faded blue-plaid shirt. As she made herself comfortable, a woman brought two cups of *chinti*, a traditional drink flavored with the bark of the white birch trees found within the forest. She bowed politely to them and then left the building. He stared at its contents for a moment, before holding the cup aloft. Julie imitated him. "To those who watch over us," he chanted in his native tongue.

"May their lessons continue to guide us through all our days," Julie finished in Amendu.

Keanu paused. "I see that your guardian took the time to educate you in our language," he commented in English, as he brought the cup back down to his face.

She sipped her *chinti*. "I educated myself, Keanu. As my guardian taught me, one cannot be an effective problem solver if one doesn't understand or make an effort to learn anything about whom they are talking to, and what motivates them to act the way they do."

They continued to drink in silence. Julie sensed Keanu's eyes on her, as well as the tension and fear flowing through the air. It didn't seem to be coming from one particular person or thing. However, her presence had increased it. She gazed about the place, staring at its decorations again, taking in as much information from the thoughts of the others. "How have you been, Keanu?" she asked aloud.

"The sky children have blessed me, Miss Warren. How are you? How is your guardian? Have the sky children healed his injury?"

"He's fine, Keanu, and, no, the sky children have not healed him, nor have the doctors, for that matter. I think he's stopped asking them to."

"Why would he do that?"

"I believe he's grown use to it. He thinks it gives him . . . character."

Keanu laughed heartedly. "He has not changed then."

"No, he hasn't, and I don't think I'd want him any other way."

Keanu took another sip of his *chinti*. His face became more serious. "I should apologize for Kinshan's behavior toward you. He didn't mean to treat you with disrespect."

"There's nothing to forgive. Kinshan acted appropriately, considering what I've heard." She looked at Keanu and adjusted her seating position. "The reports you've provided are extensive, but I don't believe they reveal the whole picture," she continued. "I want to hear it from you. Tell me about those who came here and threatened you, your people, and this land. What did they look like? What did they say?"

Keanu shook his head, not wanting to recall anything about the representatives who had traveled to speak with him these past few months, and their efforts to purchase their holy land. "They were cold, unflinching men and women. For more than five years now, they've come here in their fancy clothing, flashing their briefcases of money, trying to convince us to sell our land. They had no respect for our culture or our ways. They even refused to drink the *chinti* that we offered them. This past harvest cycle, they've become even more persistent. They belittled us and they told us that we are foolish to keep it the way it is, that there were better uses for it. They talked about the money it could be bringing to us from those who wish to gamble, wander the woodlands, or sail on the water."

He gestured to the left toward the open door and Julie gazed out. Past the numerous structures that made up the town, there was nothing but lush green trees and clouded gray sky as far as the eye can see. "What more could our land be used for except to honor the sky children for their knowledge, their beauty, and the protection they provide? We have no wish to violate the promise that they made to my ancestors, to my children and to the future generations of our tribe. Why would they believe that we would do so?"

"The promise they made?"

Keanu gave her an inquisitive stare. "Your guardian has not told you about that?"

"A little, but it's always confused me. Will you tell me the story, in your own words?"

Keanu set his cup down, sat back, and closed his eyes. Julie watched. To her, it was as if entered another realm and called on some unseen force for strength and guidance. When he opened them, Julie stared into his face, and saw such clarity and peace within it. He turned his head to his right and Julie followed his gaze. His black eyes focused on the wall hanging Julie had been admiring earlier. His voice took on a solemn tone, and he began to speak:

"The legend tells of several unforgiving harvest seasons, when my people fought for their survival. The weather would turn bitter cold, and then blazing hot. We asked for rain, and received locusts. We asked for food, and watched the yellow gold crumble and wilt. The animals fled the woods, and the fish begged for water to swim in. Many died during that time, so many that it was feared that our tribe would be lost forever."

He closed his eyes again. When he opened them again, he refocused them onto her. "Then one day, they say a dark woman with clear eyes, and six figures bathed in white, descend from the sky. They promised to help us to survive and to grow, to help us keep the corn from dying, and to protect us from the cold and the heat. They offered us food when we were hungry, nursed our sick, and comforted our dying. They asked for nothing in return, except for us to keep this land as you see it."

"Did you tell these visitors about our agreement?"

"Yes. They seemed quite versed in it, if I recall."
Keanu leveled his gaze to hers. "As you are aware,
Miss Warren, we have both honored that agreement,
and neither of us would violate it," he said in a low
tone. "Your company has no reason to follow the wishes
of the sky children, yet you have chosen to do so. We
told this to those who came. We also told them that we
would not go against the wishes of those who protect
us, for the prospect of a quick buck. They said that we
would regret our decision."

"What happened next?"

"At first, nothing. We didn't believe them, until . . ."

Julie looked at him. "Until what?"

"Over this past harvest, they have taken us to their
courts to force us to break our agreement with you. A
month ago, two of our members were beaten when they
went into Okanogan to buy kerosene for our lamps.
Another of our tribesman disappeared last week. We
have been unable to locate him. Then, something even
more disastrous occurred." Keanu closed his eyes and
hung his head. "Our coming of age ceremony was a
few days ago. Many of my people became ill after it,
but especially the children who participated in it. Our
healer, Ronan believes that they were poisoned."

Julie set her cup down. "Poisoned? Do you know
how?"

He shook his head and looked down at his cup.
"The only food or drink they shared in common that
night was the special *chinti* they drank. Ronan believes
that he mixed the ingredients wrongly. He has offered
himself for punishment."

Julie quickly rose to her feet. "The children who were poisoned? Where are they?"

Keanu stared at her. There was a look of anxiety about her that he didn't understand. She acted as if she had been the one who had caused this tragedy. He gestured toward the door again. Off in the distance, just a few yards away from the start of the forest, Julie saw a small building. A steady stream of people flowed up and down its steps. "In the medicine house. Ronan has tried everything, but he hasn't found a way to defeat its effects. Four children have died already, including a tribal councilman's son, and seventeen more are seriously ill. One of them is Ronan's grandson." His chin fell to his chest. "We do not know what else to do for them," he added in a whisper.

"Please, take me to them."

Keanu rose as quickly as his aging body would allow him. He shuffled his way out of the meetinghouse, and led Julie toward the medicine house. As they crossed the yard, Julie gestured to the back doors of the limousine. They opened, and a dark-haired white female wearing a white lab coat over a black dress and carrying a black medical bag emerged. A curly blonde-haired woman and a Hispanic-looking male climbed out behind her. "Alexandra, would you and your assistants follow us, please?" Julie instructed her.

"Yes, Miss Warren," the woman with the bag replied.

Keanu stared at her. Rarely did they allow doctors from outside their tribe attend their ill. Julie met his gaze. "I heard reports that something bad had happened here. Alexandra is one of the best physicians I know.

I brought her in case we needed her assistance." She looked down at the ground. "It may go against the wishes of your people, and of the sky children, but I know they would want your people to have the best of care."

Keanu nodded and led the Julie and the others inside the building. The crowd gathered near the door parted, making way for their leader. They crossed their arms and glared at the strangers who followed them. Julie understood their reaction, but said nothing. She would leave it to Keanu to explain who she was.

They made their way through the crowded hallway into the main treatment room. Keanu stepped out of her way, and Julie looked at the scene, dismayed. There were nearly two dozen beds filled with victims, most of them children in their pre-teens. Members of the tribe moved around them, placing cold cloths on their heads or holding their hands, talking to them, attempting to keep them awake, alert, and as comfortable as possible. Off in the corner, one man looked up from his work. Keanu gestured to him, and he approached, his light brown eyes focused on the strange woman with him. "This is Ronan, our healer," Keanu said. "Ronan, this is Juliana, Lord Simon's daughter."

The wary look on Ronan's face disappeared. He studied the woman who stood before him. "How much you have grown," he commented. "The last time I saw you, you were a small blur that raced through here and knocked over a tray filled with my best herbs."

"My behavior today will be more ladylike, I promise."

Julie watched as the memory of that day and the happiness it brought fade quickly from his face. He looked back at the beds filled with his kindred. His head fell to his chest. She touched his hand and traveled through his thoughts to recall his actions that day. She reached out to cup his face, and stared him in the eye. He began to tremble. "You did not do this," she told him in a firm voice. "What has happened here was not your fault."

"The sky children do not think so," Ronan rasped. "We went against their wishes. Why else would they have harmed them?" His gaze fell on one of the children in the middle of the group of beds. "Why else would my grandson be lying there?"

Julie followed his gaze and shook her head. "The sky children may be powerful, Ronan, but they're not perfect. Her voice dropped to a whisper: "Sometimes, even the sky children are wrong."

Something about the way she spoke the words gave Ronan solace. He thought on her comment as he and Keanu turned to watch Julie and the others who accompanied her. The nurses with them paused at each bed. They checked each victim's blood pressure, and drew blood. From her bag, Alexandra pulled out a clipboard and her stethoscope. She checked each patient's breathing and heartbeat and pretended to make notes on the clipboard, while she studied the readouts that the hidden scanners obtained. Meanwhile, Julie touched each of their foreheads, speaking words of comfort. Ronan's herbs had kept whatever they ingested from doing serious damage, but the effect was beginning to wane. Julie's hands began to tingle. She made a fist with her free one. Alexandra glanced up, her smoky gray eyes watching Julie's actions. Julie met her gaze and nodded. She forced the urges back by closing her eyes, picturing herself in a room 50,000 light years from here that glowed in a surreal green-orange-blue color. *NIK? What's your analysis?*

It is a complex poison, Ambassador. However, based on the readings, I believe an antidote can be synthesized with ingredients from the Illani gardens. With their assistance, it should be ready for the humans to digest within 24 Earth hours.

Julie left the little girl she was examining and went to the boy lying next to her. His thin face, similar to Ronan's, was covered in sweat. He gripped her left hand tight and gasped for breath. His huge brown eyes pleaded with her to provide relief. *Do they have that long?*

All except the child you are touching, Ambassador. He will die if we do not help him now.

Julie looked at Alexandra, who studied the readout on her screen and sent Julie a telepathic thought of agreement. Julie frowned. She knew the Eldar wouldn't like what she was doing, but she didn't care. These children would not become casualties in this land tug-of-war. She laid her right hand on his forehead and stroked it. "Hello," she whispered. "What's your name?"

"B . . . Baldan," the boy rasped.

She gripped his hand tight, sending a slight surge of energy through her left hand to him. "Don't worry, Baldan. We're going to find an answer to what's making you ill. I promise this, but you need to try and get some rest. All right?"

Baldan gave her a small nod. The others watched as the boy's breathing eased and his grip on Julie's hand relaxed. He settled back into his bed, closed his eyes, and drifted off to sleep. Alexandra rechecked the readings. *He is stabilizing*, miandi. *He should be fine until we return with the antidote.*

Shuffling footsteps filled their ears and the women looked up. Ronan was approached them. Tears welled in his eyes, as he stepped around Alexandra and sat down by Baldan. He stroked his head. "You seem to have the touch of a healer, Miss Warren," he murmured, staring up at her. "Perhaps the sky children smile on you."

"Perhaps they do," Julie agreed. She turned to Alexandra. "Let's get the blood samples back to Spokane so that we can get these children healthy again."

"Yes, Miss Warren," Alexandra replied.

Alexandra motioned to the nurses who carried a small cooler filled with vials of the victims' blood. They followed her out of the building toward the waiting limousine. Keanu watched them leave, and then turned to Julie. "You truly believe you can help us?"

"Simon already has our legal staff on it. We'll keep working until we're sure that those who did this are punished. Once they are, you and the tribal leaders will meet with us and the other board members to see what we can do to prevent this from happening again."

At once, the room filled with a sense of hope. The others who had watched them nodded their approval of the dark woman with the clear eyes. A few of them took note that her appearance was very similar to one of the sky children. Keanu reached out a hand. Julie took it, and he grasped it within both of his. "The sky children chose well when they brought you to your guardian," he whispered. He blinked and Julie saw his eyes had filled with tears. "I shall tell them that in my prayers tonight."

"And I shall tell them about the leadership and bravery you have shown me and your people, and ask them to give you the additional protection that you deserve." She looked down at the children. "If we find an antidote, I'll have Dr. Alexandra bring it here immediately. Hopefully in a few days, these children will be causing the same mischief I caused when I was their age."

Ronan and Keanu nodded. "Thank you, Miss Warren," they chorused.

Julie acknowledged their thanks and glanced out the window. "If you'll excuse me, I need to make some calls."

She made her way out of the clinic, taking in the words of peace and gratitude from the citizenry. She stepped back into the afternoon sunshine and walked purposely toward the waiting limousine. She reached into her purse to pull out her mobile phone. She believed she knew what had caused their illness, but she wanted an unbiased second opinion: *NIK, trace that poison, please.*

I already have, Ambassador. Many of its ingredients are from plants indigenous to Earth, but its base is sorja root, a plant native only to the planet of . . .

"Gemina," Julie finished aloud. She stopped and turned back to the clinic. She closed her eyes and shuddered inwardly. "How many more? How many more lives will be taken because of my one moment's loss of self control?"

VII

Botsworth Real Estate agent Terrance Carnegie sat behind the file-filled desk in his office and stared at the door, waiting for the knock that he didn't want to hear. He heard about Madison's assault from Barbara Livingston. The police had contacted him shortly thereafter, requesting an opportunity to talk to him. He agreed talk to them first thing this morning. For the rest of the day, he tried to work, but his trembling hands kept drifting out to touch the cellular phone sitting on the corner of his desk. It was not his phone. It belonged to the man who requested the research Madison had completed. He waited all day for a call to come in on it, but it didn't ring. Instead, it rang last night while his three children played the latest version of NFL Football on their PlayStation. He had retreated to his study and locked the door behind him. He paced the floor with the phone pressed to his ear, trying not to scream at the voice that came over it. "Do you know what happened the other night?" he whispered.

"I've been made aware of the situation. I don't understand why you're concerned."

"My assistant was mugged last night!"

"Your assistant was ready to go to the police. I made sure she didn't make it there."

"A hell lot of good that did. They're coming to see me, to talk about her and her work."

"And you will tell them nothing that they don't already know."

"That's great advice. It would come in handy, if I knew what they knew."

"You will tell them that your assistant did an admirable job researching homes to go on the market. After all, that's what she did."

Terrance sighed. "But what if they ask?"

There was a sharp pause. "What if they ask what?"

Terrance rolled his eyes into the back of his head. Did he have to spell it out? "What if they ask about . . . you know . . . it?"

"It?"

"The land up north? The land that you're after?"

"They won't ask. The police know nothing, nor will you tell them anything."

Terrance's green eyes widened with fear. He hadn't liked the sound of the man's voice as he spoke those words. "I reviewed what Madison's found out about the place. We're not playing with a great hand here. They hold all the wild cards."

"Then it's time that you showed them your best poker face, Mr. Carnegie."

Despite knowing that he was alone in the room and that he would not be disturbed, he felt like hundreds of people were watching his every move. His voice dropped to a whisper again. "What the hell's so special about this place?"

"It's special to my client, and that's all you need to understand."

"But still . . ." Terrance ran his hand through his thinning blonde locks. How long had it been since he had seen the doctor for a treatment? "Right now, I'm worried about being implicated in this. I'm the one sticking my neck out on the line for you and I don't even know who the hell I'm working for!"

"Don't worry about that, Mr. Carnegie. After all, you are being paid extremely well."

Terrance thought to the half million dollars on deposit in the offshore account. It had been set up shortly after he agreed to begin the new search on this particular account. The retainer money sent more than five years prior sat in his office safe. He never cashed the check. He had never been certain of who he had been working for, and he wasn't about to leave any evidence about that made the police believe he was on the take. However, he wasn't stupid enough to throw away $50,000.00 in instant cash. "I don't care about the money anymore. I just want this done and over, without my ass landing behind bars!"

"Your worrying may be for naught. We may be able to get at it legally now."

At those words, Terrance stopped pacing. His green eyes opened wide. "Legally? How?"

"Don't worry about that. Just know that if the last heir dies, it won't take much to get the Amendu to sell their portion to us." The voice paused, allowing the significance of what he just said sink into Terrance's brain. "You'll be able to retire with money to burn, Mr. Carnegie."

For a moment, Terrance let the picture of the boat he had been eyeing these past few months drift into his thoughts. It disappeared quickly, to be replaced by an image of him in blue prison garb and a number emblazoned on his chest. "You realize that if this backfires, and the police or these people figure out what we're doing, we'll go to prison."

"Then it would be in your best interest to make sure that nothing goes wrong."

There was a click. The connection had been broken. Terrance took the phone away from his head and stared at it. There had been no hint of a threat in his voice, but Terrance took it as such. He elected to sleep in the guest room that night instead of with his wife in their bed, tossing and turning, waiting for tomorrow to come and hating every moment of it.

"Mr. Carnegie? The police are here."

Terrance snapped out of his trance. He gazed about his office, wondering how long he'd be able to perform this activity. "How good of a selling job can you really do?" he asked himself. "Well, it's about time you found out." He stared at the phone intercom button blinking at him. He paused for moment, and then hit the speaker button. "Send them in, Barbara."

He stood and wiped his hands on his trousers, as the door to his office opened. A tall man and a slightly shorter woman entered. Their badges were displayed prominently on their jackets. The man was about Terrance's height, with dark hair and penetrating brown eyes. Terrance already felt uncomfortable around him, and the man had only been in the room less than ten seconds. He concentrated his attention on the woman. She looked a little pale, and her gaze kept darting toward Terrance's windows. He stole a glance in that direction, but there wasn't anything out of the ordinary there. "It's a pleasure to meet you, Detectives," Terrance greeting them, giving them his best smile and holding out a hand for them to shake.

"Detectives Mark Daniels and Cassie Edwards," Mark introduced them both. "We're here to talk about Madison Evans."

"Yes, please sit. Coffee, tea?" He looked expectantly at Barbara, who hung by the doorway.

"No, thank you," Cassie muttered.

She sat down in a chair and pulled out her notebook. She stared about Terrance's cluttered office, taking in as much detail as she could without glancing over toward his open windows. Before they had pulled up to the door, Mark had instructed Cassie that he wanted her to conduct this interview. Cassie felt certain that it wasn't because he thought this was some wild goose chase. Interviewing everyone and anyone Madison worked with or knew her was routine. However, because Mark wasn't planning on asking any questions, Cassie felt that this was Mark's opportunity to get a better view of her and how she worked.

Terrance dismissed Barbara with a look. She shut the door behind her, while he made himself as comfortable as he dared behind his desk. "Before we start, can you tell me how she's doing?" Terrance asked.

"She hasn't regained consciousness yet," Cassie told him.

Terrance shook her head. "Who would do something like this? Mason City is such a great place to live. Who could do such a thing?"

Cassie pursed her lips. They received the same line at every interview so far, designed to divert attention away from the real reason she and Mark sat there. She willed away her fear of Mark's disapproval and focused her attention on Terrance. "How long has she been working here?"

"A few months. She answered an ad I had placed with the university's job center. She told me she was thinking about going into real estate law, and she thought that this was a good way to get some background."

"Have there been any problems with her before this?"

"No. She took to the job really well. It was as if she was meant to do it." He settled back into his chair. "I think that she enjoyed studying the history of it and all, looking at how land transferred from one person to another, how it developed and such."

Cassie looked over at Mark. He didn't seem too concerned about her. His attention was fixed on Terrance. Cassie studied the look on his face. What was it that he saw? She stole a quick glance back at Terrance, then back at Mark. Maybe it was nothing, but whatever it was, it seemed to be making Terrance very uncomfortable. Terrance tried keeping his eyes focused on her, but Cassie saw them dart toward Mark more than once. She cleared her throat. "We learned from your secretary that she was working on a particularly difficult project for you these past few weeks."

"It wasn't really difficult, but rather time consuming," Terrance clarified. "The land was outside of my normal area, but not something that I couldn't handle."

"This research you had her doing. What was it about?"

"A client of mine has some land that he's looking to purchase somewhere north of here. He wanted some preliminary research done, to see whether it was worth the effort that he was putting into it."

Terrance stood and carefully moved a stack of files that the detectives thought would topple over from the breeze of someone walking by them. From a blue colored file, Terrance pulled out a hand-drawn map. Mark took it from him and he and Cassie studied it. On it was an odd-shaped area highlighted in yellow. There were no other markings, except for the two-lane highway that flowed through the land toward the Canadian border. "It's nothing, really," Terrance said.

"Why did you have her researching it?"

"Time, Detective Edwards, something that I have precious little of these days." He tapped the stack of files next to him. They wobbled and Terrance moved to steady it. "We're entering the start of our busiest cycle in the real estate industry. I've had quite a few closings these past few weeks, and I've been trying to make preparations for ten more that are up and coming. She had already finished the work I had given her. I thought she might like the challenge of researching land up north, where the record keeping isn't as modern as it is here."

"Do you have the results of that research?"

Terrance gave her a smile. "Unfortunately, no. I forwarded them to my client a few days ago. He also had me forward a copy to his attorney in Denver, and I forgot to keep copies."

"Why not?"

"Detective, it was just a search of some legal title. If I kept copies of every piece of land that I researched, my office would need to be three times the size of this place. I have to make some concessions." Terrance gestured to the room. Everywhere the detectives looked there were piles of files, except for one spot. In that spot sat a Boston fern that looked like it was on its last legs. Its branches drooped and the green had gone out of many of its leaves. Hundreds of wrinkled, brown leaves littered the floor in front of the bookcase, and the books and files on the floor below it.

Cassie made some notes. She could feel her fear getting the better of her. She glanced over at Mark. He didn't seem fazed by anything. His attention seemed to be riveted on the map still in his hand. He felt Cassie's stare and looked up at her. The corner of his mouth lifted up and he gave her an encouraging nod. She pressed on:

"We have it on information that you and Madison had a fight a few days before her assault."

Terrance looked flabbergasted. "Fight? Who said that?"

"Then you admit that you had an altercation."

"I didn't have a fight with Madison."

"According to your secretary, she left your office in tears."

"So that means what? I assaulted her?" Terrance's face turned ruddy and his eyes flashed. He glared at Mark. "You're here to arrest me for it?"

"You have an alibi for where you were that evening?"

"I was with my wife and children in Seattle, visiting the in-laws." Terrance fought not to rise from his chair. "You should double check your facts before you come in here accusing me of anything, Detective!"

Cassie went to make a retorting comment, when she felt Mark's arm ensnare around her wrist. She glanced over at him. He gave her an imperceptible shake of the head. Mark noticed that she was still trembling, despite the fact that she had been interviewing Terrance for more than ten minutes. Was she that nervous? He hadn't meant to put that much pressure on her. Cassie swallowed, took a deep breath, and tried to relax back into her chair. "What did you and Madison talk about that day?" Cassie asked.

Terrance kept glaring at Cassie. "Her work ethic. She seemed a little distracted. She wasn't producing as well as she had been when she started. I know that she had just broken up with her boyfriend, and that her studies were taking up much of her time. I wanted to make sure that it wasn't interfering with her job."

"So you know nothing about what happened outside your own door a few days before she was attacked?"

Terrance looked blankly from Mark to Cassie. "No. What happened?"

"One of your employees claims that Madison was accosted on the street a few days before her assault." Cassie raised an eyebrow. "He's described as being a man with a red tattoo on his forearm?"

"I know nothing about this, but that's to be expected."

Mark and Cassie both looked at him. "Expected?" Mark asked.

"We have a lot of homeless people, who wander about here." Terrance looked from one detective to the other. "I warned her about not getting too friendly with them, but it wouldn't surprise me if she gave one of them some money, and he latched onto her."

Cassie made note of this. It didn't correlate with what Mrs. Livingston had told them. Then again, Mrs. Livingston was in a lot of distress when she talked to them. If Madison had ingested drugs, they may have made her disoriented enough to wander into a situation she couldn't handle. Mark kept watching his partner. There was something else wrong with her. Whatever it was, it was interfering with this interview. He needed to come up with a creative and non-embarrassing way to get her out of here. Mark glanced at his watch and thought of one. He stood up. "Thank you for your time, Mr. Carnegie," he said.

Cassie looked at him. Anger radiated from her. "Mark," she muttered.

"I'm certain that if we have more questions, Mr. Carnegie will make himself available to us, Detective. In the meantime, let's see if Madison's awake and able to talk to us."

Cassie fought back a retort. Apparently, she had failed at her first chance to impress her new partner. She reluctantly rose from her seat. She nodded to Terrance. "Thank you, sir."

"If you need anything else Detectives, please call me."

Mark gently encouraged Cassie out of Terrance's office and through his lobby. They exited the suite and made their way toward the elevator. There were a few people already on it when it arrived at their floor. Cassie made a beeline for the corner and stared at the elevator's red-paneled wall, not acknowledging her partner's presence as he took a spot beside her. She pretended to be reviewing her notes from the interview, hoping not to get tears on them. She already knew that this pairing had failure written all over it. She might as well go home tonight, pack her bags and return to Seattle. No doubt that the number one detective in the state would be calling Lieutenant Michaels on their way back to the precinct to let her know that she didn't have the goods to make it in this line of police work, and that she should go back to walking a beat.

"Not bad." Mark said, as he watched the indicator and rocked back on his heels.

Cassie snapped out of her moment of self-pity and looked at him. "What?"

"You were a little rougher than I would've been, but on the whole, not bad."

The elevator stopped and picked up a few more passengers. Cassie began to crumble notebook pages in her hand. "Why did you stop it then?"

"Because I'm not certain that irritating the witness was the best way to go at the time."

"Mark, I think he knows more than he's letting on," Cassie argued in a low tone. "He's probably having an affair with her, and he's scared someone's going to find out. How much do you want to bet he hired the man who assaulted her in the first place?"

Mark raised an eyebrow. "Are you sure you want to be betting against me after what happened yesterday?"

Cassie opened her mouth, and then closed it again. She narrowed her gaze. "Mark, he knows something."

The elevator doors opened to the sun-filled lobby. Cassie breathed a sigh of relief as her feet hit the floor. Mark led her toward the revolving doors that led out to the main street. "I don't doubt it, Cassie. Like you said, all the evidence we have indicates that this was a robbery, and perhaps a mugging. Our best witness is in the hospital. If she's awake, maybe she can tell us something. In the meantime, we'll check his alibi and see how it pans out, and see if we got any hits from that description Mrs. Livingston gave us."

Mark went to reach for his cell phone with his right hand That's when he realized he still had the hand-drawn map Terrance had shown him. "Oops, I didn't realize that I still had this. I better give it back, in case he might need it again."

Mark turned and bumped right in the man who was right behind him. The man grunted, as his nose connected with Mark's chest. Mark took a step back. "Excuse me," Mark apologized.

The man grunted again. He stepped around him and gave Mark an icy stare. Mark frowned and took two more steps toward the door, but then he thought he caught a glimpse of something. He slowed his pace and turned to look at the man he had accidentally run into. He caught it again: the long, twisting red snake ensnared around his left forearm muscle. Mark stopped and continued to study the man walking away from them. That was when he saw the long, greasy dirty brown hair, and the left side of his pockmarked face. Could he be the man who threatened Madison the other day? Mark's eyes narrowed and he re-approached Cassie, who was still flipping through her notes. He tapped her on the shoulder and Cassie looked up. Mark put a finger to his lips and nodded toward the man walking away from them. "What do you see?" Mark whispered.

Cassie focused her attention on the man. When the man's left arm moved backward, she too caught sight of the tattoo. Her eyebrows disappeared into her bangs and she brought her eyes up to meet Mark's. "Someone I think we need to talk to," she muttered out of the corner of her mouth.

Mark nodded. He tucked the piece of paper back into his pocket. The two officers began to follow the man. They remained about five paces behind him.

Mark managed to retrieve his cell phone from his back pocket and began to dial the precinct. Just as he did so, their party of interest gazed back over his shoulder. He turned to face them and gave them a suspicious gaze. "Whadd'a want?" he asked, revealing a mouth of half-missing teeth.

"Detectives Mark Daniels and Cassie Edwards," Mark said. They pulled out their badges. "We'd like to have a word with you, if we could, sir."

His eyes grew wide. He swore under his breath and took off down the street. "That's enough for me!" Mark said, and they raced down street after him.

The man darted into the street and narrowly missed being hit by an approaching car. He knocked over a trash can and shoved pedestrians out of his way. Mark and Cassie maneuvered their way through the crowds, but Mark's longer strides soon put Cassie behind him. "Call for backup!" he screamed.

The man rounded a corner and headed toward a public park. A pewter-gray, bowl-capped tower stood in the middle it. Mark rounded the same corner and realized where the man was heading. It was Holcomb Tower, a local tourist attraction. The tower was about 255 feet high, capped by a domed structure that had several observation binocular towers, which allowed visitors to view downtown Mason City and the surrounding countryside. Mark smirked. The city closed the tower to conduct repair work on it over the winter. It wasn't open to the public yet. Cassie also spied the structure. Her pace slowed, and then stopped. Mark didn't notice. He saw their suspect take the stairs up to the central viewing tower two at a time. Mark didn't glance back to see if Cassie was still with him. He bounded up the stairs after him. "You there! Halt, and stay where you are!"

The man looked back at Mark under his right armpit. He quickened his steps. Mark frowned. If this guy had been sick or homeless, he sure wasn't acting as if he were. He heard the suspect's footsteps echoing on the metal stairs above him and then land squarely on the observation tower landing. Mark saw a flash of denim disappearing around the corner. He stopped about four steps short of the landing and pulled his gun. "Slow and steady, Cassie," he whispered, looking back over his shoulder. Then he did a double take. Cassie wasn't there. "Cassie?"

He glanced about. Around him was the remainder of the parking lot and open area that surrounded Holcomb Tower, but no Cassie. He closed his eyes and took a steadying breath. He knew that he shouldn't be going into this alone. He had no idea if this guy was carrying a weapon. His only consolation was that the suspect would have to come back this way to get away, as the stairway was the only safe way down.

Mark stepped onto the landing, making as little sound as possible. He kept his gun in front of him and took small, quiet steps. About five feet in front of him was a doorway. Mark pressed his body against the wall and dared to glance inside. He saw nothing. Mark closed his eyes and listened for breathing, a footstep, or anything to indicate where the man had gone.

When he heard nothing, he swung his gun into the room. The room was empty. He took one more step inside. In front of him was a glass-enclosed display of maps and photographs depicting the history of the tower and the development of Mason City. The only light was that streaming in from the doorway. Mark looked around for feet underneath any of the displays, but saw none.

A metallic sound echoed all round him. Mark whirled around, his gun drawn. He couldn't pinpoint where the sound had come from. He darted his eyes left and right, as he began to head back toward the doorway, looking for any sign of movement. There was no way off the structure outside of the stairway, so where did the man go? Suddenly, he felt a sharp whack at the back of his head. He flew forward and his gun went flying. His face smacked the metal grating hard and he grunted. Mark waited a few moments for the pain at the back of his head to subside and the spots in his eyes to disappear. Then he raised his head. As he went to push himself up, he heard a step to his left. Then he saw a shadow. He squinted in the semi-darkness, fighting off the pain racing through his head, and reached out a groping hand for his gun. He hoped it hadn't gone very far. That was when he realized that someone was standing over him. He was breathing heavily. It had to be the man he chased. Mark opened his eyes further and glanced around as best as he could for his weapon.

"Don't bother."

Mark felt a breeze near his left hand. Mark froze. The suspect he had been pursing was right next to him. Mark could picture him standing over him, the gun pointed at the back of his neck. Jessie's soft face and beautiful blue eyes flashed before him. He would be joining her soon, although this wasn't the way he had envisioned it. *Just the way I want to die: to be killed with my gun. Where the hell is Cassie?*

Suddenly, there was a blinding flash of light. Mark shut his eyes tight. The man holding his gun screamed as if in agonizing pain. Mark flinched, waiting for the gunshot that didn't come. A few seconds later, he heard the suspect fall to the grated floor and the sound of metal clattering to the ground. After a few moments, Mark raised his head. He opened his eyes and peeked under his left armpit. There was no one there except for the suspect he had been chasing. He lay there beside him, staring up at the ceiling. Slowly, Mark pushed himself to his feet, grabbed the back of his head, and stared around. He saw his gun, which had slid a few feet away from them. He retrieved it and checked to make sure there was no damage. Then he replaced it in his holster, reached for his handcuffs, and jerked his assailant to his feet. It seemed to snap him out of whatever trance he had been in. "Whad . . . what happened?" he muttered.

Mark had no idea, but he wasn't going to tell him that. "A well-timed punch." Mark opened up the handcuffs and pulled the man's left arm behind him. "You, my esteemed friend, are under arrest. You have the right to remain silent, and I suggest that you do so, you son of a bitch."

He shoved the man from behind toward the doorway. They emerged from the observation deck, and Mark squinted at the sudden sunlight. He gazed around the park. There was no one there. He marched his suspect toward the stairway. As they reached it, he heard a car door slam. He looked down. Cassie had just pulled up to the tower in his truck. A few seconds later, two marked cars pulled up beside her. Mark pushed him toward the stairwell. "Move!"

The man turned and glared at him, but moved down the stairwell without argument. Cassie met them about two thirds of the way down. She took one look at Mark's appearance and swallowed. "Mark!" she whispered.

Mark stared hard at her. He wanted an answer as to why she had not followed him, but he saw one of the uniformed officers moving toward them. He nodded at her and she turned and led them down the rest of the stairway. As they handed them off to the uniformed men, the senior officer also took in Mark's disheveled appearance. "You all right, Detective?" he asked.

"Yeah," Mark murmured, trying not dwell on his smarting head, or the fact that his new partner had not backed him up. He nodded to his quarry, who still looked a little dazed. "Read him his rights, get him downtown, and book him for assaulting a police officer," he instructed them. "We'll be right behind you."

The officers nodded. The herded the handcuffed man into the back of one of the squad cars. He turned and watched the detectives through the back window as the officers climbed into the front passenger side. They returned the man's stare, neither feeling very sympathetic toward him. When the squad cars had disappeared around the bend, Cassie turned to Mark. "What happened up there?" she asked.

Mark held the back of his head again and looked back up at the top of Holcomb Tower. He brought his hand down to look at it, but there was no blood. It didn't mean that it didn't hurt like the dickens. He thought back to the flash of light he had seen. He returned his gaze to her. "I don't know. Did you see anyone go up before us, or behind us?"

"No. I thought I saw a light or something coming from somewhere over there as I came up the drive." She pointed in the general direction of some nearby trees, about a thousand yards away from the tower. "It looked like it aimed right for the tower. Why?"

"Nothing. It's just that . . ." Mark's voice trailed off, as he looked up toward the platform of the tower. Someone had been there and saved his life, but whom? "Let's get back to the station."

"You okay to drive?"

Mark nodded. Cassie appraised him carefully before turning to head back toward his vehicle. He waited until he saw her hand reach out to grasp the passenger door handle. "Cassie," he murmured, dropping his voice an octave.

Her shoulders stiffened. She stared straight ahead. She knew what he was about to ask her, and she didn't want to give him the true answer. If he found out, that would mean the end of everything. She forced herself to face him. "Yes, Mark?" she asked in a small voice.

"Cassie, I could've died up there. You're my partner. Why weren't you following me?"

She glanced up at the tower. He wasn't certain, but he thought he saw her sway a little. She began to tremble, and the blood rushed out of her face. He looked toward the top of Holcomb Tower, and then thought back to her behavior this morning at the precinct, and while at Terrance's office; how she refused to look out the window, her trembling arms and hands. Suddenly he understood. "You have a thing against heights, I take it?"

"No," she gulped. "I'm terrified of them; open heights, especially." Cassie's gaze fell to the ground, and she tried to dig a hole in the concrete with her right foot. "When I was six, my parents took me to the county fair. I convinced them that I could ride the Ferris wheel all by myself. I was fine, until it got stuck, with me alone in the top carriage." She turned to lean back against the truck. She began to shake harder, and tears welled in her eyes. "It took them more than three hours to get me down from there. All I could do was grip the rail, watch as the sky grew darker, stare down at my disappearing parents and wonder if I would ever see them again." She looked up at the tower again. Mark could see the adamant fear in her eyes. She tried to laugh at herself, but it sounded more like a sob that she was forcing back into herself. "I haven't been able to stand being in a building more than three stories tall ever since. It's so bad some days that I can't even go up to my best friend's apartment on the fifth floor of her building, without fainting when I walk inside."

Mark thought back to her appearance and mannerism on the precinct floor yesterday and the look on her face today when he had commented about the view outside. He had chalked it up to first-day jitters, but she had been trying to deal with her phobia the whole time. Going to work must be torture, since the precinct was on the seventh floor. He approached her, reached out to grip her shoulders, and stopped her shaking. "What the hell made you decide to become a cop then? You had to have known that you would encounter this problem over and over."

"I hoped that it would help," Cassie argued. "I enjoy being a cop, Mark. I like the challenges it brings, the daily testing of wills, the chance to help others find justice. My desk at my old precinct in Seattle was on the ground floor and a lot of times, it didn't come up." She stared into Mark's sensuous eyes and fought the urge not to kiss him. God, he was so handsome! His looks, his personality, his warmth and sensitivity were everything she was looking for in a man, and it was just her luck that she had found them in her new partner. It was going to be torture looking at him every day, knowing that they could be nothing more than that. "Look Mark, it was either a cop or a hair stylist, and believe me, you don't want me anywhere near your hair with a pair of scissors."

He picked at a particular spot on his head. "Oh, I don't know. You might've been able to defeat this cowlick of mine."

"Huh?"

"Never mind. Let's just get back to the precinct, all right?"

He turned to head back over to the driver's side He had reached his door, when Cassie called out to him: "Mark?"

Mark looked up. Cassie watched him from over the front of the hood. Her face had a look of panic about it, and her eyes held a pleading look similar to Julie's from a few days prior. It was as if her career and perhaps her life depended upon his response to whatever she was about to say: "You're going to report this to Lieutenant Michaels, aren't you?"

Mark thought on this. They both knew that he should. However, she was barely two days into their partnership. On his way into the precinct that morning, he managed to garner some more information about her tenure in Seattle. As he stared into her face, he didn't see what her former partner did. Yes, she was quick with her words, and maybe jumping to conclusions sooner than she should, but the case was still young. What mattered was that she was trying, which was more than he could say for himself. More and more, he felt like the new guy. He looked her in the eye. Cassie took comfort in what she saw there. "No," he whispered. "I'll just have to remember not to chase suspects into buildings more than two story high, that's all."

She closed her eyes and breathed deep. "Thanks."

"You're welcome, Cass."

She opened her eyes and glared at him. "You should know I hate being called 'Cass'," she warned him.

"Don't worry. You'll get used to it."

Her mouth opened slightly. She hoped that he was kidding, although something told her that he wasn't. Instead, she nodded at him. "How's your head? Really?"

Mark reached back to touch the bump at the back of his head and grimaced. "I'll live. C'mon. I've seen your interview skills. Now it's time for me to see your interrogation technique. Let's get back to the station and find out what that idiot knows."

VIII

Later that evening, Mark sat in the living room, his bare feet propped up on the coffee table, staring at Julie's official check again. His head still hurt from where he had been whacked, but the doctor had given him a thorough examination and said there was no sign of a concussion. Once the doctor cleared him, Mark went to the hard-copy database and pulled their suspect's rap sheet. Leonard Bartman had been in trouble since he was a teenager, although he seemed to have kept his nose clean these last few years. He had just finished parole for an assault that took place five years ago. Unfortunately, it looked like he picked up where he had left off.

They let Leonard stew in the interrogation room while they watched and made their mental notes from the observation room. After an hour or two, Mark and Cassie entered the room to talk to him, or as the others put it, to let Cassie talk and Mark listen and watch. This was a tactic of Charlie's making. Charlie always told the others the twosome got their best confessions when Charlie applied the grandfather technique, and Mark stood in the corner, saying nothing. "I don't know," Charlie would say afterwards, "it's gotta be those eyes of yours. Women hope you'll fulfill every one of their fantasies, and men just freak out." Mark viewed it another way. By watching and listening, he gained more perspective as to the role this particular person played in their investigation, and what angle they should take next. He stored it all so that he could recall and apply what he had learned. It was a gift, his maternal grandmother told him, one he had inherited from his mother, who never wrote anything down, but seemed to recall things at will, like a human encyclopedia.

Ten minutes into the interrogation, Mark realized that this trick wasn't going to work on Leonard Bartman. He just leered at Cassie, occasionally letting out a grunt at specific spots, pretending he was paying attention. He ignored Mark altogether. She definitely had the makings of a good detective, Mark concluded in the end, and the interrogation room was her element. She had not been intimidated in the least, firing questions at Leonard like a 20-year veteran. When Leonard grabbed his crotch for the third time in five minutes, Cassie smiled. Then she kicked his chair from underneath the table. He had been balancing it on two legs. Not expecting it, he fell backwards and smacked his head. That was when he asked for an attorney.

Mark refocused his thoughts back to the check in his hand. He knew that Madison's assault should be his priority right now. However, his subconscious kept drifting back to two pieces of paper; the one in his hand and the one Mr. Smith had shown him at the bank today. He called his dad on his way home, who vehemently denied sending any money to the bank. He didn't dare call Judge Embry. He didn't believe it had been him, but if was, Mark didn't want to know. That left Julie. Why? If it had been Julie or her company, was he obligated to them in some way? If so, what kind of repayment would there be, and would he be willing to accept the terms?

A knock on the door brought him out his thoughts. "Just a minute," he called.

He slipped the check into the coffee table drawer and headed to the front door. Julie's beaming face greeted him. Unlike their first meeting, she was dressed in a navy blue suit, a white silk top and a pearl necklace and earring set. Her heels brought her eyes level with his. "Hi! Sorry to drop in so unexpectedly, and so late," she bubbled.

"Julie," Mark said in a stunned tone. "I was just thinking about you."

"You were? Well, I hope it was good things." She smiled warmly. "I just got back to the states, so I thought I could sign my lease now and pick up the keys, if that's okay with you."

"Sure . . . sure, come in, please."

Mark opened the door wide, and Julie stepped inside the foyer. He looked out toward the driveway. "Where's your truck?" he asked, closing the door behind her.

"In San Francisco. I flew in from a business appointment, and I had the driver the company hired bring me from the airport. He's circling the block. I know I probably should've called, but I guess my mind's a little preoccupied from the trip. I'm not intruding on anything, am I?" Julie tried to peek around the corner of the hallway and into the living room.

"No. Everything's in here." Mark gestured to the open office door. "I'll be right back. Make yourself at home."

He turned and walked into the office. He stubbed his toe on the doorjamb and cursed under his breath. He flicked the wall switch. He found the folder containing the lease in the center of the desk, right where he had left it. Then he pulled open the desk drawer and extracted the extra set of keys to the garage loft. "I hope you find everything in order," he called, as he shut the desk drawer.

He turned around and stopped. Julie had followed him inside the room. She stood in front of Jessie's painting. The fingers of her right hand just touched the outside of the frame. Mark watched her. She seemed mesmerized by it, as if someone had put her into a trance. In the dim light, he could see that her eyes had a faraway look to them, and the hint of a smile played on her lips. "Julie?"

Julie closed her eyes and took a step back from the picture. He saw her chest expand, as she took in a deep breath. "It's a beautiful piece," she whispered. "Your wife's work?"

Mark felt a lump forming in his throat and he swallowed hard. "Yes."

"The couple walking in it? That's you and Jessie, isn't it?"

Mark paused. He had never mentioned his wife's name to Julie. How did she know it? "I like to believe it is, yes."

Mark saw a shudder run through Julie's body. She hugged herself and buried her chin into her chest, her eyes still closed. "It . . . it holds special memories for you. This painting . . . the place it depicts . . . it has a special meaning . . . for both of you."

Mark took a step toward her. He glanced at the painting and then focused his attention on Julie. Is this what had happened when she saw the painting at Mrs. Johnson's place? "It's the park grove where I met her. Why do you ask?"

She suddenly straightened. Julie opened her eyes and looked at Mark. The clouded look that he had seen in them moments before was gone. Instead he thought he could see his reflection in the brown eyes behind the lenses. "No reason," she replied in a clear voice. "Your wife was very talented." She nodded toward the picture. "I'd like to see more of her work someday, if you don't mind, of course."

"Someday," Mark repeated, his mind still on what he had witnessed.

Julie gestured to the folder in his hand. "I take it that's the lease?"

So entranced with what he had just witnessed, Mark had forgotten her real purpose for being here. "Right. Here you go."

He handed the folder to her. She opened it up, walked out of the office, and into the living room, reading as she went. Mark followed her, watching her every move.

She moved through his house as if she had been here before. The hair on the back of his neck stood on end. It dawned on him that he hadn't run a background check on her. Outside of her name, her employer, and the fact that she paid the rent in full, he knew nothing about the woman who was taking over the empty space above his garage, yet she seemed to know so much about him. Who in the hell was she?

Julie sat down on the sofa, still reading. She stopped for a moment to glance around his spacious living room, painted in a soft pink rose color, and accented with walnut trim. The ivory-colored sofa, loveseat, and chairs complemented the room. A wood-and-glass curio cabinet in the corner stood empty, except for some framed photographs of Mark and Jessie and their friends. The walls were also bare, but Julie could make out hints of frame lines where she assumed more of Jessie's work once hung. She returned to her reading. She reached down and picked up a pen that Mark had left lying on the coffee table. She began tapping it against her right cheek. Mark stood off to the side, watching and noting her every action. "Can I get you something to drink?" he finally asked.

"No, thank you. This shouldn't take long." She read a little more. Then, content with what she saw, she flipped to the last page. "I take it you got the check," she said, as she started signing the paper.

"Yeah, I did." Mark paused, unsure whether he should do what he was about to do. He rushed forward: "And thank you for the other thing."

"What other thing?"

"My mortgage note? You paid it off."

Julie stared at him. "I paid it off? With the check I gave you?" She shrugged. "Okay."

Mark walked over to her and sat down, his gaze meeting hers. He knew the best way to tell if a person is lying is to look them in the eye while they're doing it. A flaring nostril, a look in the wrong direction, a twitch here or there was all he needed to detect. It was one of his hard-core rules when dealing with suspects and it rarely failed. He was the best on the force at finding out when a suspect was lying to him. "No. Someone paid the loan off with a wire; a wire that came in from a bank in San Francisco."

"I don't understand, Mark."

"Well, your company has an office in San Francisco."

"And in New York, Chicago, London, Stockholm, Cairo, Tokyo, Melbourne, and Beijing," Julie countered. "I don't see the connection."

"You're the only person outside the bank and my dad who knew about my . . . situation." Mark purposely left out Judge Embry. He still didn't believe that he had anything to do with it, and he didn't want to give Julie any indication that he thought another third party might have done it.

"What situation was that?"

"That I was having issues with the bank."

Julie just gaped at him. Then she put down the pen and stared at him hard. "And because of that, you think *I* paid your mortgage off? You actually think that I sent a wire to your bank, and told them to use it to pay your mortgage off?"

"Did you?" Mark retorted, his tone firm.

From the look of her face, Mark thought she was going to punch him. She shook her head. "Mark, officially, I've known you less than an hour," she began. "That's hardly enough time to know every little detail of your life, let alone your finances. Even if I wanted to know anything about them, it's really none of my business." She bit her tongue and fought to keep her voice in check: "Unofficially, I don't have the authority to tell my bosses to pay off other people's debts, let alone the time to find out anything about them, nor do I have the money to do it myself. My job keeps me busy enough and outside of that, I have enough responsibilities, like packing, rearranging all of my accounts, moving!" She stood up and gestured to the lease. "Look, if this is another way of telling me that you don't want me to sign this, fine. You can keep the money I gave you, since I'm certain that you've already spent it to pay this so-called mortgage debt, and I'll just go find someplace else to live."

Mark reeled. He had gone too far. She had given him no ticks. He rose and held up his hands in defense. "Julie, I'm sorry," he apologized. "I'm not trying to accuse you of anything. I'm just trying to figure out who did it and why, so I can thank them, and make some sort of arrangement to pay them back, that's all."

At first, Mark wasn't sure that Julie believed his sincerity. Her eyes still had a look of distrust about them. Finally, she sighed and sat back down. "Maybe it was a mistake, Mark," Julie said, turning her attention back to the document in front of her. She picked up the pen again. "Or, maybe someone realized that you were struggling, wanted to lend a hand, and wanted to do so anonymously. Whatever the reason, it was very nice of them. They could do that for me anytime."

Mark heard what she said, but didn't believe it. He knew better. Everything these days came with a price. He could only hope that whoever had done it didn't want too much in return.

She signed the last page of the lease just as a horn sounded outside. Julie looked up. She sighed in frustration. "That would be my driver. No doubt the bosses told him to do that. They need my report." She stood up and handed him the signed lease. She pressed the pen into Mark's hand. Her fingertips tickled his palm, and she stared him in the eye. "So? Are we settled?"

Mark took the pen and lease from her, still wary. The hairs on the back of his neck had gone down, but he still had an uneasy feeling in his stomach. Things were still uncertain in this relationship and he didn't know how to proceed. He met her gaze. "For now," he answered.

Her facial expression suddenly softened and she smiled. "Then I'll see you in a couple of days with my things."

Julie snatched the keys from the table, stepped around him, and made her way to the front door. As she opened it, Mark grabbed it. She turned to look at him. "Is there something else, Mark?"

Mark chose his words carefully: "If you did do it, would you ever admit it to me?"

Julie crossed her arms, thinking. "Probably not," she finally replied. "I wouldn't want you believing that you're somehow in my debt." She jingled the keys. "Thanks, again. I'll see you later."

"Yeah. 'Bye."

Mark watched her while she entered the back of the black Lincoln Town Car. The black male Kinshan saw earlier that day tipped his cap to Mark, before walking around the front and climbing into the driver's seat. Mark watched until the car pulled away from the curb and headed back down the street. He put a hand to the back of his head. To his surprise, it didn't hurt anymore, and the lump that was there a few minutes ago seemed to have disappeared. He shrugged. Arguing with her must've taken his mind off the pain. He closed and locked the door behind him, turned out the downstairs lights, and made his way to bed.

Inside the vehicle, Julie leaned back into the seat and breathed a sigh of relief. The driver checked for any oncoming traffic and then shifted his gaze to his rearview mirror. He studied her posture. A look of concern came to his face. "Are you all right, *miandi*?"

"Just too many close calls, that's all, Thomas. I see you got my message. Did anyone see you?"

"No, *miandi*."

Julie watched the flashing lights of the houses as they sped out of town, her mind drifting back to her conversation with Mark. Despite a stellar performance on her part, she was disappointed with herself. "The payoff of his mortgage? We did hide the money trail, correct?"

"Yes, *miandi*. NIK has taken care of that."

There was silence for a few moments. Julie recalled her initial assessment of Mark, and compared it to what she had just experienced. "I have to admit, Thomas. He is a challenge. Keeping my true nature from him may prove to be tougher than I thought."

"His deductive skills are very high. We warned you of that when you first selected this location."

"I know."

Julie leaned deeper into the seat. She wondered if had noticed that his head had stopped hurting. Julie sensed the injury before she walked into the door. She healed him when she handed back the pen. She chewed on her bottom lip. If he already had figured out that she had paid off his mortgage, how long would it be before Mark figured out the truth about her? More importantly, how would he react when he did? She pushed the thought aside. She had other things to worry about. "Let me know when we've reached the outskirts of the city, Thomas. I don't want anyone to catch our disappearing act."

*   *   *

Sophia Evans paused in her reading. Her solemn brown eyes shifted to her daughter who lay beside her. *She shouldn't be lying there*, Mrs. Evans thought again. She had not wanted Madison to go to school so far away from their home in Oklahoma City, but Madison had longed to return to Mason City since the day the family relocated to Oklahoma while she was still in junior high school. Besides, Madison was always a cautious girl. There was no way she would have ventured out of her apartment at night, and experimented with drugs? The news of her assault shook her parents to the core. Mrs. Evans had jumped on the plane in a rush, not even bothering to grab a toothbrush. She still was in the clothes she had been wearing three days ago. Her husband, Kenneth was due in tonight, and together they hoped to coax Madison awake.

She continued to watch the subtle rise and fall of her daughter's chest. Earlier that morning, Dr. McFadden had stopped in to check on her. She seemed happy with the latest results of Madison's vitals and blood work. Madison's condition was upgraded from critical to serious, but stable. She was recovering, and had started to show signs of regaining consciousness. The detectives handling her case had stopped by last evening to check in on Madison, and informed her of the capture of a man they believed assaulted her daughter. Mrs. Evans liked the two of them instantly and sensed their true determination to find their daughter's attackers.

Mrs. Evans stretched her arms and glanced at her watch. It was going on 9:00 a.m. She reached out to pat her daughter's left hand. "Sit tight, honey," she told her. "I'm going to get some coffee."

Mrs. Evans set the book down on the table and stole out of the room. She remembered that the cafeteria was two floors below Madison's room, as she headed for the elevator bank. Thirty seconds after Mrs. Evans had rounded the corner, a blonde woman wearing clothes similar to the rest of the hospital staff, emerged from the nearby stairwell. She glanced about, walked toward Madison's door, and entered the room unnoticed. From her lab coat pocket, she withdrew a syringe filled with a clear liquid. She reached for Madison's IV line, and inserted the needle into one of the ports. She pressed the plunger and injected it through the line, watching Madison's reactions. She didn't move and the nurse smiled. It would take about four Earth hours for the drug to have its full effect. When it did, her death would be quick and almost painless, or slow and drawn out. The nurse hoped for the latter. She loved it when her victims suffered.

She stared at the Earth woman unconscious on the bed. This woman would already be dead if her brother had done as she and her brother had wished. That was not their master's plan. He wished to accomplish two goals: to locate the elusive Illani, and draw out their fabled *miandi*. This human's death would only add to the guilt she already carried, and ensure that she remained on the planet until her master's human help could kill her.

She glanced at her watch and headed toward the door. She stepped back out into the hallway, smoothed out the front of her dress, and made her way toward the stairway. The door to it closed just as Mrs. Evans rounded the corner, a hot cup of coffee in her hand. She walked back into her daughter's room and smiled at her sleeping form. She looked so peaceful there, just as she had when she was a child. "Should I continue reading?" she asked her daughter, as she retrieved the book from the chair and settled back into it.

IX

"People of the State of Washington vs. Leonard Maurice Bartman."

Mark and Cassie straightened in their seats, as the bailiff led a handcuffed Leonard Bartman into the courtroom. He gave a chilling stare to the detectives before taking his spot on the opposite side of the room where the defense sat. The female public defender assigned to him whispered something in his ear, and he gave her a begrudging nod. Mark's attention turned to the bench. Judge Embry was there, as it was his turn in the circuit for arraignment hearings. His green eyes pierced the room, and his black robe set off his white hair and moustache. The hint of a white collar shirt and red tie poked out from underneath it. "Mr. Bartman," Judge Embry read in his deep voice, "the charges against you are two counts of assault in the first degree, and the attempted murder of Madison Suzanne Evans." He looked at Bartman's public defender, an olive-skinned, dark-haired woman named Claire Ilam. "Ms. Ilam, how does your client plead?"

"Your Honor, my client pleads not guilty, and we move that these charges be dismissed," she replied.

Judge Embry raised an eyebrow. "On what grounds?"

"Your Honor, the police have no physical evidence tying my client to the alleged victim. Their sole basis for arresting him was that he ran when the police went to question him."

Judge Embry moved his line of vision from the public defender toward the prosecutor's table. "Do the people have a rebuttal?"

"Your Honor, one of the people he assaulted was a police officer," argued the assistant district attorney, a Hispanic woman named Diana Courtade. "The people feel that there is enough evidence to warrant holding him with substantial bail."

"The people fail to inform His Honor that my client's actions were in self defense," Claire corrected her. "The defendant plans to file charges of his own, and possibly file a civil suit for the injuries he suffered as a result."

"What!" Diana exclaimed.

"The suspect was only picked out because they saw what they thought was a red tattoo, when in reality it was red paint from . . ."

"The officers identified themselves before he fled, Your Honor!"

"The suspect felt in danger for his life!"

"Your Honor, the officer had done nothing to him . . ."

Judge Embry held up his hand to silence them, although there was a slight thrill to watching two women going at it in his courtroom. He gazed back at the district attorney's table. "Is the officer who allegedly assaulted him in the courtroom?"

"Yes, Your Honor." Diana turned to Mark. "He's right here, sir."

Judge Embry looked toward the back of the courtroom. "Approach, sir," he ordered Mark.

Mark didn't understand. He had attended these before and they were usually routine. He looked at Cassie and then stood and made his way toward the front of the courtroom. Everyone there could see that Leonard may have a case for assault against Mark. He was half of Mark's height and build, looked like he hadn't eaten for weeks, and from his pockmarked face, was still recovering from some type of serious illness. He glanced over at the woman sitting behind the defense table. She was an attractive blonde, who had the same nose and cheekbones as him. It was probably his sister. She sat there, wringing her purse strap as if it would drip water, her chin trembling. Mark returned his gaze back to Judge Embry. "Yes, sir?"

"State your name for the record, sir."

Mark was slightly insulted. *Fine, I'll play the game.* "Detective Mark Daniels, Serious Crimes, and lead investigator. Your Honor, I wish to state for the record that I and Detective Cassie Edwards did not harm this suspect in any way."

"Was your partner was there when this alleged assault took place? Can testify to this under oath?"

Mark swallowed and tried not to look back at Cassie. He already knew that she was cowering even further in her seat. Diana took over: "Your Honor, the People contend that we have the man who assaulted Madison Evans, and if you let him go, you'll be letting the prime suspect and possibly a potential killer on the street."

Judge Embry shuffled papers on his bench. "That may be your opinion Ms. Courtade. However, I've reviewed the evidence that the officers have presented." He rubbed his head. "Right now, the defense motion is warranted, and I'm inclined to grant it."

Mark was incensed. The blow he had taken to the back of his head had been for nothing? "What!"

Diane put a restraining arm on his forearm. "Detective," she murmured.

Mark jerked his arm away. He glared at Judge Embry. "Your Honor, this man assaulted me while fleeing a lawful arrest, and he was seen accosting the victim just days before her attack!"

"You're out of line, Detective," Judge Embry warned him.

Mark didn't care. His case was tighter than the yarn in a baseball. Now he had to watch while the prime suspect walked. "Your honor, our victim was beaten within an inch of her life, my partner and I almost die, and you're going to believe this bullshit he's feeding you?"

At those words, Judge Embry straightened. His green eyes were afire. He pointed his gavel at Mark. "In my chambers, Detective. Now!"

Mark looked at Diana, who stared back at him, baffled. He looked back at Cassie, who had sunk so low in her seat that she nearly disappeared. Mark straightened and made his way to the front of the room. He fought to bring some of his anger back into line as the bailiff escorted him down a narrow corridor, where he saw the back of Judge Embry's robes disappear into a room. Mark took a deep breath and followed the judge inside a room filled with various law books. His desk was immaculate, save for a few files that he had not yet read. All of his law books stood in a line on their bookshelves, occasionally broken up by a decorative vase or photograph. Mark had been in here more than once to get warrants signed by him. Judge Embry nodded to the bailiff, who shut the door behind them. He walked behind his desk and turned to face Mark. "I would be citing you for contempt and throwing you into jail, if you weren't who you are," Judge Embry told him in a solemn tone.

Mark was aware of that and was surprised that wasn't what the judge was doing. "Then why am I here, sir?" Mark asked in a low voice.

Judge Embry crossed his arms and looked Mark in the eye. "I thought I'd spare you the embarrassment of being dressed down in front of a packed courtroom and, based on the way the woman in back was slouching, your new partner."

Mark's protest died in his throat. He gave the judge a blank stare. "What?"

Judge Embry shook his head. "Mark Daniels, you're a better detective than this. Granted, I don't believe the story about you assaulting Mr. Bartman, but you really had no reason to arrest him. His description probably fits a number of men in this town. Also, I studied the evidence that you've collected regarding his alleged attack against Ms. Evans, and it's weak at best. You have no physical evidence to tie him to the scene, no fingerprints, and no eyewitnesses. The only way that you can tie him to your victim is the statement of a woman claiming that she may have seen the two of them talking outside of her workplace a few days prior."

"Sir, I disagree. Based on the evidence we have, we feel he's more than likely her assailant. Once the victim awakens . . ."

"If the victim awakens," Judge Embry quietly countered, "she might be able to help you tie him to the crime. Until then, you have nothing."

"He was seen outside her workplace two days before the assault, and when we went to question him, he ran."

"And when did running turn into assault?" Judge Embry raised a white eyebrow and narrowed his eyes. "I'd like to give you the benefit of the doubt, Detective, since you're just returning to work, but unless you can bring more proof to charge him with, the defense's motion is warranted. I have no choice, Detective. I have to let him go."

Mark stared at the judge. He didn't want to listen to him anymore. The best suspect that they had would be leaving the courthouse in a few minutes, probably for parts unknown. Although Madison looked like she was recovering, the doctors couldn't tell them when or if Madison would wake up. Mark took a deep breath. "Then I guess I should get out there and look for it," he murmured.

He turned to leave the judge's chambers. Mark's hand had just touched the doorknob, when Judge Embry asked, "I've been meaning to ask you, Mark, how's your mortgage situation?"

Mark stiffened. Did he know? Possibly, since he had been the one who signed his eviction papers. He had to know that the papers were never served, and that there had been no need to. Sandy wouldn't have told him, but he could have other contacts in the Recorder's office. All Mark knew was that he hadn't called the number on that business card. He found the tattered remains of it in the office trash can this morning, just where he had left them. He had been hoping that his hunch about Julie paying it off had been right. Her reaction last night had dismissed that notion. He tried to relax. "Fine, sir. Thanks for asking."

"Good, good. I knew that it would be. My friend can work wonders on short notice. Oh, and I trust that everything has been arranged for its repayment?"

Bile rose up in the back of Mark's throat. It was the response that he had been praying he wouldn't hear. "Not yet," he whispered. "I'm certain that they'll be in touch soon."

"I'll certain they will. Now, I think I need to get back to work, and so do you."

"Yes, sir."

Mark opened the door and left the judge's chambers. The walk seemed interminable. Somehow, he made it back into the courtroom. Diana gazed at him, trying to determine what the judge had told him, but Mark only shook his head. He made his way to the back and took a seat next to Cassie, trying not to give her any indication of how he felt right now. Cassie noticed that Mark looked pale and distracted. She put a hand over his. "Mark? Are you all right?"

"All rise."

Their attention returned to the front of the room. Judge Embry had returned to the bench. His face was the perfect poker face, as he stared at the assistant district attorney and picked up his gavel. "The charges against the defendant are dismissed. I grant leave to the prosecution to re-file, once they have obtained sufficient evidence."

Mark closed his eyes as the gavel came down. Leonard turned to his attorney and gave her hand a vigorous shake. Then he turned to the woman behind him, and gave her a bear hug. As he did so, he looked over the woman's shoulder, and gave Mark and Cassie a toothless sneer. Cassie's eyes were afire with anger. "Bastard," Cassie murmured, her gaze turning toward Judge Embry. "We had him dead to rights."

Mark's gaze refocused on the bench. The judge had already moved on to the next arraignment. He hadn't bothered to look Mark's way. Mark gave him a hard stare, and then he turned and left the room. He headed toward the crowded hallway, filled with attorneys, police and court officials. He stared off through the glass at the cityscape before him, Judge Embry's words ringing in his head. He didn't want to be here. He didn't want to be a cop anymore. For the first time since Jessie died, he didn't want to go home tonight. He would only be waiting for the phone call that he didn't want to take. Everything he believed in and fought for had just become corrupted and stained, slick with tar and grime. His life would not be the same, there was nothing he could do to change it, and he felt sick to his stomach about it.

"Mark?"

He looked up. Cassie had taken a position beside him. She still didn't like what she saw or sensed from him. "Mark? What happened back in chambers? What did the judge say to you?"

Mark shook his head. "C'mon, Cassie. Let's get back to work."

"What about him?" Cassie gestured toward the departing Leonard Bartman, who had walked past the two of them, clutching his sister as they departed the courtroom and heading toward the elevator banks. "We're just going to let him go?"

"We have to. We don't have the goods yet. Now, let's go find them."

Cassie gave him a look of exasperation. "All right, where do we start?"

"First, let's get away from the theory that she was just a victim of a routine mugging."

"Okay. Which angle do we take now?"

Mark reached into his jacket pocket and stared at the sketchy map of the area Madison had researched. Like the business card that had once been there, it burned against his chest. He had once unfolded it in front of Leonard during the interrogations. He had seen Leonard's eyes drift toward it, and Leonard didn't correct his gaze quick enough for Mark not to notice it. Mark chewed on his lower lip. "Let's assume that there's another reason why Madison was attacked. Let's assume that it was Madison's research, and that this land is the key," he said, tapping the piece of paper. "We need to get more information about the work she did without going back to Terrance for it." Mark frowned. "Too bad Tyler's in L.A."

"Tyler?"

"You haven't been introduced to Sergeant Martin from the tech room yet?"

"No. Why?"

"Just meet him first. That's usually enough for most people."

Cassie took the paper from him, reading it. "Well, we could try the land records office for Okanogan County. Maybe they can help."

"Land records?"

Cassie shrugged. "It's a starting point, at least. Maybe someone there can tell us something, or at least give us some direction as to where to start looking."

Mark thought about what Cassie said. Then he smiled. "Good idea, and I know just the person who can help."

He took the paper from her and headed around the corner toward the elevator banks. Curious, Cassie followed him. She reached him just as he hit the "Up" button on the elevator panel. Cassie took a step back.

Her face took on a look a fright. "Mark? Where are you going?"

"Upstairs to the land records office and you're coming with me."

She pointed a shaky finger at herself. "Me?" she squeaked.

"C'mon. It's your idea."

Her eyes widened and a thin line of sweat began to break out across her brow. "But . . . it's upstairs," she whispered.

Mark leaned down. "Yes, Cassie, and we're in an enclosed building, not an open tower," he murmured. The elevator doors opened and he stepped inside. "It's perfectly safe. It's only a couple of floors from the precinct, and I'll be with you the entire time."

Cassie hesitated. Already, her hands had started to tremble. Mark stepped back out, took her hands, and guided her into the waiting elevator. The doors closed and it began to move. They were the only ones on it, but it was little comfort to her. Cassie watched and swallowed repeatedly as the indicator moved upward. She began to sway a little and she closed her eyes tight. Mark reached out and gripped her left hand with his right. "It's all right, Cassie," he whispered. "You'll get through this."

"Right," she murmured, fighting the urge not to vomit all over him. The courtrooms were on the fourth floor, but the counter had already moved past the tenth, and the elevator still climbed. "'Only a couple of floors', you said."

"Hey, this was your brainstorm. I think it's only appropriate that you explain it."

They approached their destination floor. Cassie's grip grew so tight, he thought she was going to break every bone in his hand. "Hey, no hurting the gun hand," he teased.

"Can I hurt another part of your anatomy for making me do this?"

Just then, the doors opened. Cassie stumbled out and felt her way to the non-windowed wall, breathing heavily. Then she slid down to sit on the floor. Her eyes were still shut tight. She trembled from head to toe, and Mark thought that she might to pass out. Mark squatted down next to her and put an understanding hand on her shoulder. "Hey, partner, you did it."

She managed to crack open one eye to stare at him. "Great," she croaked. "For this, you are permanently off my Christmas card list."

Mark chuckled, cupped her elbows, and helped her to stand again. Then he led her into the office. They had to wait a little bit, as there was a line. Finally, Sandy's window opened up, and Mark and Cassie approached it. "Back so soon?" Sandy greeted him. "I thought I gave you good news the last time I saw you."

"You did Sandy, and thanks." He motioned to Cassie. "This is Cassie Edwards, my new partner. Cassie, this is Sandy Youngblood."

Cassie was still pale and trembling, and she couldn't raise her eyes to meet Sandy's. Sandy gave her a quizzical look. "Are you all right?"

Cassie managed to nod. She kept her back to the windows behind them, and grabbed the counter so she wouldn't sink to the floor. Mark patted Cassie on the shoulder and then turned his attention back to Sandy. "Sandy? Do you know anyone at the Okanogan County Recorder's office?"

"No, but I can call up there. Why?"

"Could you request a search for us there?"

"Sure. What're you looking for?"

Mark pulled out the piece of paper they had been reading earlier from his shirt pocket. He unfolded it. "We're trying to track down the owners of a piece of property up near the Canadian border. It looks like most of it falls in Okanogan County."

Sandy studied the information on the paper. "Why? What's going on?"

"We're just curious. It's become a focal point of our investigation. We'd just like to know a little more about it and its owners, if possible."

"That's fascinating, but what does this have to do with you? I thought you dealt with assaults and killings."

"You heard about the woman who was beaten in the park?"

"It's been all over the news. Why?"

"She was doing research on this land before she was attacked."

Sandy gasped. "Man, that's awful." She studied the map and the notes Madison had made in one of the corners. Her brow wrinkled, as she tried to estimate its location, and the amount of land it referenced. "Okanogan County's way north of here, and they're not that big of a county government," she cautioned them. "Most of their county is huge countryside and Amendu reservation land. On top of that, their records may not be on computer yet. It could take some time."

"Just try, Sandy." Mark winked at her. "Please?"

Sandy gave Mark an admiring look and winked back. "I will, for a price."

Mark gulped and stared at Cassie. Cassie gave him a vengeful smile. In her mind, a date with Sandy was a small price to pay for the torture he had just given her.

*   *   *

Ambassador?

Julie was in one of the Illani laboratories with Alexandra, Patrick, and Eliza, the Illani scientists who had accompanied her on her trip to see the Amendu children. They were concluding the final tests of the antitoxin they had developed to combat the *sorja* root that the Amendu had ingested. She and Alexandra were leaving for the reservation shortly to help Alexandra administer it. At the sound of NIK's voice, they all looked up toward the ceiling. "Yes, NIK?" Julie answered.

A new inquiry has been launched.

Julie and the Illani stopped their work. "By whom?"

It was initiated in the Mason County Recorder's office. However, all information is to be forwarded to

Detective Mark Daniels or Detective Cassie Edwards of the Serious Crimes unit.

The white figures with Julie stared at her. The expression that showed in their black eyes was the same. Julie drummed her fingers on the immaculate counter. Events had started to move faster than she had anticipated. She thought back to the day in the courtyard with the Caretaker. "NIK, the woman who was beaten? Didn't you say that she worked for a real estate agent?"

Yes, Ambassador. She was the person who initiated the last inquiry six weeks ago on behalf of her employer, Terrance Carnegie.

"What's her condition?"

Her condition is slowly improving, but she is still unconscious.

"What about Antoinette? Has she sent a response out?"

No, Ambassador. She is waiting on instruction from you.

"Good. Tell her to delay sending out the information on the land ownership as long as she can. Also, keep an eye on the woman in the hospital. Inform me the minute that anything changes with her. In the meantime . . ." Julie stared back at the Illani with her. "I'll come up with something."

As you wish, Ambassador.

Julie turned away from the Illani scientists and walked a few steps away. She stared at the pristine space and reached out to sense the heartbeats of the 300-plus spheres in the nursery. Their future emergence was in danger and Julie didn't understand how or why. The Illani with her watched her body tense. Finally, Patrick spoke: "You're worried, *miandi*."

Julie sighed. First the Amendu were attacked, then a humanoid woman who had done research about this land. They didn't seem to be connected, but instinctively Julie knew that they were. They had to be. "I don't understand why this is happening. Has someone else discovered you're here? If so, how?"

"There are two Narcalonians who know we are here," Alexandra countered.

"Yes, but they couldn't tell anyone without severe repercussions." Julie shook her head. Telepathically, she instructed NIK to alter the communication codes with the Illani, and to limit contact with their systems until further notice. She also instructed NIK to inform all of their outside contacts to limit communication with the farm to an absolute necessity. She then turned her attention to her newest concern: Detective Mark Daniels and his ongoing investigation. She had not made mention of it to him the night before when she retrieved her keys. His pursuit of information regarding whether she had paid off his mortgage had driven the thought from her. Now, she realized that she needed to pursuit it in earnest. She stared at the vials of antitoxin waiting to be given to the Amendu. Their poisoning was only one small part of the puzzle. She needed more. "I need to talk to him," she murmured. "I need to ask him about the case, and how it's proceeding."

"How will you do that without drawing more suspicion, *miandi*?" Eliza inquired.

"I don't know, but I need to know what he knows."

"But according to NIK, they have very little to go on," Patrick offered.

"That's true. Right now, he just has a woman who was beaten. To him, it's probably still a robbery case." Julie frowned. She knew the best way for her to find out what Mark knew would be to "read" his mind. She hated this particular gift of hers: the ability to interpret the lightning-fast brain signals and chemical reactions a humanoid brain produced to create thought. All the immortals possessed it, but she was the best at it. When she was younger, Simon used to take her to planets that did not know they were immortal, especially those planets where the people had exceptional telepathic skills. Simon's limited strength made it difficult for him to engage in it as readily as he used to. He quickly discovered that no humanoid could block their thoughts from her. She didn't mind probing people's minds when she had to. It was sorting the thoughts from the intense, sometimes overwhelming emotions that accompanied them that she hated.

Julie began to pace the laboratory, trying to think of another way to get the information she needed from Mark. Her stomach rumbled. Absently, she patted it. Yes, she could live forever, but she was also humanoid. It was this part of her that she felt gave her advantages over the others. First, it meant that she needed to eat. Second, she could indulge in all the exotic food tastes that her traveling had to offer. Being on Earth meant that she could overindulge on her favorite food. She tried to recall how long it had been since she had eaten and the answer to her question came to her. Julie turned to the white form to her left. "Alexandra? Can you and the others handle the distribution of the medication? I think I need to go to lunch."

*　　*　　*

"I'm getting a headache from reading all of this. Are you?"

Cassie grunted. Mark's new theory on the case had turned into the worst day of reading either of them had experienced as police officers. While Sandy waited for a further response from the Okanogan County Recorder, she had done a little of her own. She brought down the results to them an hour ago, with much thanks from Cassie. Sandy determined that the Amendu, the native tribe that had settled in the area owned more than ninety percent of the targeted land, some two million acres of woodland. However, the Amendu shared ownership of about 10,000 acres with someone else. Along with the land information, Sandy found another document related to the land. They were at their desks now, trying to decipher it. "I don't recognize any of the words in it, except one: sale," Cassie commented. "We should have someone at the district attorney's office look at this. What this thing is talking about is way beyond me."

Mark had to agree. It was a complicated document, written in the tribe's native language, although the English word, "sale" was in the document. According to the date of its signing, it went back to the early seventeenth century, before European explorers had entered this part of the country. He turned his attention to the numerous maps. Among them was a color photograph of the land in question. He tilted his chair and rocked on its back legs, studying it. It looked like a nice area. It appeared to be acres and acres of evergreen and hardwood forests surrounding pristine blue lake water. There looked to be a clearing as well with a couple of structures sitting on it. Off in the lower right corner of the photo was a piece of land that looked to be dead. He could see the toothpicks passing for trees still standing on it. "I wonder if this area of land falls within the provisions of that agreement," Mark mused, circling the dead area of the picture with his index finger. "It's probably really close to the Canadian border. Even if it isn't, it doesn't look like it's worth much."

As the two of them continued to read, Mark's desk phone rang. He glared at it over the photograph. Frowning, he set the legs of his chair back down on the floor, and casually reached for it: "Serious Crimes, Detective Mark Daniels."

"Hi, Mark."

Mark's eyes opened wide. After what he said last night, he was surprised she even wanted to talk to him: "Julie?"

Cassie looked up from her reading. A quizzical look came across her face. "Who's Julie?" she whispered.

"My new tenant," he mouthed back. "I'll explain later."

"I'm not interrupting you, am I?"

Mark turned his attention back to the phone. "No, I thought you went back to San Francisco."

"I did, but it's only an hour by airplane. Anyway, I wanted to thank you for everything that you've done so far, and I was wondering if you were free for lunch today?"

Mark stared at Cassie. In all honesty, he needed to stay at work. Madison Evans was still unconscious. There still was no clear motive as to why she was attacked, and her suspected assailant had just been set free. They also had to plow through the remaining results of Sandy's search. However, a burning curiosity lingered about the woman who would soon be virtually living in his home. The obsessive cop knew that he needed to get to know her better. Then again, what if she wanted something more? He cupped his hand over the mouthpiece, forcing back the wave of panic that had begun to build. "My tenant's inviting me to lunch," Mark whispered to Cassie. "What do I do?"

Cassie shrugged her shoulders. "Is she attractive?"

Mark stared. "I . . . guess . . . I don't know. She's just a kid."

"What do you know about her?"

Mark shrugged. "She's black."

"I'm certain she's aware of that fact. What else?"

"Well she's employed, and she travels a lot, and . . ."

Cassie gave Mark an incredulous look. "I don't believe what I'm hearing. The man who's so thorough about his cases rents a room to a complete stranger, without bothering to find out anything about them? Good work, Mark Daniels, ace detective."

Mark swallowed. So much happened these past few days, he hadn't bothered to run a background check on Julie. Then again, when you are desperate to save your home and someone takes a room and hands you $10,000.00 with no questions asked, why bother? *Perhaps because she took the room and gave you a $10,000.00 check with no questions asked*, the cop reminded him. He gave her a sheepish smile. "I guess this is my chance, isn't it?"

"Uh, yeah, especially since she's buying. After all, don't forget the first rule of life."

"The first rule of life?"

"Never pass up any opportunity for free food." Cassie smiled, stood, and grabbed her notebook. "I'll go talk to Madison's ex-boyfriend. Apparently, he's back in town. I need a break from this anyway," she added, gesturing to the reading before them. "Just remember your starving partner, all right?"

Mark winked at Cassie. He took his hand away from the mouthpiece and settled back into his chair. "Sure, Julie. I'd be happy to join you. Where at, and what time would you like to meet?"

X

Scordalia's was an Italian restaurant in the heart of the retail and restaurant section of downtown Mason City, about six blocks from the precinct. Rumor had it that reservations were required just to get a seat at its bar. Mark had been past its black-and-gray marble entrance numerous times in his wanderings. Jessie and Mark decided to eat there once, until a friend told them how expensive it was. They promised each other that they would save the trip for a really special occasion, like her first gallery opening at the San Francisco Museum of Art. As Mark approached, he suddenly realized that day had never come. Instead, he was dining here with a woman who was still a stranger to him.

Julie waited for him by the canopied front door, dressed in a gray tweed suit and black mock turtleneck sweater. Her eyes danced behind her glasses. "You're right on time."

"I haven't kept you waiting, have I?" he asked, reaching for the silver door handle.

"No. I just arrived myself."

Julie gave her name to the hostess. "We've been expecting you, Miss Warren," she told her, as she turned and led them through the tomato red and Italian black-leather accented restaurant. Mark felt underdressed, walking in just wearing jeans, a black polo shirt, and his leather jacket. Everyone else inside were in either expensive business suits and ties, or the newest spring fashions. The couple received more than a few curious stares from patrons while their hostess led to a corner booth and handed their menus. Mark did a quick glance about to see if recognized anyone. In one corner, he saw Judge Embry with one of the city's prominent business people. He seemed to stare at Julie more so than at him. She didn't seem to notice. Mark wondered if the judge knew her from somewhere, of if she reminded him of someone.

They settled into their seats and their server was there almost immediately, pouring them glasses of lemon-flavored water, and informing them of the specials. He left them for a few moments while they perused the selections. "I'm treating today, so order what you want," Julie said, "and don't look at the right side, please."

Automatically, Mark's eyes drifted to the right side of the menu. The prices started in the $50.00 range, and only went up. He tried not to raise an eyebrow. This was just for lunch? He didn't even want to think about how much dinner would cost. He struggled to make out what the dishes were, but the menu was in

Italian, or so he thought. He glanced up at Julie. "Any recommendations?"

"Don't ask me. I'll recommend everything."

Frowning, Mark skimmed the menu with his finger, hoping to recognize any word on it. His eyes fell on a dish that looked like it had chicken it. He moved his lips, trying to sound out its name. Julie noticed where he was pointing. "It's grilled chicken breasts, marinated in a white wine, garlic and rosemary sauce, topped with fresh pesto," she explained.

Mark looked at her. "Is it good?"

"It's wonderful. It's what I'm having." She handed the menu back to their server, who had returned to take their order. "Along with a salad."

Mark shrugged. Nothing else caught his fancy, not that he understood a word on the menu. "Then make it two," he replied, handing his menu back.

"And to drink?"

Mark sighed, as he turned back to gaze at the bar. A golden opportunity was going to waste because he was still on duty. "I'll stick to this," he said, tapping the water glass.

"And for you, madam?"

"Water's fine for me, also," Julie replied.

Their server collected the menus and walked away. Mark looked at her with amusement. Julie was drinking water in a restaurant that had the best wine cellars in the Pacific Northwest. It was the main reason most people entertained clients here. Her company didn't seem to care where she dined. "No liquor on the job?" he teased.

Julie unfolded her napkin and placed it on her lap. "No liquor, period. It tends to do nasty things to me."

"Oh? Like what?"

She shrugged. "Heart palpitations, hives, and dizziness."

"Whoa! What do you do when all they're serving is alcohol?"

Julie smiled. "I manage."

They paused in their conversation when someone delivered their bread basket. Mark inhaled the scent of fresh-chopped garlic and chives coming out of it, and reached for a loaf. He ripped it in half, and took a bite. It was good. In fact, it was fabulous—fresh from the oven and no butter necessary. He chewed and pondered the woman who had so abruptly entered his life. *No, not woman—girl,* Mark thought. He knew that it was chauvinistic to think that way, but there was no way that Julie was out of her mid-twenties. He felt certain that she wasn't much older than Madison was. "So? Officially, when are you moving in?"

"Tomorrow afternoon, I hope. I'll have to beg off some assignments." She closed her eyes and rubbed her head. "I need the break, though. I feel like I haven't been able to think straight these past few days."

"I know that feeling." Mark took another bite of his bread. "Mrs. Johnson said that you stopped by to see her."

"Mrs. Johnson?"

"Ruth Johnson, one of my neighbors . . . our neighbors," Mark corrected. He finished his first loaf and reached for a second. Forget lunch. He could skip his meal and live on this, it was that good. "She lives across the street, in the yellow house?"

Julie thought for a moment. Then a smile broke out. "The one with all the flowers?"

Mark nodded. Julie's expression turned reminiscent. "She's a wonderful woman. I don't think her dog likes me, though."

"Nipper? He just has to get used to you, that's all." He wanted to ask her about what she had said to Mrs. Johnson about her husband and the fifty-year-old broken plate, but he pushed it aside. It was a fluke.

He finished the remainder of his bread, brushing his fingers off in his lap. After a few moments, their server returned with their salads. Mark stared at his plate, tossing the lettuce about. Then he looked at her again. He rubbed his chin with his free thumb and thought back to everything he had done in the days before her arrival. He knew that he had pulled the advertisement at least two weeks before she appeared on his doorstep. His place was not near a major street, and you couldn't see the sign just by driving by the place. *How did she find me? How did she find my place? She must have researched me ahead of time, and acted from that. That can only mean one thing: she needs something or wants something from me.*

Julie felt the intensity of his gaze and looked up from her plate. She tilted her head, trying to read his face. It showed warmth and sensitivity, yet those eyes of his seemed determined to penetrate through to her inner self, and extract the secrets within. She wondered if this was what he looked like when he was questioned a suspect. "What?"

Her eyes—even behind the glasses, they're so clear and focused, and yet so . . . old. I always like to pretend that I can see right to a person's soul. Why do I feel like she actually can? He smiled. "Nothing."

"It's more than nothing. You look like you want to ask me a question."

Mark set his fork down and leaned forward. "Can I?"

"Sure."

Mark thought quickly. First, the most burning question: "How did you know my wife's name?"

"Your wife?"

"Jessie? You mentioned her name when you looked at her painting. I never told you what it was. How did you know it?"

Julie thought for a moment. She must've done it again. She became so absorbed in the painting, she lost touch with where she was and whom she was with. She did the same thing at Mrs. Johnson's house when she sensed the guilt her husband carried over breaking that plate, but never admitting to it before he died. She picked up her glass and took a sip of the lemon-flavored liquid. "I saw a portrait of the Johnsons when I entered their home. The artist had signed it in the corner. I saw the same signature on the one in your office. You mentioned at our initial meeting that she was a painter. I assumed that she painted them both, and that's what her name was."

Mark stared at her. Inside, his stomach did a flip flop. She lobbed his first serve right back at him, a volley that landed right in the corner. He cleared his throat and tried again. "The check that you gave me? You know it more than covers the rent for a year."

Julie took another sip of water and nodded. "I'm like that. I always like to pay my bills well in advance. That way, I know that everything's taken care of. I know you can do much of it online these days, but my schedule changes constantly and I don't like to rely on others to pay my debts for me. Also, given your initial impressions of me, I didn't want you to also think that I'm a deadbeat."

He studied at her appearance. She wore minimal makeup and jewelry, but he could tell that her gray tweed suit, like the one she wore the night before, was custom tailored. A driver came to pick her up the other evening, and one probably picked her up at the airport and dropped her off here. Despite the low level her position carried, her employer took very good care of her. He often wondered what it was like to have no worries about how you were going to pay for something. "So I take it that you come from money?"

"My employer pays me well, but not so well that I could pay someone's mortgage off, like you claimed I did."

Mark hung his head. "Yeah, well about that . . ."

"Don't worry about it. I'm over it. You should be too."

Mark picked up his glass and swirled the water in it. "On you business card, you listed yourself as a consultant. So who and what exactly do you consult?"

Julie reached for her fork and picked at her salad. "I counsel everyone from world leaders and business people, to rival tribe factions and would-be murderers." She took a bite, chewed for a few minutes, and swallowed. "I'm more of a mediator than a consultant," she clarified. "I try to help people search for diplomatic means, rather than reaching for a weapon, real or otherwise, to solve their problems."

"Real or otherwise?"

Julie pursed her lips. "There're many ways to hurt people that don't involve bullets or knives, Mark—like with words, or deprivation of food, water, or medical care—or the chance to be with loved ones."

Mark thought on her statement. When put that way, it made a lot of sense. He gave her a sardonic grin. "Building a stronger universe one life at a time, huh?"

"You like our slogan?"

"I have to admit it's unusual." Mark picked up his fork again and took a bite of his salad. "And pretty lofty."

"I don't think so. I mean, do we really know whether we're the only ones out here?"

"Who knows?" Mark ate a few more bites of his salad. The house dressing was incredibly tasty. Jessie would've loved it. *Stop it, Detective. You're here for information. Treat her like a potential suspect. Don't let your baggage get in the way.* "What about humanitarian things? Does your company do anything along those lines?"

"Yes. Actually, that's why I was in Somalia." She reached for a loaf of bread, picked up her butter knife, and sliced through it. "It's been an ongoing project these last ten years or so. Our corporation sends someone at least twice a year to see how it's progressing. This year was my turn."

"It sounds like your work keeps you pretty busy."

Julie took another bite of her salad and dipped a piece of her bread into the dressing that had formed a puddle on the side. She savored the taste of the bread and the dressing. She glanced at the kitchen door. From the cook's mind, she extracted the recipes, and transmitted them to NIK. If she ever had the chance, she would try to make both of them herself. "Yes, but I like to stay busy."

"It doesn't leave much time for a social life." He raised an eyebrow. "So, is there anyone?"

"Anyone?"

"You know, boyfriend, fiancé, significant other? Is there another face I should be keeping an eye out for?" He picked up his glass again and stared at her through the condensation and ice. He gave her a teasing wink. "You know? Can I expect someone walking into your place when you're not there?"

"No, there isn't." She paused, as if she just realized what he had asked. She looked up at him. "This isn't your way of making yourself available to me, is it?"

She took another bite of her salad and winked back at him. Mark nearly spat out the water in his mouth. He spilt even more as he tried to set the glass back down on the table, hoping he wouldn't choke on what he had swallowed. His eyes watered and he gaped at her. A broad grin crossed her face and her eyes sparkled with mischief. "Gotcha."

"Funny," he sputtered, reaching for his napkin. "At least now I know that you have a sense of humor."

They finished their salads just as their server returned with their meals. They settled down to eat, take in the people, the atmosphere, and the conversations around them. Mark fought to savor every bite. He could taste the hint of garlic and white wine in the sauce, and the pasta melted on his tongue without tasting floury or doughy. Then Julie asked: "So, what about you? You told me the day we met that you're a detective?"

"Yes, with the Mason City Police."

"What type of crimes do you investigate?"

"Mostly murders, assaults and kidnappings. I worked vice for a year or two before moving up."

"How long have you been a police officer?"

"Fifteen years."

"That's such a long time to do one thing! Are you good?"

"I'm told that I'm one of the best."

"No, I mean seriously."

Mark took another bite of his meal before answering. He didn't like to brag about how good he was. "It was a team effort," he insisted whenever Charlie gave him the credit for breaking a tough case. "I have a case closure rate in the 95th percentile," he replied in a low tone. "Highest in the state."

Julie sat back in her chair. "Wow! You really are good!"

"I just do my job, Julie. I do it well, but I couldn't do it without my partners."

"Partners?"

"Charlie McKenzie, for one." Mark took another bite of his meal. He chewed and swallowed before continuing. "You probably won't get a chance to meet him. He moved to Arizona some time ago. He was shot in the line of duty."

"Charlie." Julie remembered that name from the research on Mark, but Mark had said partners. "Who's the other one?"

"Cassie Edwards. We've only been paired up a few days, so we'll have to see what happens there."

"I'm sure it'll be fine. One of these days, you'll have to tell me more about them. In the meantime, I'll need to make sure to steer clear of you if I do anything wrong."

Mark gave her a devilish grin and took another bite of his meal. "You? Do anything wrong?"

"I don't mean that I would purposely go out and break the law. I just mean that if I was one of the bad guys and I saw you coming, I would definitely run." She twirled her pasta around her fork with her spoon. "What about your family? Do they like what you do?"

Mark bit into his chicken, saying nothing for a moment. "My mother's dead," he murmured. "My dad's an attorney. He lives in Seattle."

"Do you see him?"

Mark glanced up at her quickly. "No . . . not that I mind."

Julie swallowed what she had eaten. There was no need to read his mind to realize this subject was off limits. She reached for another roll, wondering how to recover. "So, your work? Do they frown upon you talking about your cases with an outsider?"

"No, not that I really have any I could talk about. I just came back on the job." Mark stared out toward Judge Embry's table. He was just getting up to leave, and he glanced over at the two of them and nodded. Mark didn't nod back. What happened in and outside the courtroom earlier that morning still irritated him. "The one I'm investigating right now is proving troublesome. Cassie and I are still trying to pin down a motive for it."

"Why? What's going on with it?"

Mark took another loaf of bread. "You might not have heard, since you've been in and out of town. A woman was beaten and left for dead in a park this past Sunday night."

Julie set her fork down, stunned. "What? But why? How?"

"We're not certain. At first we thought she was just a mugging victim, but from what we've been able to gather, it looks like she found out some information regarding a property sale that might not be as legitimate as it seems. Someone threatened her life, or at least to keep quiet about it."

"Over a piece of land? Where at?"

He picked up his water glass again. "Up in the northern part of the state somewhere. We haven't pinned down the exact location. It's a huge parcel, from what little we've been able to find out about it. From the pictures, it appears to be acres of forestland. It also looks like there might be some structures there. I think it might have been abandoned by its owners. We haven't been able to track them down."

Just then, a cellular phone rang and Mark's ears perked up. He relaxed when he realized that it wasn't his. It rang again. He stared at her purse. "I think that's yours," he commented.

"Mine?"

The phone rang a third time. Julie looked down at her purse, tucked under the table. "Oh. Excuse me."

She picked up her purse, pulled out a silver flip phone, and answered it: "This is Julie . . . . Yes? Yes, I sent it an hour ago." She positioned her elbow on the table, rested her forehead in her left hand, and gave Mark a look of exasperation. "I'm at lunch right now. Can't it . . . I understand the importance of it, but . . ." Julie sighed, sat up, and rolled her eyes. "All right, all right! I'll go back to the car and resend it to you . . . when I'm done with my lunch, please!"

She hung up and snapped the phone shut. Mark grinned. "Paperwork, I take it?"

She made a face and slipped the phone back into her purse. "I hate it. It never seems to end, but in my job, it's just a part of the routine."

As they finished their meal, their server brought over the dessert tray. Mark passed, but he gave Julie a curious stare as she ordered one of everything that included chocolate. She caught his amused smile and despite her dark skin, he swore she blushed. "I love chocolate," she admitted.

"I noticed."

The server packaged all five of her desserts neatly in a carryout bag and delivered them along with the bill. She perused it quickly and then pulled out her wallet. *Titanium level*, Mark noted, as she retrieved a credit card and handed to the server. *Yes, her job pays her well.* She looked up at him. "I hope you enjoyed lunch," she said.

"More so the company. I'm glad I got the chance to get to know you a little better."

"Me too."

He nodded to the carryout bag. "I take it you're staying in town tonight?"

"Actually, I'm not. I have to head back to San Francisco. My guardian wants me home tonight." She sighed again. "He's having a hard time adjusting to the fact that I'm moving out. I guess he didn't believe I was serious about it."

"His little girl's growing up. It's a hard thing for any parent to adjust to."

"I guess."

Julie paid the bill and they stood up and made their way out of the restaurant. Julie's limousine waited for them at the corner. As they approached it, a black Taurus pulled up alongside the curb in front of the limousine, cutting off their path. A red light flashed in their eyes. Mark recognized the figure in the driver's seat. She rolled the passenger window down. "Cassie?" he asked. "What's going on?"

"We need to go, Mark," Cassie said, her tone somber. "On my way back to the precinct, I got a call from the hospital. Madison's taken a turn for the worse."

"Great." Mark turned to Julie. "Julie, meet Cassie Edwards, my new partner. Cassie, this is Julie Warren. She's renting the space above my garage."

Cassie extended her hand out the window and Julie shook it. Cassie glanced up at the name on the building, and at the dress of some of the people emerging from behind them. She looked back at her. "I'm not going to try and pronounce it," she said. "I'll just assume that the food's very good, and really expensive."

Mark opened the passenger door, and folded his tall frame into the passenger seat. He gazed up at Julie. "Thanks again for lunch."

"You're welcome, Mark, and good luck with your case."

Cassie took off away from the curb. Julie waited until he had rounded the corner before turning and heading toward her limousine. The door opened from the inside and she climbed in. She looked down at the bag of desserts, too depressed to even think about eating them. "NIK," she said in a stern tone, "contact the Caretaker, and have Patrick go to the hospital. I want a full report as soon as he can get it. Make sure he takes care to not be seen by Mark or his partner."

As you wish, Ambassador.

Thomas watched her from the rearview mirror. He had never seen this look on his protector's face, but he sensed that it meant something terrible threatened him and his people. "What is it, *miandi*?"

She stared out the front windshield again, watching Cassie's car disappear into traffic. Her expression turned malevolent. "We were right, Thomas," she murmured. "It *is* our land that's the focus of the investigation. I won't be able to hide it much longer. Sooner or later, he's going to figure it out, and discover my interest in it."

XI

Mark leaned up against the wall opposite the doors of Mason City General's ICU unit, his eyes fixed on the small windows. Inside, Dr. McFadden and the rest of the emergency team continued their struggle to save Madison's life. He had been here since he left his lunch with Julie, and now it was approaching 10:00 p.m. A few feet away, Cassie paced the hallway, her cell phone pressed to her right ear. She avoided the anxious glances of Mr. and Mrs. Evans, who huddled nearby.

He closed his eyes and rubbed his forehead, fighting to stay awake. To distract himself, he reached into his shirt pocket and pulled out the hand-drawn map he had received from Terrance. The theory that Madison had been a victim of a robbery returned to him, but he dismissed it just as quickly. He traced the outline of the land with his finger. The research she just finished was the key. What did she discover that set these events in motion? Was there something valuable, that the person or people seeking it were willing to kill to get it? Or did the people who truly owned it set these events in motion?

Mark saw movement behind the doors and motioned to Cassie. She hung up the phone and approached Mark, just as the doors swung open. Dr. McFadden came out of the room. She met Mark's eyes long enough for him to know that the news wasn't good. The detectives watched as she turned and walked to the end of the hall, where Mr. and Mrs. Evans clung to each other. She took them down the hall a little bit, out of Mark and Cassie's eyesight. Then Sophia Evans let out a strangled cry. Cassie stiffened beside him. A few minutes later, Dr. McFadden rounded the corner and walked back toward the officers. She wore a defeated look on her face. She shoved her hands into her lab coat. "She was a trooper," she told the detectives. "She fought against it as best she could."

"What happened, Doctor?" Mark asked.

"That's the problem. We don't know. There was nothing to indicate that she was not having any type of reaction to her medication, nor does she have a history of these things. Then suddenly . . ." She hung her head. "We gave her at least ten different blood thinners. Every time we thought we had found one to counteract the blood clots, they would strike again, until they finally overwhelmed her system."

Mark and Cassie glanced at each other, and then at the doctor. "You're saying that this may have been deliberate?" Cassie asked.

"I'll get our laboratory working on the toxicology report. If she was poisoned, I've never seen any kind of drug work like that. Whoever did it must have given it to her when she was alone in her room." She nodded to the two of them. "Anything you need detectives, let me know."

He glanced at his watch. He knew that he and Cassie weren't going home tonight. They needed to pull the security tapes and interview every doctor and nurse who had been in contact with Madison in the last 24 hours. One of them had just become an accessory to an assault and potential murder. It was time to find them. He forced a smile to his face. "Thanks, Doctor."

Dr. McFadden nodded and headed back into the ICU unit. Mark turned his attention to his new partner. She studied him. Procedure wise, their path was set, but something told her that Mark wasn't going to follow procedure when it came to this case. "What do you want to do?" Cassie asked.

He pointed to the phone still in her hand. "Call the precinct. See if they've found Leonard. I want to talk to him again."

"Mark, it couldn't have been him. He was either in jail or being arraigned."

"Yes, but if it hadn't been for him, Madison wouldn't have been poisoned."

"Mark, you heard the judge. Until we have more evidence to link him to the crime, we can't touch him."

"It'll make me feel good to know that I know where to find him, and that I can pin murder charges to him if he's any way responsible." Mark glanced at his watch again. "I'm going down to the security office. Maybe our killer slipped up and was caught on tape coming and going from this place."

Cassie started to dial the precinct again. "One can only hope," she murmured.

Mark turned to head down the hallway toward the security office. About a third of the way down the hall, he stopped. "Cassie? I meant to ask you something."

"What?"

His eyes narrowed. "What do you see now?"

Cassie stared at Madison's parents, who had come around the corner holding each other tightly. Then her gaze went to the door where the body of Madison Evans laid. She faced Mark, her expression stoic. "I don't see a mugging anymore, Mark. I see a murder."

*   *   *

At that moment, Julie and four of the Illani council members, Alexandra, Thomas, Russell, and the Caretaker were in the main observation chamber. Patrick was now outside the hospital, parked away from the building, reading them his analysis report. "The poison is similar to that administered to the Amendu, but at a much higher concentration," he informed them. "The human's medication could not prevent the blood clot that lodged in her left orbital lobe."

"Which means their toxicologist will be able to break it down, but not be able to trace the *sorja* root that is its base," Alexander added.

Julie fumed. "It still means another human is dead, and we're no closer to finding out who's behind all this, and why. Patrick, get back here as soon as you can. We'll need those tissue samples. Hopefully, there's a clue in them."

She stared at the dish in her left hand: a white chocolate mousse pie with a thin strip of dark chocolate on the crust. The chef had drizzled chocolate on the top and made strips of it into curls for garnish. When she returned from her lunch with Mark, she went to visit the tribe again. Alexandra and the others had distributed the antitoxin and the poisoned children were beginning to recover. Seeing the children walking about restored some of Julie's appetite, and she had thought back to the desserts waiting for her at the farm. This was the fourth one she had eaten since she had returned from seeing the Amendu less than an hour ago. She continued to pace, and thought back to all she knew so far. "There are too many irregularities," she murmured. "There are just too many missing elements to form a clear picture. Caretaker, are you certain that no one's tried to enter this place?"

The Caretaker watched her, his black eyes unmoving. "Yes, *miandi*, nor have we detected outside technology of any kind monitoring us."

I have run a thorough diagnostic of their systems, Ambassador, NIK's voice echoed throughout the chamber. *The Caretaker is correct. No one has entered this place, nor has there been any sign of outside technology scanning the area.*

Julie looked at the eldest of the Illani. NIK must've thought that Julie didn't believe him, but she knew not to doubt his word. She gave the Caretaker a smile of understanding and he nodded in reply. Thomas took a step forward. "Why do they wish to do this?" he asked. "Why do they want to hurt us?"

She stopped pacing and stared at the screens, watching the humans interacting on it. "I don't think that they want to hurt you per se," Julie answered. "It's this planet now. Its inhabitants are driven by money, power, and greed. It's the money that we collected in the past that keeps you safe now. They feel that with enough of it, they can do anything. We learned that lesson with Jack, but who would want this place? How did they find out about it? Do they know that you're here?" Julie tapped her foot, her face concentrated in thought. "NIK, give me the name of Madison's employer again."

His name is Terrance Carnegie. He operates a real estate agency in downtown Mason City.

"Display his information please."

On another screen, NIK called up biographical information and the business records on Terrance Carnegie. Julie read it quickly and nodded. "This human has the information that we need," she announced in a firm tone. "We need to talk to him, but more importantly, we need to get inside his office." Julie paused. "*I* need to get inside."

The council members watched as their protector resumed her pacing and eating. None of them wanted to say what she needed to know and understand. Finally, Alexandra took a step forward. "It'll be difficult, *miandi.* This planet, especially this country, is obsessed with security. As we warned you, they have cameras and sensor devices in nearly every building here. There's nowhere that you can appear or disappear without someone seeing you, or detecting your presence."

Julie took another bite of her dessert. "I know I can't go myself. It'll only draw suspicion, and we have to assume that he'll recognize me. What level of technology is Earth at right now?"

"Level Two," Alexandra replied.

"They're fascinated with it, and they know the basics of it. Thankfully, we know more. Alexandra, is there a way to send a signal to me, through my link with NIK?"

The Illani looked at each other and then back at their protector. She stared at the screen again. She sensed their confusion and tried to find a way to explain her plan. "These security systems? Most of them run on computer technology, correct?"

"Yes, *miandi*," Russell replied. "However, many of these places have cameras or other devices that don't run on such technology."

"Let's assume that Mr. Carnegie's systems do," Julie muttered through another bite of her dessert. "Have NIK run a thorough check on that building's systems. When we're ready, NIK can go in and disable their security systems, and then I can use a separate link established within the building. That way I can appear without anyone seeing me."

The Illani gathered in the room looked at each other and nodded. "That is possible, *miandi*," Alexandra said.

Julie smiled and looked toward the view screen. "NIK?"

I am forwarding the specifications to the Illani computers. I have also secured access to the security system within that building and Mr. Carnegie's office. Once the device is installed, you will be able to enter at anytime.

"Good. Now we need is someone to go in and place the link inside. It'll have to be someone who'll catch our opponents off guard without drawing too much attention, but how do we do that?"

Julie began to pace the floor again. She took another bite of her dessert and sucked on her fork, savoring the mixture of the creamy white and bitter dark chocolates melting on her tongue. She looked at the Illani in front of her, perusing them carefully. She paused at the tall one in the middle and pulled her fork out of her mouth. "Russell? How would you like to purchase some real estate for me?"

*   *   *

Terrance fumbled to hang up the phone, resisting the urge not to fling it out the window. It was the police, calling to inform him that Madison Evans had died from her injuries. They were on their way to talk to him again. He had known that this would happen. Sooner or later, the police would come back and when they did, he wouldn't be able to hide it any longer. He stared at the cellular phone on the corner of his desk. The phone had not rung and this time he wanted it to. He wasn't certain why, but he wanted reassurance from the voice on the other line that he wasn't next in line to die.

"Mr. Carnegie, your 11:30 appointment is here."

Terrance froze. He didn't want to see this man. He wanted to jump in his Mercedes, leave town, and not look back. However, this Russell Webster had flown in from Dallas. Although this appointment had supposedly been on his electronic calendar for about a week, he didn't remember even speaking to the man, let alone gathering information about him or his company. He stuffed the cell phone into his center desk drawer. Then he hit the intercom button. "Bring him in, Barbara," he ordered, hoping the terror he felt didn't show in his voice.

Terrance stood, straightened his tie, and wiped his hands on his tan pants. He managed to regain his composure, just as Barbara led a tall, African-American male into Terrance's office. He wore a three-piece black pinstriped suit, right down to the silver vest chain, and carried an attaché case that looked like it ran in the thousands of dollars. There were only touches of gray in his tightly curled, black hair. His brown eyes were solemn and he wore an austere, yet comforting look on his face. "Mr. Carnegie, I presume?" he asked.

"Yes? How can I help you sir?"

My name's Russell Webster." He handed Terrance a business card. "I'm a real estate attorney from Dallas. I help out-of-state clients find and purchase land for potential development."

Terrance gave Russell his best Cheshire cat smile, as he studied the name of the company on it. He had never heard of it. He reminded himself that he needed to jump on the Internet and see what they were like, and how much they had closed in the past few years. "Wonderful. What brings you here?"

"For some time, I've been looking for a piece of land in the Pacific Northwest, one with lots of room to expand, as well as plenty of lakeshore views. I've been having some problems, so my client asked that I enlist some local help with the search. Your firm comes highly recommended."

Russell sat his briefcase down on the empty chair, opened it, and pulled out a sheet of paper with list of names. Terrance took it. He immediately recognized nearly all of them. They were high-profile clients that he had closed in the last year or so. Apparently this man had done his research. His heart skipped a beat. Perhaps the solution to his problem had just wandered through the door. "Well, you've come here at a great time. I have one piece of land that just came on the market. The sellers bought it a few years ago, but their building project fell through. They need to sell it quickly and they aren't quibbling about the price." Terrance leaned forward over his stacks of files. "Can I ask who the potential buyer may be?"

Russell took the chair in front of Terrance's chaotic desk. "I can't disclose the name of my client, Mr. Carnegie. Privileged, you understand. However, I can tell you that this company is interested in starting a major building project in the northeastern part of Washington."

Terrance's delight with Mr. Webster's client grew by the second. "Oh? What type of buildings? Residential? Commercial?"

Russell smiled, crossed his long legs, and straightened the crease in his pants. "Residential homes, Mr. Carnegie, huge homes on the waterfront with multiple bedrooms, lake views from nearly every room, and water access to all those who purchase one. Their price tags will start roughly in the two to five million dollar range."

Terrance sat back in his seat. Two to five million? Already he was doing the math. "Well, I think that the land that my client is looking to sell might be right up their alley."

He stood and moved toward the teetering stack of files and moved a few of them to the floor. "You'll have to excuse the mess. My regular secretary is out ill."

He opened the blue folder that he had taken the hand-drawn map out of for Mark, and retrieved a photograph, some pamphlets and brochures he had made up for the person who had first initiated the research. He handed them to Russell. "How's this one?"

Russell reached for them while pulling out a pair of gold reading glasses from his right breast pocket. He slipped them on and stared at the photos. Terrance saw the man's thick, graying eyebrows rise toward his receding hairline. It was an exceptional aerial view of a parcel of land. In the center of it was a deep blue lake, surrounded by lush forests of evergreen and hardwood trees. It looked like it was nestled in a valley somewhere with hills rising in the distance. There looked to be a red barn and a old farmhouse in a clearing about 1,000 yards off the lake, but they could probably be torn down. If houses were built on this land, they would be able to sit on at least three sides of the lake, yet still have access to the inlet and the utmost level of privacy available. "Yes, I believe this will be perfect," he said, a smile breaking out on his face.

Terrance enjoyed the look that came across Russell's face. He had him. "I thought so," he commented. "From what I've been told, there's lots of virgin timber on it, waiting to be sold to the highest bidder, plus it's prime acreage, just begging to be built upon. There's also several gorgeous view of the hillsides and nice deep waters for people to bring their yachts right up to the house, if they wanted. Your client would more than triple their profits if they invested in it."

"Yes, this will definitely pique their interest." Then the smile began to disappear. Russell's dark forehead wrinkled as he spotted something in the lower right hand corner of the picture. "What's this land off to the side?" he asked, pointing to another part of the picture.

Terrance leaned over his desk to look at the spot where he indicated. From the photographs, it was obvious that the trees there were dead and stripped of their foliage. It abutted the two-lane highway that flowed nearby, but it was more than that, Russell thought. To him, it had an almost haunted look about it. He tried not to shudder. "Is this also part of the sale?"

"Oh? Unfortunately, yes." Terrance sighed, as took the photograph back. "As you can see, it's not much for home development, but then with technology these days, it might be suitable for a shopping center or something like that."

"That will drive down the price my client is willing to pay considerably."

"Well, it could, but since my sellers are just looking to get rid of all of the land as quickly as possible, breaking even will make them happy." Terrance sensed that Russell was quickly losing interest. "I'm certain that we can work out something so that part of the land is not included," he added quickly.

The intercom buzzed. Terrance shot daggers at his phone. He was about to land the commission to a multi-million dollar sale, get rid of a pesky real estate project, become an even richer man than he already was, and Barbara had to pick now of all times to interrupt him? "Excuse me." He picked up the receiver. "Yes," he said through clenched teeth.

"I'm sorry, sir. It's Mrs. Bluewater again," Barbara Livingston's voice rang in his ear. There was another shrill voice behind her. Terrance plugged his other ear to hear the rest of Barbara's conversation. "She in the lobby right now and she won't leave. She insists on talking to you, face to face."

Terrance sighed and rolled his eyes in his head. "Fine. I'll be right there," he muttered, hanging up the receiver and giving Russell an apologetic smile. "Excuse me, I'll be right back."

Terrance stepped out of his office. "Mrs. Bluewater? What can I do for you?" Russell heard Terrance say in a cheerful tone, as the door shut behind him.

He heard the disturbance outside grow louder. Apparently, Mrs. Bluewater wasn't very happy with Terrance, either. Russell waited a beat and then stood up.

From his pants pocket, he withdrew a off-white contact lens case. He unscrewed the left cover and extracted a disc that appeared to be a white shirt button. He gazed about the room and then walked over to the fern on the far bookcase. He stroked the leaves, saddened at its near-dead appearance. He held the disc up to inspect it, before slipping it inside the fern's dirt, making sure the soil completely covered it. He reached for the handkerchief in his breast pocket, brushed his hands on it, and slid it back into his jacket, positioning it so that the triangle points were as perfect as before. He placed the case back into his pants pocket, sat back in his chair, and picked up the brochure Terrance had handed him to read just as Terrance walked back into the room. His ears and cheeks were bright red. "I'm sorry about that sir. An irate client. You know how it is."

"A sad part of our world, unfortunately."

Terrance settled back behind his desk and gazed at his savior, the anticipation plain in his eyes. "So, Mr. Webster, what do you think?"

"Well, as I informed you, I'm just preparing the proposal for the potential buyer," Russell replied. He held up the photograph, brochures, and portfolio that Terrance had given him. "I'm sure that the information that you provided me with today will be most helpful. May I kept these?"

"Certainly, sir. Keep anything that you feel you need to help you and your buyer reach a quick decision on this."

Russell stood and glanced at his watch. "I should leave you. I'm sure that you have other clients that you need to attend to." He reached for his briefcase. "I thank you for taking the time to see me today."

He turned and headed for the door. Terrance scrambled to his feet to rush after him. "Mr. Webster, wait please!" Terrance called out.

Russell paused, his hand on the doorknob. Terrance sidled up next to him, trying not to let his anticipation show. "I know that you probably don't know the answer to this, and it's probably presumptuous of me to ask, but . . ." Terrance's voice dropped to a whisper. "Just how much are they willing to pay?"

"I'm not allowed to disclose that, sir. As you are well aware, my client hasn't had the opportunity to inspect the land. Also, I don't know if they'll be so keen to buy it, once they realize that dead area of land near the roadway may also be included. However, if they remained interested, and are willing to invest in it, you can rest assured that whatever is offered, my client can offer double."

Terrance looked at him, thunderstruck. Double? Based on his initial figures, he predicted offers in the tens of millions. Mr. Webster's client was willing to pay double that to get it? "Well, I'm sure that we can work our way around that minor detail regarding that unusable part of the land. I have a friend who can help us out with that."

"I'm certain that you do." Russell smiled in reply, and opened Terrance's office door. "I'll be meeting with my client in the next day or so. If they are interested in continuing, I'll contact you in the next few days with their terms and conditions."

Russell gave Terrance a slight bow as he left the office. He felt Terrance's gaze on him the entire way as he strolled toward the elevator bank. When the doors opened, a man and woman stepped out. The woman looked a little pale to Russell, but she held her head high as they headed directly toward Terrance. Russell stepped into the elevator and rode it down to the ground floor. He kept his eyes fixed on the revolving front door. In front of the building sat a white limousine similar to the one that had picked Julie up these last few days. The door opened from the inside and he stepped in. He smiled at the young black woman who waited inside for him. Once he was inside, she nodded to Thomas. He made to join the afternoon traffic.

Julie watched the congestion out the window. She dropped her mental shields a little, so she could concentrate on the thoughts of the commuters traveling beside them. She shook her head. So much had changed, she realized, as their thoughts and emotions shifted with every stop and start of their vehicles. She had seen the effects of evolution too many times not to recognize the pattern. She turned her thoughts from the world outside her vehicle and stared at Russell. "Is it in place?"

Russell's black-suited form dissolved in a flash of light. In front of her sat the tall Illani councilmember from the previous night. His black eyes blinked once at her. *Yes,* miandi. *He will not find it. You'll be able to enter his office undetected.*

"Good." Julie glanced out the limousine's tinted window toward the top floor of the building. "Did he seem keen on selling you your home, Russell?"

Most enthusiastic. However, I like our home just the way it is.

Julie smiled. "Is there anything else that I should know?"

He mentioned that he has a friend helping him. He didn't reveal his name to me.

"That's all right. Perhaps he left something in the files."

There's something else, miandi. *Detectives Edwards and Daniels are in his office. I watched them emerge from the elevator as I left. They may be preparing to search it.*

Julie straightened. She thought she recognized the Explorer that had pulled up just before Thomas had parked the limousine. She stared up toward the floors that housed where she would be traveling to in a few hours. "Russell, work with NIK in delaying Mark and Cassie. Do so as long as you can. Thomas, pull into that parking structure. I think I'll wait and watch from here."

XII

In the lobby of Botsworth Real Estate, the cherry mantle clock tolled seven times. There was no one about to hear it. Its regular occupants had gone home hours ago, saddened by the news that Madison had died from her injuries. Barbara was inconsolable, and Terrance wound up sending her home and closing the office early. This also insured that he wouldn't be here when the cops came back to search his office with the warrant they promised to bring at his insistence.

Inside Terrance's main office, the security sensor device in the northeastern corner failed to detect Julie's sudden appearance. It was as if she entered through an invisible door, created specifically for her. She gazed about the room and smiled, thanking those who had created her for endowing her with this power. When she was younger, it bothered her that she could not change her form at all like the others. However, she had an ability that they didn't: she could transport herself anywhere within the universe. All she had to do was concentrate on the place that she wanted to go and she was there, instantly. It allowed her to come and go as she wanted without worrying about finding a ship to carry her or using an intergalactic portal, which she hated. The power had one drawback: she needed to have visited the place once before, to coordinate her body rhythms to that of the planet, and to determine how to appear and disappear without detection.

She continued her observations while gathering her bearings. Then she walked over to the dying fern that Russell visited earlier in the day. She unearthed the small button disc out of the soil. Inside if it was a signaling device tuned to her telepathic link to NIK. She looked up in the left corner of the office and saw a white, odd-shaped object in the corner. "That must be the motion detector that Russell mentioned," she realized. NIK had already made her way through the office security system and reprogrammed the detectors within it. As far as it knew, no one was here.

She walked over to Terrance's cluttered desk, easily avoiding the files scattered about the floor. Her powers not only protected her humanoid form, they also enhanced her senses. She could hear conversations of people from a mile away, pick up scents that even the most sensitive of noses could not detect, and see in pitch blackness what most couldn't see even in the light of day. She frowned at the stacks of files on top and around it. There looked to be hundreds of them. "He's not going to make this easy," she murmured.

She held her hand over each stack. In her mind, the contents of each flashed through her brain like film in a motion picture camera. In the fourth stack, about a third of the way down, she found what she was looking for. She levitated the stack of files on top of it in the air and pulled the file out. Then she set the stack back down on the desk, making sure that it maintained the delicate balance it had before she had moved them.

She held her right hand up and a flashlight appeared within it. She really didn't need it, but it felt good to have it in her hands. She clicked it on and it emitted a soft glow. She held the flashlight up and began to page through the file. She laid the photographs and papers across the small empty space on Terrance's desk and began to analyze them. There were dozens of pictures of the land, all shot from above, as well as maps, graphs, and other information outside what Madison had gathered from the Okanogan County Recorder. Madison had done a good job. When Antoinette had thrown up her obstacles, Madison circumvented her by visiting some of the public websites. Julie searched the documents thoroughly, but the name of Terrance's source was not there. "Well, Russell was correct in his assessments," Julie admitted. "Terrance Carnegie doesn't leave information this important lying around. Now I have no choice. I'll have to visit him."

She lifted the pile again with her thoughts and slid the file back where she had found it. As the remaining folders settled down again, she scanned the walls of Mr. Carnegie's office with her flashlight, looking for anything hidden within them. Toward the far right corner, behind a black-and-white photo print, there looked to be something. She turned off the flashlight and stared at the wall. There was a huge metal container recessed deep within the wall. Curious, she walked toward it and lifted the print away from the wall. It revealed a metal door with some type of electronic lock. She placed her hand on it. She scanned its circuitry and deciphered its code within seconds. It beeped and the door unlatched. She tugged on the handle and held the flashlight up to gaze inside of it. A stack of manila folders, a beat-up white envelope, and a tightly-wrapped wad of money rested inside. She placed her hand on the white envelope and evaluated its contents. Intrigued, she took the envelope out of the safe and walked back to the desk. She pulled the documents out and examined each one carefully. The right corner of her mouth twitched. Apparently, Mr. Carnegie had researched the land before. The documents and the cashier's check within it were dated from five Earth years' prior. There was also an English copy of the Foundation's agreement with the Amendu. Attached to it was a Foundation business card from Jack Adams, the Foundation's former director. Jack would have a copy of the agreement, because it was part of the Foundation's archives. How did Mr. Carnegie get a copy?

She continued reading. One of the documents was a real estate contract between the Amendu and an overseas corporation known as Liverpool & Antioch, bearing the same date as the check. One of the officers had already signed it, but there was no name printed underneath it. She thought back to the events that had caused her to remove Jack from his post. At that time, Jack had been working with a company deeply interested in purchasing the land. He had assured them that he could convince Julie and Simon to sell the land, or so Julie had pulled from his thoughts the day she confronted him about it. Julie had not really pursued the company or any of its members. Jack's actions had been her primary concern at the time, and interest had quickly waned after Jack's arrest. "NIK?"

Yes, Ambassador?

"Could you do some research on this corporation for me?"

Julie transmitted the name of it to NIK. It was a few seconds before NIK responded: *It does not exist, Ambassador.*

Julie held the flashlight higher and picked up the document. "Doesn't exist? How's that possible?"

I am trying to backtrack it now to see if I can match it up to one that does exist. However, it will take some time and you cannot wait there.

"Why?"

A vehicle has pulled up to the front of the building. My readings show that belongs to Detective Daniels. Two marked police cars and a police van are with him.

Julie abandoned the documents and walked quickly over to the windows. She parted the blinds without touching them and looked down. She saw Mark and Cassie below her. It looked like they were giving instructions to some other police officers. They must intend to search this place, she realized. She moved the blinds back into position, replaced the file back inside the safe, closed it, and re-hung the picture. She made one final glance about the place to make sure everything was the way she had left it. As she did so, her eyes returned to the wilting fern. She heard its cries for help. She stole a glance at Terrance's main door, and then walked over to it. She reached out to stroke one of its branches. Then she placed her hand over top of it. Soothing rays of energy flowed invisibly from her hand to it. In seconds, the limp fern began to straighten and stand taller. Its fading green leaves darkened in color and the brown tips that had touched its edges disappeared. When it was back to full strength, its branches waved merrily at her. She pulled her hand away and smiled. "You're welcome," she whispered.

There was a click outside the door. Julie glanced over at it. She focused her thoughts on the farm and disappeared just as Mark's hand touched the doorknob to Terrance's office. He leaned his ear against it. Cassie looked at him. "What is it?" she asked.

Mark put a finger to his lips. When he had been outside giving instructions to the officers, he thought he saw Terrance's window blinds part and a flash of light. Now, he was certain he heard movement in the room. He drew his gun from his holster. Cassie nodded and she and the officers with him did the same. He turned the knob and quickly opened the door. They pointed their guns inside. One of the officers flicked on the light. Mark gazed about. The office was empty. He shrugged and re-holstered his gun. It must have been his imagination. There was no way in or out except through the door, and the security alarm was on when they entered the main office. His eyes fell on the fern on the bookshelf. He raised an approving eyebrow. It looks a lot better than it did the last two times he saw it. Someone must've finally watered it.

"Mark!"

Mark walked over to the desk, where Cassie had already rifled through the stack of files on Terrance's desk and found the blue folder they had seen the other day. "Mr. Carnegie lied to us about keeping copies of his research. There's a boatload of stuff on the property in here." She pulled out one completely covered in wavy lines that varied in width and length. Her brow furrowed. "What is this?" she asked in a disgusted voice.

"It looks like a topographical map," Mark answered, taking it from her. He held it up and stared at it in admiration, remembering his high school geology teacher. "I used to like studying these things when I was younger."

"Had other ambitions than being a cop?"

"A seismologist, but I couldn't get past trigonometry."

"Detectives?" a new voice called to them.

Mark and Cassie looked up from their map reading. One of the officers had found the safe hidden behind the black-and-white photo print. "Can you open it?" Mark asked.

"It'll be a few minutes, sir."

After about five minutes, the lock beeped and the door swung open. Mark reached inside, and pulled out the stack of wrapped-up hundred-dollar bills, manila folders, and the envelope that Julie discovered just a few minutes before. He parted the envelope with his left thumb and forefinger. Cassie approached him. "What do you have there?"

Mark shrugged, walked over to the desk, and laid the envelope down. He pulled the contents out without noticing Jack's business card, which had caught on one of the documents and drifted to the floor. Cassie picked it up, stared at it, and then slipped it back into the envelope. Mark began flipping through the papers. He saw the official check. Then he saw the real estate agreement. He paged through it and noticed the signature at the bottom of the last page. Unlike Julie, he recognized it. He had seen it too many times not to. Cassie noted his look, and raised an eyebrow. "Mark? What is it?"

"I'm not certain," he told her, blinking his eyes hard. They were beginning to sting and his body suddenly started to ache. It dawned upon him that he and Cassie had been going at it for longer than 24 hours. "Let's get some sleep before we tackle these," he told her, slipping the documents and its envelope into the bag that one of the technicians held open. "Hopefully we can find something in them to make Mr. Carnegie more talkative."

"And what if we don't? We don't have anything to tie him to Madison's assault. Not only that, no one's been able to find Leonard. It's as if he's disappeared off the face of the earth."

Mark rubbed his eyes, but the image of the signature on that document continued to float stubbornly in front of his vision. "Let's just see what these tell us. Hopefully, we'll know more by morning, and we'll have the energy and strength to do something about it."

*　　*　　*

Mark slept little that night. His mind kept drifting from Meghan Danvers's sleeping form; to Jessie's passive face in her hospital bed; then Charlie's bleeding chest in the warehouse; then to Nelson Chambers, the man he nearly killed. His dreams then turned to the gibberish of numbers he saw at the bank and the signature at the bottom of that real estate contract. He sat up in bed at about 5:00 a.m., wondering whether he should even bother going to work. Then he thought of Madison, the Amendu, and to the people who owned that mysterious property up north. Madison would not want him to give up so easily and from what he could tell, the Amendu and their co-owners had no idea what was happening. Mark didn't understand it completely, but he knew that he had to at least try and do something, if only to bring Madison's killer to justice. He continued to dwell on it during his morning jog, and as he dressed for work. That morning, he sat quietly in Lieutenant Michaels' office, allowing Cassie to update their boss on how the case was proceeding. More than once Lieutenant Michaels' attention turned to Mark. He in turn stared either at Cassie, the floor, or the lieutenant's desk. She sensed that he was holding something back. "Anything you want to add, Mark?" she asked when Cassie had finished.

"Only that Cassie's right in her hunch about Terrance Carnegie holding something back. We need to get him in here and talk to him again on our terms."

"Well unless you have some way to pin the murder of Madison to him, you can't get near him without his attorney," Lieutenant Michaels informed the two of them. "He's already screaming about filing harassment charges against the two of you. Go through that paperwork you found in his office with a fine-tooth comb. If there's something there you can use against him, get him back in here and use it."

They walked back out to the center of the precinct. Cassie had taken over Charlie's old desk. She tried to position it in a way that prevented her from looking at the blinded windows, but there was very little room to maneuver. Now, she faced them. As they approached, they noticed a brown folder labeled with Madison Evans' name. Cassie picked it up and the two of them began to leaf through it. "The preliminary autopsy report is in," she said.

"What does it say?"

"Well, the initial toxicology report supports the theory that Madison was poisoned. Because of the medications the doctors used to try and combat whatever she had been given, it would take some extra time to sort out what had been used." She looked up. "Have you heard from the district attorney's office?"

"Only that they're still trying to translate that contract. I'm going to fax them over a copy of the English one we found. That should help a little."

"Good. Maybe I'll take a copy of it home with me tonight. All that legal jargon may help me go to sleep at night."

Mark shook his head and reached for the information found in the blue folder on Terrance's desk. It was mostly photographs and maps, but they gave a more precise location of the land. However, it did little to shed light as to who the other owners were. Mark shook his head and rubbed his eyes. He glanced up at Cassie. She was studying the maps and photographs. Her hair had fallen into her face, but her head was jerking up and down, as if she was fighting to stay awake as well. "Are you all right?"

"Now I remember why I hated school so much." When she looked at him, he saw traces of circles under her eyes. "I still say this is a wild goose chase."

Mark gave her a grim nod. He reached for the white envelope and emptied its contents on the desk. He didn't notice Jack Adams' business card fall out. He looked at the documents that had been in the white envelope, forcing himself not to look at the real estate agreement. He paid particular attention to the dates on the check and at the top of the remaining documents. Then he did a double take. "Cassie?"

"What?"

"I think I found out what Terrance was hiding." He looked at her, gave her a devilish smile, and held up the papers. "And, I think I know how to get him to talk to us."

* * *

"What's on that land, Mr. Carnegie?"

Mark tossed the document-filled envelope in front of Terrance Carnegie, who sat in the main interrogation room along with his attorney. Mark noticed that Terrance's eyes looked much like his when he had first started his leave. Terrance tried to look at him as if he didn't recognize the envelope, but Mark saw through the façade easily. "What?" Terrance managed to say.

Mark tapped the envelope. "The research Madison did for you? This wasn't some random mugging. She was attacked because of what she really found out about this place, wasn't she?"

Cassie took a seat next to Mark. She had no idea where Mark was going, but she liked the effect that the furious look on Mark's face was having on Terrance. Terrance's attorney straightened in his chair. "Wait a minute," he interrupted. "You're not charging him with her murder? He already told you that he had nothing to do with it."

"We're not, although being charged as an accessory before the fact is still in the picture. We're just trying to find out who's behind this." Mark leveled his gaze at the now trembling Terrance. "If he cooperates, there may be something we can do."

"But I've told you everything!" Terrance cried.

"We found Madison's research in your office, Mr. Carnegie. Unlike what you told us, you did keep copies of it. In fact, you had another search done to verify what she had found. You told us this research project was a recent one, but according to the documents in here, you've known about this place for a lot longer than that." He faced his chair so that the back pressed against the table, straddled it, and leaned forward. His eyes narrowed, and a rueful smile played on his lips.

"So tell me, Terrance? What's so special about this place? What's on it that makes it worth more than a person's life?"

Terrance turned and gave his attorney a frantic look. "I don't know what's there! I've never seen it, except on paper!"

"The documents in there seem to indicate otherwise."

"No! You have to believe me! I don't know anything!"

Mark's expression didn't change. Cassie hardly blinked. His attorney turned to him, wondering what his client was holding back. Terrance realized that there was no way out of his predicament. His head fell into his chest and he covered his face with his hands. "She was just doing a little research for me," he whimpered. "That's all it was, I swear. I didn't expect this. I didn't expect any of this."

Terrance's attorney placed a hand on his shoulder and stared at the detectives. "He tells you everything that he knows, and you don't charge him with Madison's assault or murder," he offered.

Cassie gazed at Mark. He blinked once. "That's up to the district attorney. For right now, let's hear what he has to say," Mark answered.

Mark righted his chair, sat back down, and leaned back. His hands fell casually in his lap. He stole a glimpse at his new partner, who looked at him with a mixture of awe, surprise, concern, and perhaps a touch of merriment. He pulled his notebook out of his pocket, clicked open his pen, and he returned his gaze to his prey. "Talk to me, Mr. Carnegie. What's so special about this place?"

Terrance looked over at his attorney, who bent down and whispered something in his ear. Terrance frowned, and then nodded his assent. He took a deep breath. "More than five years ago, I received some documents in the mail," he began. Terrance swallowed, and then gingerly put a hand out to touch the envelope. "These documents you found? When I first received them, I had no idea what it was about and I threw them away. Before I left the office that afternoon, a call came into me. The voice was male. He didn't mention his name, but he asked me if I had received this envelope. Then he instructed me to do some research on it."

Terrance paused and looked at his attorney, unsure if he should continue. His attorney nodded at him. "Tell them, Terrance," he instructed him. "Tell them everything you know."

Terrance returned his gaze to Mark and Cassie. "I should've thought it suspicious then, but I didn't come across anything illegal. I located the land, which was somewhere near the Canadian border, in Okanogan County. I did the initial research and sent it to a post office address that he gave me in Colorado. A few days later, I received an official check for my services, and a separate check in the amount of $50,000.00."

Mark nodded. That much of his story seemed to be true. Cassie didn't entirely buy it. "That's a hell of lot of money for a little research," she chided him.

Terrance's face hardened. "The voice told me that the $50,000.00 check was a retainer fee," he argued in a quiet voice. "He intended to use my agency to sell the land once he had located a suitable buyer. A few days later, he called to tell me that the project was on hold. He instructed me to keep these documents and the money, so I locked them in my office safe. After a while, I forgot about it."

Cassie raised an eyebrow. "For five years?"

Terrance gave her an icy stare. "Normally, I would have refused to keep such an amount. However, there were . . . special circumstances regarding this particular piece of land, so he told me . . . that and I didn't want to know anything more."

She crossed her arms. "So we noticed."

Mark looked at her, and then back at Terrance. "Why you? Why your firm?"

"I specialize in researching and closing large land purchases, especially land where the owners can't be determined or traced. I've helped out-of-state law firms, even state and local officials find the information that they need to help terminate the interest of deceased parties, and no heirs can be established. If there's no one who can raise a claim, the land reverts to the state. They sell to whomever they want, leaving them free to do whatever they want."

"So why the sudden interest now?"

Terrance paused. He looked about as if he expected the gunshot that would kill him to be fired at any minute. "About six weeks ago, I receive a cell phone in the mail with instructions to wait for a call on it. It came that night. It was that voice again." Terrance shuddered. "He wanted a detailed search done. He wanted me to try to find the specific owners, and any information regarding them. I didn't have the time to dedicate to it. I still thought it was a wild goose chase, so I had Madison do it." His face took on a pleading look. "Honestly, I didn't think that she'd find anything new. From the initial research I did, I determined that the Amendu tribe owned the majority of the land. It being tribal land, I knew that any chance of my client getting their hands on it were slim. I told them that the first time I had researched it. When she showed me the updated results . . ." Terrance's voice trailed off. "I should've gone to the D.A. then," he continued. "I knew that there was something weird going on."

"The conversation you had with Madison in your office a few days before she died. What was that about?" Cassie inquired.

"I'd gotten a call the night before from the same man. He wanted even more information. I let it slip that someone helped me with the research and he threatened her. I was just warning her, nothing more! I wanted her to be careful. I thought I was dealing with the mob or something."

"And the man who accosted her outside your office?"

"I don't know anything about that. I'm telling you the truth."

Mark reached into the manila folder he had also brought with him. He pushed Leonard Bartman's photograph into Terrance's face. "You've never seen him before," he stated.

Terrance stared at the photograph. "No, never," he rasped. "Please, I didn't think that she would be hurt! I had nothing to do with what happened to her."

Mark's gaze on him did not waver. His instincts had already determined that Terrance played no role in Madison's assault and death, but he needed more to go on before he could get the D.A.'s office to charge Leonard again. He leaned forward. "This voice? How many times have you heard it?"

"A few. He only calls me at night, on the phone he sent me." Terrance shook his head. "I've already tried to trace the number and the phone. I have friends who work in the industry, but they haven't even been able to find the store that sold it to him."

"Do you think you'd be able to recognize the voice if you heard it again?"

Terrance looked at his attorney and then back at the detectives. "I think so." He paused and a look came onto his face, as if he just realized something. "You know, for people anxious to build, they dropped a few balls."

Cassie raised an eyebrow. "Meaning?"

"I've been at this for a while. There're a lot of people at the federal, state, and local levels that you have to convince if you want to take on any major type of building project. You don't even think about doing something as big as they seemed to be planning without a ton of research, but there were some things that they didn't ask me to do."

"What do you mean? What kinds of things?" Mark asked.

"Well for one, they didn't ask for the usual testing, like the geological surveys, environmental impact studies, soil samples, the oil and gas research." Terrance managed a smile at the detectives' blank looks and continued: "It's standard procedure. In most cases, those rights go to the state or federal government, or back to the tribe. Then there's probably a whole host of state and federal environmental regulations that would apply to the land when they got hold of it. To my knowledge, they didn't even ask me to check around to see whether anyone would be willing to buy the thousands of acres of timber that would become available if they managed to snag it." Terrance chuckled. "Not that they could. I think there are other things protecting it."

"Other things?" Cassie asked.

"Yeah. According to Madison's research, it's the Amendu's holy land."

"Holy land?" Cassie challenged. "You're telling me this man was willing to steal land, possibly kill the members of the Amendu tribe, and caused Madison's death so as to get to a place where they bury their dead?"

"No, no, not the tribe. He seemed more concerned about the heirs."

"Heirs?" She and Mark gave each other a blank stare. "I thought you said that the Amendu owned the land."

"Not all of it. According to Madison's additional research, they lease out part of the holy land to some non-profit corporation. I had an attorney friend check them out for me. From what he found, there's no way anyone could get that land away from either of them. They have resources that the most prestigious law firms would beg to have. The company and the family that runs it have been helping the Amendu protect that land for more than four hundred years. They've defeated every claim that's been brought to break that agreement."

"So what does this have to do with the heirs?" Cassie pressed.

"He said something about them dying, that if the last heir dies, then company's interest is severed. I'm not certain if I heard him right, but to me, it sounded like he planned on killing at least one of the heirs."

"One of them? Did he give a name?" Mark asked.

Terrance strained to remember anything of the conversation he had been trying to forget these last few days. "No."

Mark kept writing down notes. "The corporation that helps the Amendu protect this land? Do you know its name, or where it's located?"

Terrance looked up at the ceiling. "It's in San Francisco somewhere . . . the Fund . . . the Finding . . . the Founded . . ."

Mark tried not to laugh. "The Foundation?"

Terrance snapped his fingers and pointed at Mark. "That's it."

The detectives were taken aback. "The Foundation?" they chorused.

Terrance nodded. Mark continued to stare at him. Then he set the legs of his chair down and placed his tablet and pen on the table. He had said the name as a joke. Could it be that the person who held all the answers to his questions had just moved into his wife's studio? Cassie realized where she had seen the name of that company. It was on the business card that had fallen out of the envelope. She looked over at Mark. He looked in shock. She gazed back at Terrance and his attorney, and then tapped Mark on the shoulder. "Mark?"

Mark suddenly stood. "C'mon, Cassie," he murmured.

He headed for the door. Cassie stared back at Terrance and his attorney, who wondered what happened to trigger such a reaction from the both of them. Then she hurried after Mark. He was already halfway to the precinct door, and she rushed forward to grab his arm. "Mark, what's going on?"

Mark turned to her, remembering that she had reacted the same way he had when he mentioned the name. "What do you know about this company called the Foundation?"

"It was on the business card that fell out of that white envelope."

Cassie bent down to retrieve the dropped business card from the floor. She showed it to Mark. Mark stared at in disbelief. Cassie stood there before him, her arms crossed. "My turn. What do you know about the Foundation?"

"It's the name of the corporation my new tenant works for."

Cassie gave him a look of doubt. "You're certain?"

Mark reached for his wallet and pulled out Julie's business card. The corners were bent due to all the handling it had received the last couple of days. Cassie took it from him and read the black imprint. It was similar to the one that she just handed to Mark. "This is just coincidence, Mark," she argued, handing it back to him. "She can't know anything. She's just a paper pusher from what you've told me."

Mark sighed, and ran a hand through his hair. He remembered the signature on the bottom of the documents that now sat in front of Terrance. He stared off into space for a moment, torn about what he should do. Then he nodded back to the interrogation room. "Keep him talking. See if he can get you to tell you anything else about the heirs. Oh, and call the D.A.'s office, and see if they've finally made heads or tails out of that agreement."

"Wait! Where are you going?"

"To talk to Julie," he called back over his shoulder as he headed for the precinct doors.

"Julie? Do you think she's in town?"

"I hope so. She said she was going to try and move in today."

"Mark, do you really think she knows anything about this place?"

"No, but she might know how to get a hold of the people in charge. We need them to warn the heirs that their lives may be in danger." He nodded at the papers still left to sift through on their desks. "Keep digging, and let me know if you find something else."

"Mark, wait."

Cassie made her way away around the desks. She avoided looking out the windows as she led Mark out into the hallway, away from the ears of their fellow colleagues. Something told her that Mark knew more than he was letting on, and that he was purposely trying to keep her out of the loop. She thought back to the look on Mark's face when he had come out of Judge Embry's chambers the other day. It was the same one he had last night after he read that single-signature contract. "Mark, this wouldn't have anything to do with what you and Judge Embry talked about in chambers, would it?" she asked under her breath.

He turned to face her. To her, he looked like a man who had been defeated before he had even stepped into the boxing ring. He gave her a smile. "No, Cassie, it wouldn't."

He hit the "Down" button. The doors opened immediately and he stepped inside. He waited until the doors had closed in front of him before he muttered his follow-up response: "At least, I hope not."

XIII

Mark made the drive back home in what seemed to be record time. While driving, he thought about what Terrance said, and the signature scrawled at the bottom of the real estate contract. He knew that it belonged to Judge Embry, so he had to conclude that Judge Embry knew about the land. What else did the judge know? Had he hired the man who assaulted Madison? Was he a middleman, or was he so callous that he would kill the people who rightfully owned it? Even in his worst nightmares, Mark never thought that Judge Embry would do anything illegal. He was a respected man of the community. He donated his time to Big Brothers/Big Sisters, taught an ethics class at the university, and served as the honorary chair of the city's police benevolence fund. He knew that he should tell Lieutenant Michaels what he had discovered, but he didn't want to. He sighed. He was doing it again: obsessing. He wondered if he had "The Look" on his face as well; the one that Jessie, Tyler, Charlie and a few others often tried to describe to him, but always seemed at a loss for words. He gripped the steering wheel tight. "Judge Embry didn't do it," he told himself. "The judge is not involved. You only want him to be the bad guy because of your conversation with him the other day."

Mark turned left onto Church Street, two blocks away from his home. It was odd to see it so light out this late in the day. He wondered what he was even doing out here. "This is probably worthless," he concluded. He didn't even know if Julie was in town. He had tried to call her, but her phone transferred him to her voice mail the minute it connected. That meant that she was out of range or she had turned it off. He figured the latter. No doubt her guardian has been pestering her, trying to get her to change her mind about moving out. He knew that he shouldn't, but a part of him hoped that he had succeeded.

Mark rounded the corner to his street and gazed up at the maple trees. Their leaves had grown thicker these last few days. That meant Jessie's studio would be that much cooler for a few weeks—perfect for snuggling against the windows and watching the last of the spring sunsets. The thought made his heart feel a little lighter. As he approached the house, he recognized Julie's vehicle parked in front of Mrs. Johnson's. A huge moving van blocked access to his driveway. Its back doors were wide open. He glanced at the front end and saw the California license tags on it. He stopped in the middle of the street and sat back in his seat. The lightness he had felt moments before had deserted him. He shook his head. Was he ready for this? Maybe he was still living in a dream world, where he would walk through the studio door and see Jessie in front of her easel, splatters of fresh paint on her face and smock, her blonde curls tied away from her face, her eyes dancing when she saw him.

He parked a few houses down the street and made the sojourn back to his house. For the first time since Jessie died, he dreaded the trip up the stairs to the studio. He paused in the doorway to watch the activity inside before knocking on the door's frame. Julie was inside. She glanced up and gave him a small smile. He took that as a cue to enter. Once again, the smell of oil paint greeted his nostrils when he crossed the threshold. How long would it be before he came in here and he didn't smell it anymore? *Probably never. For me, a part of Jessie will always be in here.*

He stepped out of the way of the movers heading back down the steps and glanced around. Julie's dining room set was there; a simple maple and white table with four chairs, already laden with boxes. More boxes and plastic bins were stacked in the corners of the living room, kitchen, and on top of the empty bookcase in the corner. Toward the front window stood an oak-stained entertainment center, pulled out about two feet away from the wall. Julie was behind it, dressed in blue jeans and a red long-sleeve crewneck shirt, fidgeting with something. Mark approached her. Her glasses were up in her hair, and she stared blankly at the back of the unit, muttering to herself in a language he didn't understand. He leaned over to watch. She had at least three different sets of jacks in her hand, and it looked like she was trying to figure out how to plug them into the various electronic components in front of her. "Are you all right?" he asked in an amused tone.

"Technology! Why do they have to make things so complicated?"

"If you want some help with that . . ."

She shook her head, set the cables down on top of the cabinet, and dusted her hands off on her jeans. "No, it's all right. I'll figure it out later. I guess that's why they give you those user manuals. I was hoping to listen to some music tonight while I unpacked, that's all."

Mark gazed around again, not quite certain how to raise the topic that was on his mind. Finally, he sighed. "Julie, can I talk to you for a moment?"

Julie looked up at him. Immediately, she sensed that something troubled him. She pulled her glasses back down. "What is it, Mark?"

There was a grunting noise and they turned. The movers had brought in an area rug. Julie stood on her toes to look over the entertainment center. "Right there in the middle is fine. I think I'll put the sofa there against that wall," she instructed them, pointing to the far wall.

The men nodded and set the rug down on the floor. Mark watched while they removed the bindings and started unrolling it. He caught reflections of silver floss within the ocean blue fibers, before turning his attention back to her. "Julie, how high are you on the totem pole in your company?"

"Not very. I only started working there less than a year ago."

"So your position probably doesn't get you into much contact with the board, does it?"

"Not unless someone's asking for a lot of money, and I'm feeling either brave or stupid. Why?"

"Do you have any way to get in touch with any of the board members, or the CEO?"

"I could call our director Jennifer McIntire, and she could get in touch with them." She turned to watch as the rug unfurled. In her head, she heard the Caretaker reading the Illani scripture written with silver floss. She fought back tears. Now was not the time or place. She forced her attention back to Mark. "Is there something going on that they should know about?"

There was another noise and again, they turned. Two more men had appeared. They groaned with the effort of wedging a black cloth-covered sofa through the doorway. The other two movers abandoned the rug and went over to assist them. Mark thought one of the movers looked familiar. Unnerved, he realized that he didn't want this conversation to reach their ears. He glanced in the direction of the bedroom. "Could we?" he asked, pointing to it.

Julie turned in the direction he pointed, shrugged, and led the way toward the empty room. Mark closed the door behind them and leaned on the doorknob. He wasn't sure how to begin, or how much to tell her. He stared at her in the semi-dark room. "Julie, are you aware of any land that your company owns in this state?" he asked, his voice echoing throughout the empty room.

Julie thought for a moment. "Not really, although it's not surprising. If you believe the rumor mill, we own at least a quarter of the planet." She smiled at her joke. When Mark didn't return it, the smile disappeared and her brow furrowed. "Why?"

"You remember when you treated me to lunch, and I told you about the case I'm investigating?"

"The woman who was assaulted? Yes."

"You may remember Cassie picked me up to take me to hospital? The victim died yesterday evening."

Julie's face fell. "Mark, I'm sorry."

"There's more, Julie. She didn't die from her injuries. She was poisoned."

Julie let her arms drop. "Poisoned? But why? What did she do?"

Mark sighed and approached her. He pulled a piece of paper out of his pocket; the same one Terrance had given him. He tapped the paper against his open palm. "The victim? She conducted some research for her boss on a particular piece of land. It's a piece of land that I think some people in your company might know something about."

"Where?"

"It took some doing, but we finally managed to track it. It's in Okanogan County." Mark unfolded the piece of paper and pointed to the circled area on the map. "According to the land records up there, it's held jointly between the native tribe that lives nearby, and your corporation in San Francisco."

Julie took the paper and stared at it in the growing darkness. She walked over to the window to get a better look at it. She turned to Mark. "The Foundation owns that much land here?"

"That's not the half of it. There's another corporation out there that's trying to steal it out from underneath you."

Julie looked at him, aghast. "Steal it? Why?"

"People get greedy, Julie. It's not anything against you or your company. They see an opportunity to exploit someone and they run with it. Cassie and I think that our victim stumbled across what these people were doing. It's our theory that they threatened her, and it went too far."

Julie turned away from him, staring at the empty walls and the maple tree outside. "A woman died because someone else wants this land? I don't understand. What's there? What's on it?"

"I don't know. We've seen a few photos of the place. We know the native tribe there uses part of the land to bury their dead. The rest just looks like a lot of virgin forestland with a couple of falling down structures."

"And you're certain that it's our company that owns part of it?"

"We had someone here in our county recorder's office double-check the records. We also found out that your corporation and the tribe have some sort of agreement in place never to sell that particular piece of land. The D.A.'s office is reviewing it to see what kind of protection it offers." He chuckled. "I talked to them on my way here. They're still trying to work their way through it, but from what they've read so far, it's a pretty airtight document, except for some clause about the heirs."

Julie turned back to him. "The heirs? What heirs are you talking about?"

"Those who will inherit its wealth and responsibility once those in charge pass on."

"I still don't understand. What would they have to do with it?"

"We're not certain. It's possible that if they're already out of the picture, then there's no way for your company can fight to keep it. We're still waiting for them to get back with us with the results, but our bad guys think they might've won already." Mark pulled out another piece of paper. It was a printout of a newspaper article from a paper up in Okanogan County. "A co-worker of mine found us this. According to the article, the tribe's already agreed to sell it if your company's interest no longer exists."

Julie took the second sheet of paper from him and strained to read it in the darkness. She closed her eyes and shook her head. "No," she whispered. "They can't do this. It's not right!"

"It's not a matter of being right, Julie. It's what the law says." Mark's voice trailed off. "Is there anyone that you can contact to let them know what's going on?"

There was a knock on the door. Julie looked at Mark and then went to open it. One of the movers was outside. "Excuse me, ma'am, but we're bringing in the bedroom furniture now," he murmured.

Julie forced a smile on her face. "Thanks."

She turned to Mark and the two of them made their way back out into the overflowing living room. Mark noticed that her pace had slowed drastically. She stared back and forth at the sheets of paper in her hands. Mark thought she might have seen something, because her eyes took on a hopeful glint. "Mark, if you know the names of the people behind this, would you be able to tell me?"

Judge Embry's face immediately came to the forefront of Mark's thoughts. However, he knew that he couldn't tell her what he thought. He had no concrete evidence; only a feeling in the pit of his stomach from the signature he recognized, and it clashing with the judge's casual comment regarding his mortgage. If there was any evidence that he was behind Madison's death, it was going to be difficult to find. He had to be more than 100 percent certain that the judge was their culprit before he could even think of bringing him in for questioning. The problem was, Mark was hip deep in it. He knew a person who worked for the corporation being threatened and he wasn't certain if he wasn't Judge Embry's personal clean-up boy within the precinct. If it came down to him, whom would he protect? "No," he told her, "not until we know for certain. Even if I did, I wouldn't want you risking your neck to protect people you don't even know."

Julie's gaze fell back to the papers in her hands. In one thought, Mark confirmed what NIK's additional research had discovered. She hadn't desired a direct confrontation. Now she realized that if she wanted answers, she would have to see this judge face to face. That meant she needed to keep Mark distracted for just a little bit longer. She handed the papers back to him.

"Do you have any more paperwork that I could forward to Jennifer and the board members?"

Mark nodded and took the pages back. "It's back at the precinct, if you want to read it."

"Then I'll stop by and pick it up. I might not be good with stereo equipment, but I think I can get my computer up and running. That way, I can scan them here and e-mail them to Jennifer."

They stood there silent, watching as the movers continued to bring the last of Julie's belongings. Finally, Julie stared at the blank wall above her sofa. Mark studied her face. She seemed torn about something. "Julie? What is it?"

She gestured to the empty space. "It's . . . just my first night in town, and I was hoping to hit some of the local art stores and find something for that spot." She sighed. "I guess it'll have to wait."

Mark reached out to touch her shoulder. "Julie? I'm sorry."

Julie found herself appreciating his gesture to the point that she almost forgot how she should be acting. Her face took on a look of consolation. "It's not your fault Mark. You did your job, and I'll be sure tell Jennifer and the board that when they ask me." She glanced at her watch. "I'll call Jennifer directly. I have her number at home. Maybe there's nothing we can do, but I have to try, if not to save the land, then to protect the tribe's interests, and the heirs whose lives you believe are in danger. Let me get my computer up and working. I'll see you at the precinct within the hour."

Mark nodded in agreement. "In the meantime, I'll leave you to get settled." He looked at Jessie's studio one last time, its appearance so different from when Jessie used it as her place to create and dream. Then it dawned on him. From here on, he would need permission to enter here. He tried to hide that realization from her as he looked back at her. "I hope you're happy here, Julie," he murmured. "Try to enjoy your first night in your new place."

Julie met his gaze, understanding every bit of what he was feeling right now. Some of the happiest moments of his life happened in this very place, with the woman he loved. Now a total stranger had taken over; someone who in his mind, had not earned the right to be here. She wanted to comfort him, to tell him that he would always be welcome. Instead, she just nodded in reply. "I will, Mark, and thank you."

Mark tried to smile, but Julie saw the sadness that came to his eyes. He nodded to the movers and walked out the door. Julie watched while he climbed back into his truck and drove away. Then she closed the door, and turned to the four men standing behind her, their hands clasped behind them. The tall one in the middle that Mark thought he recognized gazed at her through his light brown eyes. "It seems that he believed you, *miandi*," he commented.

"Yes, he did, didn't he, Russell?" Julie mused. She stared into space, disgusted with herself. She was good at many things, but somewhere along the way, deceiving others had become her best ability. She turned to the jumble of boxes and furniture around her. She began to open them and moved the objects within them into place with her thoughts. The wires for the electronic components moved into their right jacks. The boxes of books opened and began to flow into the bookcase in the corner. The sofa that sat in the middle of the room rose about six inches off the floor and backed into place against the wall. The mattress, box spring and other bedroom furniture lifted up in the air and settled itself into place within it, completely made and ready for sleeping. In the kitchen, stacks of plates, bowls, cups and glasses floated out their boxes, and sorted themselves into the cabinets. The movers watched with concern. Their protector needed to do this. She had so much frustration pent up within her and she could not properly release it without it drawing attention. Having them there observing her at least kept it in check.

After a while, the moving stopped. The empty boxes collapsed themselves and disappeared. The ones that she hadn't reached stacked themselves neatly in the bedroom hallway. The remaining furniture settled into place. She stared about her new home. She had looked forward to this day, but now events outside her control had tarnished it. She had read somewhere about two trains on the same track, rushing toward each other. It was what her life was like right now—her worlds were on a collision course. She thought it would be simple to keep them in their separate corners, like she had done so often in the past. In less than a week, they were on the verge of meeting. She flopped down into a dining room chair and looked at the men in front of her, hoping to gain from them an answer she knew they couldn't provide. "How long can I keep this up?" she whispered. "How far am I willing to go to protect you?" She looked out the window toward Mark's house. "How long can I keep lying to him about who and what I really am?"

The Illani with her looked at each other. Then Russell walked toward her and laid a comforting hand on her shoulder. "As long as you feel it is necessary to protect those you care about," he assured her. "Or, as long as it takes for him to find out the truth for himself, and accept it."

Julie reached out and placed a hand over his. Tears filled her eyes and her chin quivered. "The question is, Russell . . . will he?"

XIV

Mark made his way back to the precinct, while the evidence he had gathered and the questions it had raised circulated in his head. The more he thought about it, the more he realized that his path was laid before him. Judge Embry was in some way a part of everything. How would he be able to prove it, and distance himself from the personal quagmire he had stepped into? Then he thought about Cassie. As the new kid on the block, she wouldn't recognize his handwriting. How dangerous would things become for her? How could he protect her? Mark gripped the steering wheel. She didn't deserve to be dragged into the middle of his personal problems. Mark could see potential in her. It just needed nurturing, just as Charlie did for him. He should go talk to Lieutenant Michaels about what he discovered, but what if he was wrong. He stared up at the familiar tower structure, and hoped that it wasn't for the last time. At least there was some consolation. He had talked to the one person with the ability to find, and possibly warn the heirs that their lives could be in danger.

He pulled into his usual parking spot and walked through the semi-deserted hallways toward the elevators. It zipped him quickly back to the seventh floor. Upon entering the precinct's double doors, he spotted Cassie at his desk, her ear glued to the phone. She looked up at the sound of the squeaking door and gestured to him. "Hang on a minute," she said to the person on the other end of the line. She pressed the speakerphone button. "It's Natalie Bishop of the D.A.'s office, regarding that land agreement," she informed him.

Mark smiled. Natalie Bishop *was* the Mason County District Attorney. She was a willowy, elegant African-American woman who wrestled the position away from G. Stanley Barnabus a year ago. He could see Natalie now, her long, straight black hair flowing down her back, her gold half-rimmed glasses perched on her nose, and her appearance as perfect now as it had been at 8:00 a.m. Mark took off his jacket, draped it over an empty chair, and leaned towards the phone. "Hey, Natalie, how are you?"

"Detective Mark Daniels, it's good to hear your voice again. I see you landed yourself a doozy of a case on your first week back."

"Par for the course it seems." Mark slid into his chair next to Cassie, who appreciated his subtle gesture, as he had blocked the darkened windows from her view. "What's going on?"

"Well, I've gone over this document as best as I can. This thing's a Contracts professor's dream come true. It's fascinating reading."

"Yeah?" The document nearly put Mark to sleep by it before he finished the first paragraph. "What did you find out?"

"As I was telling your new partner, it's a pretty tightly drafted document. From a legal point of view, it covers nearly every change in the law from the early 1600s. Any outside third party doesn't stand a chance of getting it overturned from any recognized legal standpoint. I called the court clerk's office in Okanogan County earlier today. He told me that the judges up there have seen more than their share of motions regarding this property. According to him, the tribe's been approached by these same people for more than five years, trying to get them to surrender their portion, and in their view, at a fraction of what it's probably worth. There've been some other issues as well."

"Issues? Like what?" Cassie asked.

"Well, they've been sued for one thing. It looks like this corporation's trying to convince the courts to overturn the agreement by saying it violates eminent domain . . . legal jargon you needn't worry yourselves over," Natalie assured them. "I also talked to the sheriff. According to her, there've been some other nastier things going on."

"Nastier things?"

"A couple of their tribes' citizens were attacked a few weeks ago. Another one went missing. They just found his body on the other side of the reservation.

They're calling it suspicious, although the guy didn't have a mark on his body. Then, someone poisoned their sacred drink during their coming of age ceremony. Four children died."

Mark and Cassie looked at each other. "Poisoned? How?" Mark inquired.

"They all died of various aneurisms or strokes. The cause is unknown, though. I'll ask the Okanogan D.A. to have their medical examiner forward their reports to you. Maybe there's a link between their deaths and the woman here."

"But why are they being so persistent? Why kill anyone if this document's so airtight?" Cassie wanted to know.

"It's not completely airtight. From what we've been able to determine, there's only two legal ways to break it. Way one is if the entire Amendu tribe dies. I don't think you have to worry about that."

"Why not?"

"According to the last census count, there were about five thousand of them, and I don't think whomever's after this place is stupid enough to commit genocide. However, Mr. Carnegie's right about the heirs. You need to put a concerted effort into finding them."

"Why? What's so special about them?" Cassie asked.

Mark and Cassie heard paper rustling over the speaker. "Apparently, only direct descendants or their adopted children can be the CEO of the company, but that's only the half of it," Natalie continued. "The Foundation's interest is immediately severed if the child or children of the current CEO die before them. Their interest transfers to the Amendu, and all restrictions regarding its sale are removed."

"What about the company pursuing the land? Any leads on them?" Mark inquired.

"We're still digging. They're working under a lot of shell corporations and alternate names, but one that popped up is noteworthy; a company called Lemont-Bay Industries."

"Lemont-Bay Industries," Mark murmured. "I know that name. Are they local?"

"Nope. They're based out of Delaware. I found a website there that gives you information about the corporations incorporated there, which is what makes this connection so interesting."

"How interesting?"

"Well, for one thing, its treasurer is locked up in a California mental facility. He was convicted of embezzlement and tax evasion more than five years back, but suffered some sort of head trauma in a car accident shortly before his trial. He went a little loony after he went to prison. The president is someone we both know, Mark—J. Jacob Embry."

Mark picked up the documents taken from Terrance's safe. It hadn't been his imagination. It *was* the judge's signature. The feeling he had in his stomach was replaced by confusion and anger. Then he remembered where he had seen Lemont-Bay Industries before. It was on the business card the judge gave him; the same day he met Julie. The judge told him that they would have the money he needed to help pay off the mortgage.

Mark tore the card up and in retrospect, was glad he had. The man who allegedly paid of his mortgage was involved with the corporation looking to steal this land. "Anything else, Natalie?"

"Nope. However, if you need me for anything else, I'll be home all evening."

"Thanks, Natalie."

Mark broke the connection and held his finger on the button. He stared at the device as a cloud came over his face. Cassie gave her new partner a curious stare. There was something different about him now, as if he had figured out the puzzle already. "Hey, partner, care to clue me in on what you're thinking?"

Mark sat back. The family friend who had tried to reach out a hand to help him was behind all of this? He couldn't believe it. He didn't want to believe it. He glanced over at Lieutenant Michaels's blinded window. He needed to tell her, to give her ample warning of the path he was about to embark on. He was hesitant to tell her because he wasn't even certain that he wasn't on the right one. He wouldn't be, until he inserted at least one more piece of the puzzle.

"Mark? Are you all right?"

Mark snapped out of his reverie. Cassie was staring at him. He forced a smile to his face. "I'm fine. I'm just trying to work some things out, have them make sense."

Cassie didn't like what she sensed from Mark. He knew something, but he didn't want to tell her. She also recognized the name of the man Natalie Bishop had mentioned. J. Jacob Embry was the name of the judge at the arraignment hearing. What was Mark's relationship with him? She sensed it was more than just a judge and a cop. Something had happened when Mark had gone back into chambers that day Leonard was released. Was Mark somehow involved with this attempt to snatch land that didn't belong to them? Cassie immediately dismissed it. He wouldn't be working this case as hard as he had been if he was. Then what was it? She tried another tactic: "I meant to ask you? Did you talk to Julie?"

"Yeah."

"What did she know about the place?"

"Not much. She said that she's not at the office much, and she doesn't have a lot contact with the brass. She's on her way here to see what we have, so that she can show it to them." Mark toyed with the coiled cord, thinking hard. "Let's assume for a moment that Judge Embry and his corporation are our bad guys. We need to find the person or people he's threatening to kill. Julie's working on that from her end. Let's work on his finances. See if we can squeeze both ends against the middle?"

Cassie nodded and made herself cozy at the computer, while Mark made a few discreet phone calls to pull Judge Embry's phone records and finances. As he hung up the phone, he remembered the look the judge gave Julie that day at Scordalia's. It was as if the judge knew who she was. However, Julie said that she hadn't been there long, and that her position in the company wasn't that high. An uneasy thought occurred to him. "Hey, Cass?"

"Yeah?" Cassie answered without halting her typing.

"Have we done any research on Julie's employer yet?"

"I was just getting to it. Why?"

"I wonder if we can help Julie out. Maybe there's something there that can give us a clue as to whom we should be looking for."

"There's an idea. I'll start with their website. Do you still have Julie's business card?"

Mark fished out his wallet and pulled it out. Cassie took it, stared at the front, and keyed in the Foundation's Internet address. Their website came up on the screen. Her fingers moved across the keyboard. Mark watched her and raised an eyebrow. She was far more adept at using this thing than he was. He'd have to take advantage of that in the future. After a bit, she clicked on a link. Ten seconds later, a list of the board members and their biographies appeared. Cassie began to read them carefully. She gazed back at the card again and her jaw dropped. "Mark?" she asked in a hesitant tone.

"What?"

"This one biography I'm reading? It's the CEO's. His children are listed." Cassie pointed to the screen at the top name on the list. "Look."

Mark rolled his chair around her desk to see. His eyes went wide. He read it three times to make sure, but he still didn't believe what he read. The current CEO, a man named Simon Birmingham III, had held the position these last forty years. He also had an adopted daughter named Juliana Lynn Warren who worked as a consultant for the company. Cassie looked at him uncertainly. "It can't be," she muttered. "There's no way she could be."

The wheels in Mark's mind turned a mile a second. There were no pictures so they couldn't be certain, but in his heart, he knew. The custom-made suits, the limousine, the credit card and the brand-new car should've been dead giveaways. Then he thought back to their lunch at Scordalia's. He had gone there to try and find out more about her. Apparently, she had the same idea, except she had been cleverer, and far more successful. Now he understood the questions she asked him at her place. She wanted to know if he had found out who was behind it, and probably how close he was to truly finding out about her. "But why?" Mark whispered. "Why would she lie to me about who she was?"

"Perhaps to protect herself," Cassie answered. "Then again, maybe she did it to protect you."

"Protect me?"

"Well, if you knew who she really was, you would've had to remove yourself from the case. This way, you get to do your job and you can't be accused of any wrongdoing. Of course, she's also not a blood relative, so she mustn't think that she's in that much danger."

"But Nat said that the termination clause covers adopted children as well. She's the child of the current CEO and as that child . . ."

The realization of the clause hit him full force. He glanced around the room. Julie should've been here by now to pick up the information. Where the hell was she—unless she had already figured it out—and was going after the judge herself. He slammed his hands against the desk and cursed. "Get a squad car over to my place right now, and put an alert out on her and her vehicle! We need to find her!"

He snatched the business card from Cassie's hand and pulled out his cell phone. He flipped it over and called the number printed on the back of it. There still was no answer. There wasn't an answer at her new home number, which she had given him the day prior. Frantic, he called the number in San Francisco. "Miss Warren should be at her residence in Mason City," the female voice he heard at the beginning of the week told him. "Is there something wrong?"

"I need to reach her." Mark paused. His voice took on an authoritative tone: "I know that she's the daughter of the CEO. I also believe that she may be danger."

"Danger? What's wrong?"

"I don't have time to explain. Do you have another number that I can reach her at?" "No, sir. However, her guardian's here. You may want to speak to him."

The woman placed Mark on hold for a moment. Then the phone picked up again. "This is Lord Birmingham," a voice said in a distinct British accent.

"Lord Birmingham, my name's Mark Daniels. I'm a detective with the Mason City police department. Your daughter just rented an apartment from me."

"Yes, she's told me about you. Why are you calling here?"

"Sir, your daughter's in great danger. I need to find her, but she's not answering any of her phones. Do you have any idea where she may be?"

"She should be at her new home. Why?"

"I'm working on a homicide here. My investigation has led me to some men who are attempting to steal some land that your family and corporation own. Do you know anything about this?"

"Yes, she told me." There was a pause. "I sense that there's something she didn't tell me."

"It's possible that she might be trying to go after them herself," Mark explained. He mentally punched himself for what he had told her, and for not picking up on what she hadn't told him. His detective skills had really slipped during his leave. It was high time to get them back in gear. "I know the identity of the man who's after your land, and I think she does too. I think she's gone to confront him. The problem is he knows who she is, and he'll kill her if she goes anywhere near him."

"No, Detective. She can be foolhardy, but she wouldn't knowingly expose herself to such a risk."

"I'd like to believe that, sir, but I've tried calling her, and I can't reach her. Do you have any idea where she could be?"

Mark heard him sigh. "She's been trying to establish herself on her own for some time. She doesn't like to tell me everything that's going on in her life. She thinks I worry too much. However, as her guardian, that's my job." There was another pause. Mark heard him say something to the receptionist. Then his voice returned.

"I'm contacting my head of security. I've had someone following her ever since she was a child, even if she didn't want it. They'll find her, and I'll contact you when they do. You have my word on that, Detective."

"Thank you, sir."

Mark hung up the receiver, and then realized what her guardian had just told him. He had someone following her since she was a child? Granted, there was a real danger to her until she had children of her own, but no wonder she was anxious to get away! He looked up at Cassie, who had plunked herself back down at the computer. She was typing furiously on the keyboard. "Cassie?"

"Wait a minute, Mark."

The monitor light had changed color. Apparently, Cassie had gone to another website. The screens were changing too fast for him to figure out where she had gone. Finally, the screens stopped shifting. She read what it displayed and sat back in her chair again. Mark studied her body posture. She looked to be in shock. "What?" he asked.

When she didn't answer, he walked over to her desk. The glow of the monitor lit up his face. He read the top of the screen. Cassie had overheard his conversation, and directed her research to a secure website. It listed the certified registered gun owners in the state. It also stated whether they had permission to carry a concealed weapon. In front of them was a name he had become intimately familiar with: "Warren, Juliana Lynn, 5485-A East Pine, Mason City," he mumbled. He closed his eyes, trying to will away what he had read. "Oh my God."

Cassie turned and stared. She had only jumped onto the website on a hunch, not thinking that she would actually find something. "Mark?"

Mark opened his eyes. A steely look had come to them. "C'mon, Cass."

Cassie glanced over at Lieutenant Michaels' office. She knew that they should be telling her what they had found, and the lieutenant making the decision that Mark was making now. "Mark, where are you going?"

Mark reached for his jacket. "To confront Judge Embry and hopefully, to stop Julie from walking into certain death."

"Mark, she wouldn't. She can't be that stupid."

Mark slipped his jacket over his shoulders. "I don't know her that well, Cassie, and she's been lying to me throughout this investigation. If she is the heir, and she's going after him, then I have to try and stop her before she gets herself killed."

Mark headed for the double doors that led out of the precinct. Cassie stood up. Didn't he realize there was a lot more at stake than a woman's life? She raced after him and grabbed him by the arm just as he reached the elevator. "Mark, wait and think about this!" she warned him. "If you go and confront him, and you're wrong, he'll have your badge."

Mark turned and gave her a stare. Cassie took a step back, her eyes wide. It was a look that she didn't understand and couldn't translate, but in her heart, it meant something ominous. "Then let him have it," he muttered in a low voice. "I'll gladly give it up. I'll give up my life, too, if it stops an innocent woman from being killed in cold blood."

He turned and walked away from her. He hit the "Down" button and the elevator doors opened. He stepped inside and turned around to gaze at his new partner. If she wanted to demonstrate how good she was, now was the time to do it. "Are you coming?"

Cassie noticed that the look in his eyes had not disappeared. She fought not to show any sign of fear. "No. You find Julie," Cassie assured him. "If what you're thinking is true, helping her guardian and their security team protect her should be your first priority. I'll type up the warrant and get D.A. Bishop to get a judge sign it. I'll meet you in front of Judge Embry's home in an hour."

"Then I'll see you there."

The elevator doors closed. Cassie let out a sigh. Inside, her stomach felt queasy, but not the queasiness that she had been experiencing being up on the seventh floor. It was from the expression on Mark's face. Two people in the precinct had warned her about it before she even met Mark. They also instructed her to notify them at once if she saw it appear. She bit her bottom lip. Should she go to them now, or should she be loyal to her partner? She looked back at the closed door of Lieutenant Michaels's office, and then back to the elevator doors. With a great effort, she turned and headed back into the precinct. She gathered up the papers from Terrance's office, their notes and Julie's business card, and walked up to the door of Lieutenant

Michaels' office. She hesitated, and then rapped on the glass. "Come in," she heard her superior call out.

Slowly, Cassie opened the door. The lieutenant was on the phone. She looked up to see who was there. "Just a minute." She cupped the receiver's mouthpiece. "Yes, Detective?"

"Lieutenant, I need to talk to you." Cassie swallowed. "I need to talk to you about Mark."

Lieutenant Michaels didn't like the tone of Cassie's voice. She pushed her hair out of her face, so that she could better study her. "Detective? What is it?"

Cassie glanced down at all of their notes and then back at her boss. It took a moment for her to speak. "I saw it," she whispered. "I didn't think that I ever would, but . . ." She struggled for the words. She wasn't certain how to describe what she had seen, except to use the words the lieutenant had used. She took a deep breath and raised her chin. "I saw the Look, Lieutenant," she answered in a firm voice.

Lieutenant Michaels frowned. She put the receiver back to her ear. "Chief? Can I call you back? Thank you." She hung up the phone and nodded to a chair. "Sit down, Cassie. Tell me what's going on."

*   *   *

In the Foundation's San Francisco office, Jennifer McIntire's assistant Elise Carpenter gazed at the distinguished-looking man known on Earth as Lord Simon Birmingham III. He leaned heavily on his silver-tipped mahogany cane, and handed her back the receiver.

She replaced it in its cradle and noted the concerned look on his face. "Is she all right?" Elise asked.

Simon closed his eyes and reached out to search for her. When he sensed her reply, he smiled. "Yes. However, I don't know how long she can keep up this masquerade with the human detective."

"The *miandi* is very clever, sir. She will keep her secrets from him."

Simon opened his eyes and gripped his cane tighter. From here, he and Elise had watched as Julie and NIK manipulated the information that Mark and Cassie read on Cassie's computer screen, right down to the fake handgun registration permit. "I know, but I fear the cost may be too much; not just for her, but for the human as well."

XV

The fourth movement of Beethoven's Ninth Symphony boomed out of the ceiling-mounted speakers, as Judge J. Jacob Embry sat in his study rereading a particular paragraph in a land ownership agreement. The contract dealt with a piece of land up near the Canadian border. For four hundred years, others had struggled to break it. He shook his head in disbelief. How could no one have seen the one way to this land, defined for all to see in the document they cursed? Or, had they seen it and were too morally just to act on it? Judge Embry smiled. When billions of dollars of untapped wealth were yours for the taking, morals be damned.

The doorbell chime rang out over the soaring chorus. Judge Embry set down the contract and glanced at his watch. It was after nine in the evening. He wondered who would be gracing his door this late at night. Perhaps it was Mark Daniels coming to try and pay him back for the loan that he did not make. He chuckled. A part of him had hoped that Mark would take him up on his offer of assistance. However, Mark thinking that Judge Embry had helped him seemed to be just as effective. Having a man like Mark under his thumb would come in handy, especially if the people who were really after the land came back to visit. He shuddered at the memory of them. He assumed the potential buyer had sent them to check on his progress. The woman had been an attractive blonde, but the man had no face, as if he wore a gray mask to disguise his features. They gave him a vial of clear liquid and instructed him to give some to Terrance. Judge Embry never got the chance. Terrance was now in protective custody at the police station. Judge Embry wasn't worried. Terrance couldn't identify him. He only had a voice to go by and the phone he sent him was untraceable.

The doorbell rang again and Judge Embry frowned. He reached for his suit jacket. When all was in place, he walked down the dark hallway and peeked out the peephole. He paused and then opened his front door. The last person he expected to see stood on his stoop. She wore a jeans and a long-sleeve crewneck shirt instead of the tweed suit she wore when he first saw her in Scordalia's. Her brown eyes held a determined look behind her glasses. "Judge J. Jacob Embry?" she asked.

He hid his shock and delight with his best courtroom face. He wouldn't have thought it possible. Was she that desperate to protect a piece of land that she would risk her life to confront him directly? "I am," he replied in his deep voice.

"I'd like to talk to you, please."

"Of course. Please, come in."

Julie thanked him and stepped through the doorway. She waited for him to close the door behind her and followed him into his study. She took two steps inside and paused to listen to the music, before turning her attention fully on him. "I'm sorry to disturb you at such a late hour, but this could not wait."

"I understand." He appraised her carefully. All Julie carried was a black messenger bag. Would she be so brazen to accost him without any means of defense? He wondered if she even bothered to tell anyone where she was going. He doubted it. If she had, she would not be here right now, not with the security her guardian drowned her with, and if Mark had finally figured out exactly who she was. Once she was inside, he closed the door and made his way back to his desk. He reclined back in his chair. "I apologize for being rude, but, who you are?"

Julie took a position in the center of the room. She recognized him now. She saw him in Scordalia's when she lunched there with Mark the other afternoon. She had felt his stare on her, but she had ignored it. At the time, her mind was preoccupied with Mark and his potential dangers. Now, she turned it toward her new enemy. "I'm certain that you already know, but if it'll satisfy your curiosity, my name's Julie Warren. I work as a consultant for a non-profit group in San Francisco. You may have heard about the Foundation?"

"Why should I know anything about this Foundation you're talking about?"

"I'm also the daughter of its current CEO?"

"Oh. In that case, you have satisfied my curiosity." He leaned forward in his chair. "Although I must admit I expected you five years ago."

"Five years ago? Why so long?"

"Because Jack said that you might come looking for me. Sooner or later, I knew that you would." At her confused expression, he continued: "Jack Adams, your former director."

"You know Jack?"

"Yes, before his accident. He hasn't been the same since. Tell me, what did you say or do to him?"

"Pardon me?"

"Before his sentencing, he was involved in a car crash. I saw photographs of the wreckage. It's a wonder he escaped with only a mild concussion. However, he went berserk when he spotted you at his sentencing, and the mere mention of your name sends him into a rage that only the strongest sedatives seem able to quell. The few times I have seen him, he mutters the same thing to himself: 'You don't know what she is. You don't know what she is.' What does he mean?"

"I have no clue. Perhaps it's his guilt and remorse talking."

"I doubt that. If it were, you would've come after me much sooner than now. I am curious to know what you said to him the night you went to fire him."

"I just showed him the error of his ways. It's a lesson he learned quite well, albeit too late to rectify things with the Foundation."

"I see. It's too bad you won't be able to teach me that lesson."

Judge Embry slid his right hand into his jacket pocket and brought it forward. Julie realized that there was a gun within it, and that it was pointed directly at her chest. She stared at it for a moment, then at him. "You intend to kill me, sir."

"Yes. Thank you for making it so easy. I have to admit it would be a shame, considering that you're the last surviving member of the family who has protected that land for such a long time."

Julie considered her surrounding and the circumstances she found herself. Then to his surprise, she sat down in one of the chairs before her, and rested her bag against the left legs. He gave her a bemused smile. "You seem very calm for someone who's about to die."

"Do not mistake my calmness as a lack of fear. I knew that by coming here, I was placing my life in your hands. However, I have an overwhelming curiosity that must be satisfied before I die. You will answer some questions for me?"

He leaned back in his chair, his weapon still aimed at her chest. "How I discovered your land, perhaps?"

"Among other things."

He caressed his mustache, thinking. "Jack told me of it," he answered finally. "We went to college together, and struck up a close friendship. He and I were good at making money, and taking money away from others. While we went separate ways for a time, we never stopped seeking out opportunities to increase our holdings. Then on a stroke of luck, you hired him to take over as director of your corporation. You should have checked him more carefully than you did, or at least not granted him the carte blanche discretion he had over your funds. It would have saved you quite a bit of hassle, not to mention millions of dollars if you had."

"Millions?"

"Yes. He tucked away quite a bit of money before he showed me that contract. He also stumbled across research done on the property back in the early 1950s. It indicated that the land harbored vast mineral deposits, not to mention the millions of dollars of virgin timber. We hired Terrance Carnegie's firm to update the findings. The corporations we created were just ways of hiding what we stole from you; money that we would use to purchase it once the time was right."

"But something happened to change your mind; else you would've come after me back then."

His face turned cross. "My wife divorced me. She took all the money she could find. I barely had enough money to run for a second term as judge. Also, Jack became greedier than he needed to be. I warned him that if wasn't careful, he would be caught. Inevitably, he was. Your accountant's evidence was most thorough. Had he lived to testify, Jack's punishment would have been far more stringent. With my main source of information gone, and my personal life in ruins, I decided to forgo any further pursuit of it. Then I received a phone call. Someone wanted me to renew my interest in it. He provided me the capital I needed to begin anew. He also pointed out some things within the contract that I had overlooked."

"Had you read the agreement before then?"

"I gave it a cursory glance. After my new benefactor had hung up, I devoured it. It left me with many questions that you can now answer for me."

"I shall endeavor to try."

He rose from behind his desk and made to sit in front of her. Now his gun was at point-blank range. He expected her to flinch or cower. She remained relaxed and congenial, as if she were having a chat with a long-time friend. "I've been a lawyer for more than 30 years," he admitted, "and I've never seen anything like it. It's a marvel of legal drafting, so brilliant in its structure, in its attention to detail. It's so ahead of its time, I believe it'll continue to protect that land, even after the children of your children's children are dead. Tell me, how did your guardian's forefathers come up with some of the conditions to cover events that did not take place for hundreds of years?"

"I don't know. I've never asked him."

"Oh, I don't believe that for a minute, Ms. Warren. You're an astute businesswoman and a licensed attorney. I'm certain that when you were a child, your guardian read you that document to lull you to sleep. You above anyone else must know the risk you're taking in confronting me alone and unarmed."

"I do know, sir. However, I'm being truthful when I tell you I don't know how they came up with the provisions. I've always assumed that they guessed."

"Or they had incredible insight, almost as if they could see the future. Tell me, Ms. Warren, can you see the future?"

Julie's eyes floated from his face to the gun and back again. She wasn't sure if she should give an honest answer to that question. There were those rare days when she could. The problem was when she did, there was little she could do about it. "If that were true, then I wouldn't have come here knowing that I might die. However, it was a risk worth taking. I thank you for filling in the gaps. Now if you don't mind, I need to inform Detective Daniels of what you told me."

She rose from her chair and retrieved her bag. The judge rose as well, his gun aimed at her heart. She heard the click of a bolt sliding into place. Her eyes drifted to his face. There was no mistake to his actions or thinking. "You seem certain you're leaving here alive," he said in a low voice.

"I am. You see, while talking to you, I learned a few other things. I know you were the behind the tactics used to bully the Amendu into breaking the agreement. When they refused, you became furious. I've yet to locate the person you hired to poison the Amendu's *chinti*. Did you know that four children died as a result? That's a total of five counts of murder when you count Madison Evans. That's not an auspicious way for a judge to operate."

"But it's so deliciously rewarding. I call it my just desserts for having to protect the scum that traipse through my courtroom each day. Besides, why retire just a lowly judge when I could retire a billionaire, with an ocean-side home, acre of land at my disposal, and no way to be prosecuted for my actions?"

"I doubt you'll have that opportunity, sir. Detective Daniels will be here shortly. I'm certain that he's figured it out as well, and will be coming to arrest you."

The judge took another step forward. The barrel of the gun grazed Julie's chest. "You haven't known him as long as I have, but I admire your faith in him. He's an excellent detective, when his mind is on his job and not his grief. Even if he has figured it out, he won't be able to arrest me. You see, by the time he gets here, he'll find you dead. When he figures out where I've gone, I won't be anywhere near here."

"Why not?"

"I have a plane waiting for me at the airport. I plan to leave Mason City for a country with no extradition treaty with the United States. I'll be able to oversee everything from a place where he can't touch me."

"I wouldn't count on that, sir."

"You forget you didn't recover all of the money that Jack and I took. I still have quite a bit of it, in places you and your company can't touch."

"Not for long."

Her brazenness shocked and delighted him. "You sound extremely confident for a woman who's about to die."

"I am, sir." She gazed at his weapon again. Then she raised her chin. Judge Embry saw a touch of anger flash in her eyes. "I'm confident in the knowledge that Mark has figured out your role in all of this. I'm also confident that this scheme of yours will be exposed and that the citizens of this city will soon see you for the greedy, self-serving killer you are. If my death aids in that discovery, so be it. I have no fear of death, so go ahead. Kill me."

Judge Embry took a step back and raised the gun. "As you wish."

Before she could react, he fired. Within a second, the bullet entered her heart. Julie let out a sharp gasp, recoiled, and fell backward into the bookcase behind her. A few books tumbled from the shelf. Her bag flew from her shoulder into a glass vase that sat on a nearby table. It fell and shattered into pieces. She slumped over to her left. Her right hand twitched involuntarily. She stared at him in shock. Then her eyes drifted closed. Judge Embry smiled manically. "No, Ms. Warren, there's no recourse for the Amendu. You see, your death severs the relationship. They don't have the money or the will to stop me. Their tribe will be scattered to the four winds, and I will be rich beyond any man's dreams."

He walked toward her still form and bent down to take her pulse. Just as he did, her eyes opened, and she blinked. He stepped back, bewildered. She had a wicked grin on her face. He stared down at her chest. It was still moving. Then he saw something else and he took another step back. It had to be the lights playing tricks on his eyes. There was blood on the front of her red shirt, but it wasn't red. It was almost black in color. She pushed herself away from the bookshelf, stood up, and lifted her shirt. He stared in horror. The blood that splattered her chest was evaporating back into her skin, and the bullet wound he had placed in her chest was healing. All that remained was a black ball less than a quarter inch in diameter. She reached up and plucked it from her chest. He watched in growing disbelief as the hole disappeared, and replaced by chocolate brown skin. There was no sign of a wound. She discarded the used bullet and stared at him. "It seems you failed. Would you care to try again?"

With a shaky hand, Judge Embry pointed the gun at her and fired again, aiming for her head, her chest, any part of her. None of the bullets struck her. Instead, a white ball of light seemed to envelop her. Panicked, he grabbed the gun with both hands and emptied the clip. He tried to continue firing, even as he heard the clicking of the empty cylinder. The light that had surrounded her disappeared. After a moment, she held out her right hand. The remaining eight bullets were in her hand. They were in the same condition as when he had loaded them in just minutes prior to her arrival. Suddenly, they disappeared from her palm. The gun slipped from his hands. It fell to the floor with a thud. He backed away from her until he collided with his desk. He tried to climb backwards over it. His mouth was moving, but no sound came out. "No," he managed to gasp. "This . . . this isn't possible!"

"Oh, but it is, Your Honor. You are right about one thing: when the last of the heirs die, the agreement between the Foundation and the Amendu will be severed. The problem for you is that I can't die. I think the proper term to describe its impact on you is . . . bummer?"

Judge Embry regained his bearings and searched for his discarded weapon. That was when he realized that he had risen in the air. He saw his Oriental rug below him, but nothing between him and it. He flailed his limbs and twisted his torso, trying to see what held him up, but there was nothing there. Panic flowed into his face. With great fear, he looked down at Julie. There could only be one reason, and one cause for what was happening to him, but the unanswered question was how she could do it. He fought for his words. "Who . . . what . . . are . . . you?" he croaked.

Julie looked to her right. With a second, the shattered vase repaired itself. The judge watched in growing horror and fascination as it floated in the air while it waited for the table it sat on to settle itself into place. She held out her left hand. Her bag flew right into it. She waved her right over her shirt. The blood that once stained the front of it vanished. She adjusted the strap against her shoulder, and returned her focused gaze back to the man floating above her. She sensed him quaking with terror. An evil glint came to her eyes. "If you studied the Amendu and the agreement as well as you claimed, you would know who and what I am," Julie said in a throaty tone. "I'm one of the sky children, Judge Embry. In fact, I am the sky child . . . the *miandi*, as the other tribe that reside on that land call me."

He stared at her. "Other tribe?"

"Yes. That's the tribe you've been really threatening, sir. It's also the tribe that you'll never meet."

Judge Embry suddenly fell to the floor in a heap. He scrambled backwards while struggling to get to his feet. Julie did not move. She continued to gaze at him, a devilish smile on her face. He fumbled back toward his desk and reached for the phone. He held the receiver to his ear, but there was no dial tone. He clicked on the cradle several times, but still heard nothing. Then out of nowhere, a force that he could not see thrust him back into the bookcase wall behind him. Books tumbled on top of his head. He struggled to move, but he couldn't. Julie stood there. The look in her eyes had not changed. "What are you doing to me?" he gasped.

"You asked, so I thought I would demonstrate."

"Demonstrate what?"

"What I did to Jack."

A shock of electricity raced through his body. He screamed in agonizing pain. It started at the top of his head, and traveled to the soles of his feet. He twisted his body to escape from it, but he had once again risen into the air. He struggled against the invisible force that held him captive, but couldn't move. Then he thought he sensed something enter his mind. His eyes rolled into the back of his head. Julie stood below him. "Tell me Judge Embry, who aided you in your attacks on the Amendu? Who ordered you to kill Madison?" he heard her ask.

"I . . . don't . . . know!" he screamed.

Julie scanned his thoughts again and saw Jack Adams' face swimming in them. As she ransacked his brain, she realized that he had not been lying. Judge Embry's knowledge of the termination clause had only come recently, not five years' ago, when he first heard about the place. Then an image of a blonde woman and a man with a gray face came to the forefront, but they had no names or voices. There was another presence too, one that Julie didn't recognize, but seemed intent on eluding her probes. Julie tightened the force on Judge Embry's neck. It was against her nature to do what she planned to do next, but the thought of what happened to the Amendu children and to Madison, combined with the threat to the Illani, seemed to kindle something within her. She delved deeper into his thoughts, trying to get closer to that mysterious presence. As she did, she began to expose the judge's hidden nightmares and fears, and events in his childhood long forgotten. She began to use them against him, so as to help drive the secrets he held from his mind. She sensed various levels of his body functions rising to dangerous levels. His mind was also becoming unstable, but she didn't care. *Who, Judge Embry? Who helped you? Tell me!*

Judge Embry only screamed louder. The memories Julie had awakened flowed into his brain, too fast and with too much fury for him to shut out. Her voice echoed in his head. The pain deepened. He felt as if his insides were melting and ready to explode simultaneously. He didn't want to know what she was now. He only wanted to get away from her. Even death would be welcome, if it stopped the agony his mind was experiencing right now. "Stop!" he begged. "Stop, please!"

A new presence tickled the back of her mind and Julie straightened. There was a vehicle heading directly toward the judge's house. She reached out and recognized the approaching human signature. It was Mark. She relinquished some of the hold she had on the judge. He fell back to the carpet in a sprawling heap. She closed her eyes and collected herself and her thoughts. She opened her eyes again, reached into bag and retrieved her phone. She pressed a few keys, and waved it over the spot on the rug where she had landed and swept it over the nearby bookshelves. "NIK?"

There is no trace of your presence, Ambassador.

"Good. Scan the room for a safe or some other hidden storage space. There has to be more information here about who helped him."

I have already done so, Ambassador. I have found no such structure.

Unconvinced, Julie turned back to the desk. Spread across its surface was copies of the research that Terrance and Madison performed for the judge. She turned her attention to the drawers. In the pencil drawer, she found a clear vial of liquid. She held it in her palm. Its contents began to bubble. Her face turned cross. "Sorja root, NIK," she said aloud. "It's the same concentration as the poison that killed the Amendu children and Madison. Now, all I need to know is who helped him."

Ambassador, Detective Daniels has entered the inner perimeter. He will be at the judge's home within two Earth minutes. Also, the human's vital signs are beginning to fluctuate.

Julie returned her attention to Judge Embry. His hands were around his throat and his eyes bulged out of his sockets, as he fought against the force that he believed was choking him to death. He stared blankly at her. She knelt beside him and reached out two fingers to touch his left temple. Instantly, his facial muscles slackened and a glaze came over his eyes. She scanned his thoughts again. The image of the man and woman she had seen earlier came and went quickly. "NIK, take these codes I'm transmitting. I believe they'll lead us to our missing money."

Confirmed. They are passcodes and bank account numbers to his corporate accounts throughout the world.

"And backed by money that doesn't belong to him. NIK, make sure that those corporations are closed down at once, and those funds transferred back to where they belong. Now as for you, Judge Embry."

She pressed her hand fully against his forehead. Her eyes closed and her hand began to glow. She began to move through the judge's brain, deleting certain images, and reprogramming his thought processes. Julie mentally kicked herself. She had let her emotions get the best of her, and she had caused some damage. "NIK, contact Alexandra. Have her stop by the jail and confirm my readings on Judge Embry. If they're correct, have her begin preparations."

As you wish, Ambassador.

Satisfied with her results, she pulled her hand away and stared Judge Embry in the eye. "Like Jack, you'll live these last few moments for the rest of your life, Your Honor," Julie whispered. "You'll never tell anyone what happened here, what you learned, or that you spoke to me. However, you will tell the police and the district attorney about your role in this property scheme and everything you did to try and accomplish it. Do you understand?"

"Yes," Judge Embry replied in a monotone.

Julie stood and scanned the room, this time taking note of its disorderly appearance. Immediately, the books that had fallen flew back into place on their shelves. The still-floating vase reassumed its position on the table. Judge Embry's gun hovered into the air. His center desk drawer opened and she guided the gun inside of it. Like a marionette, Judge Embry rose from the floor and sat down in his chair. He still had a distant look on his face, but it would be gone before Mark walked through the door. She retrieved her bag and gave the room one more glance to make sure that nothing was out of place. Then she focused in on her vehicle, which she had left parked a few blocks away, and disappeared.

XVI

Mark gritted his teeth as he wove his way through the late evening traffic down Warren Avenue toward the exclusive neighborhood where Judge Embry lived. "Damn it, is it just me, or is there an unusual amount of traffic for this time of night?"

He looked at the dashboard clock for the fourth time in less than a minute. He felt certain that if Julie had done what he feared, she would stick to the side streets to avoid detection. Although Julie may not know the area well, it wouldn't take her long to realize that Warren Avenue was the most direct route to the judge's home.

While he drove, he kept one ear tuned to his scanner, hoping that someone had spotted Julie's vehicle somewhere around town. The other one was pressed to his phone, on which he repeatedly dialed Julie's cell phone number to no avail. Frustrated, he threw the phone down into the passenger seat and began to scrutinize every vehicle he passed, looking for her

Escape. He saw one with Washington tags, but he was certain that Julie's still had California license tags. After all, she was moving from her guardian's place, and they lived and worked in San Francisco. He shook his head, disgusted with himself. "She lied to me! She lied to me and thought that I wouldn't find out. Why? Why would she do such a thing, unless she was tired of being coddled by her guardian and wanted to show him that she was more than capable of taking care of herself. Well Julie, this wasn't the best way to go about it."

The scanner squawked, breaking Mark concentration for a moment. He reached over to turn it up. It was a routine call: someone's cat was stuck in a tree again. Mark reached over and snapped it off. He gripped the wheel tighter and felt his sweaty hands slide around it. "Let me get there first," he prayed. "Let me get there, and let Julie be found before Judge Embry kills her."

Ten minutes later, he reached the corner of Fisk and Warren avenues. Judge Embry had the corner townhouse, a three-story brick structure trimmed with black shutters, and an ebony black door with brass handles. He parked around the block and shut off his headlights. If Julie had somehow made it here before him, he didn't want Judge Embry to know he was coming. He climbed out of his truck and headed toward the judge's house. He had been here a few times with his father, when they still had some semblance of a relationship. Not much had changed on the street, except that the oak and maple trees that lined it were taller and more mature. Mark stared at the front door. To his left, he saw a light on in one of the judge's cream-draped front windows. The judge was home. He walked up the steps and went to rap on the door, but it swung open on its own. The hair on the back of Mark's head stood up and instinctively, Mark drew his gun. Had Judge Embry expected him, or someone else? He gazed down the dimly lit hallway, listening for any sound that seemed out of place. All he heard was the roar of traffic from the distant highway, the rustle of the spring breeze in the newly forming leaves, and choral music. He took a step through the doorway. "Judge Embry?"

There was no response. Mark pushed the door open wider. He saw light emitting from an open doorway on the left. He took another step inside. "Judge Embry?" he called out again.

"Detective Daniels, is that you?"

Mark didn't dare quicken his pace. He kept his gun at the ready, taking determined steps toward the room at the end of the hall. Mark assumed that Judge Embry had help with this scheme, and that the person or people responsible may be waiting for him on the other side. "Judge Embry? Are you all right?"

"Come into the study, Detective. I've been expecting you."

Mark poked his head around the corner and looked into the book-filled room. He glimpsed Judge Embry sitting at his desk. He looked like he had just arrived home; he hadn't even taken off his suit jacket. The judge looked up from his reading and his moustache twitched. He took his reading glasses off and stared at the man before him. "Detective, how nice of you to visit. Please, come in."

Mark glanced about the book-filled room. Judge Embry noticed the suspicion in his eyes. He was entering the room the way a cop expecting an ambush would enter one. He laughed. "It's all right, Detective. I assure you I'm quite alone."

Mark stood tall in the doorway and continued to look around. Sure enough, the judge was alone. He dropped his gun arm to his side and stepped fully inside the room. His nose wrinkled. He thought he picked up the distinctive scent of spent gunpowder. Judge Embry watched him, a serene look on his face. His eyes were bright, but seemed distant. "Detective, what brings you by on an evening like this?"

Mark stared at Judge Embry, remembering the signature at the bottom of the documents they had seized from Terrance's office, and the look on his face when he had seen Julie at the restaurant. For five years, he had been after the land. A young woman, and possibly others had died in the process. Now he threatened the life of his new tenant. How could this learned man be responsible for all of it? Mark took an uncertain step forward. "I'm here to ask you a few questions, sir," Mark answered.

"About what? Your repayment plan for your mortgage?"

"No. About some new evidence I've come across in relation to the Madison Evans case."

Judge Embry raised an eyebrow. "Oh?"

Mark stopped and stood in the same spot that Julie had occupied just moments prior. "We have proof that Madison Evans was deliberately targeted because of that research that her boss asked for. We've also talked to Terrance Carnegie, the real estate agent whom you initially hired to help you. He's been most cooperative in respect to what he knows. However, I'm more interested in what you know, sir."

Judge Embry set his papers down and leaned back in his seat. "What I know?"

"Yes. I need to gain more information about some of your extracurricular activities, especially in a company called Lemont-Bay Industries."

"Oh, that." Judge Embry stood up and retrieved a book from the shelf behind him. He opened it and flicked through the pages. "What do you want to know, Detective?"

Mark regarded him silently. For a man who was about to go to jail, he seemed very confident. Mark took another step, but he kept his gun at his side. He stole a glance at the papers on the judge's desk. They were copies of the documents that they found in Terrance's office. He swallowed and returned his attention back to the judge. "Why is your company so interested in a piece of holy land? What's on that land that your company feels that it's worth killing for? Most important, what's your role in all of this?"

"My role?"

"It looks like that you might have initiated all of it." Mark paused. "And from the looks of it, you may have been at it for at least five years. There's evidence to suggest that you're responsible for the deaths of several people, and may be attempting to kill at least one more person."

Judge Embry replaced the book back on the shelf. He turned to face Mark, his arms crossed. The serene look had not left his face. "And if it was, and I admit to you that I sanctioned it, what would you do?"

Mark fought not to gape. Was the judge actually going to admit that he was responsible? Mark took a deep breath. "Then I'd arrest you, sir."

"Arrest me? On what charge?"

"The murder of Madison Evans to start, sir."

Judge Embry threw his head back and laughed heartedly. He recovered himself quickly. "Murder? You're awfully brave to come here and accuse me of that. Do you have any evidence that I ordered people killed, or tried to take this land? Even better, do you have an arrest warrant with you?"

Outside, Mark heard squealing brakes and the squelch of tires on the pavement. A red strobe light cut across his vision. He stole a look out the window to his right. Two unmarked police cars had pulled up in front of Judge Embry's place. He thought he saw Cassie alight from one of the vehicles. A few seconds later, more police cars had pulled up, along with a television van. Mark frowned. How did the media find out already? If he was wrong, the last thing he needed was to have his mistake blared across tens of thousands of television sets throughout the area. He turned his attention back to the judge. "I should have a warrant here any minute now."

"Well son, I'll be surprised if you found a judge in this county willing to sign it." Judge Embry argued. "Even if you did, you better be able to show that your new evidence can stand on its own merits. Otherwise, you're going to be looking for a new line of work so that you can pay that loan back. I can assure you of one thing, Detective: my payment terms won't be in your favor."

"You can't intimidate me that way, sir. I'll just add bribery to the list of charges."

"Bribery? If I recall, I didn't twist your arm to take out that loan, Detective."

Mark stared the judge in the eye. Protecting Julie was his only task right now. Whatever came out in the media about him and his relationship with the judge didn't matter. "I never called you sir, and I didn't ask for the money. You forced it on me, and you know it."

"And how will you prove it, son?"

Mark thought back to the piece of paper Mr. Smith had given him. "I'll find a way sir," Mark assured him in a quiet voice. "One thing I do know is that if I am to repay that money to someone, it won't be to you."

"And you're certain of that?"

Mark hesitated to answer. The judge gazed at him, his green eyes unwavering. "No," he murmured. "I didn't think so."

"Detective Daniels?"

Mark turned slightly toward the sound of the new voice. Cassie had walked into the room, along with Lieutenant Michaels and two uniformed officers. The lieutenant had spoken to him. When he didn't reply, she walked up behind him. "Detective Daniels," she whispered, "let me do this."

Mark's gazed hardened on the judge. "No, Lieutenant."

Lieutenant Michaels looked at Cassie. Cassie stepped forward. "Mark, we still need to find Julie," Cassie reminded him. "If she's in danger, she may not be out of the woods yet."

"It doesn't make a difference, Cassie. She's probably already dead, and everything I did to try to protect her may be for nothing."

Lieutenant Michaels placed a hand on his shoulder. Mark finally turned to meet her gray eyes. She saw traces of the Look still in his eyes. She gave him a reassuring nod. "Mark, someone came in after you left and dropped off some more papers," she said in a comforting voice. "With them, we got enough evidence to bury Judge Embry and everyone who helped him. Whatever he has on you, whatever you think he's holding over you, he can't. It's over."

Mark swallowed. He saw the conviction in his boss' eyes. She was telling the truth, but what about Julie? Had she been found? Was she safe? He turned to face the judge again. The uniformed officers had already moved behind him to place handcuffs on him. The serene look had not left his face. It was almost as if he was in a trance. Mark tried to let loose some of the tension in his shoulders, but he knew it would never fully disappear until he knew for certain that the judge could never threaten him again, and that Julie was truly safe. He turned to look at Cassie. He gave her a small smile. "Make sure the cuffs are nice and tight, all right?" he asked.

"Extra tight. I promise."

Mark turned to his boss. Lieutenant Michaels nodded at him, and then stepped toward the judge. "J. Jacob Embry, you're under arrest for murder, bribery, solicitation, and conspiracy," she stated in a firm voice. "You have the right to remain silent . . . ."

Mark holstered his gun and made his way out of the room. He didn't bother to look back. He felt the judge's eyes on him as he made his way out of the study and the townhouse. As he opened the front door, a television camera light flashed in his eyes. He raised a hand to block it out and made his way down the steps. He walked a few paces away, ignoring the frantic voices calling after him. He forced himself to take deep cleansing breaths, but the fury he felt against himself didn't lift. Cassie was right about one thing. If she and the lieutenant were there, it meant that they hadn't found Julie. What if Judge Embry hired someone to find her, and Julie already lay dead in an alley, or at the bottom of the river? If that was the case, then everything he had just done was for nothing. The Amendu would have lost their land and Simon Birmingham his only child; a woman that Mark had barely begun to know, except in the fact that she was someone truly special.

He turned in the misty rain to watch the scene unfolding behind him. Then his phone rang. He didn't want to answer it. It could only be bad news. He retrieved it from his coat pocket, and took a deep breath before speaking: "This is Detective Daniels."

"This is Simon Birmingham," said the voice with the British accent he had heard earlier. "My security team has found my daughter."

"They did?"

"Yes. Apparently, she went on a drive and got herself and the car following her quite lost. Her ramblings temporarily took them out of phone contact range." Mark heard the man chuckle. "My daughter never did have a good sense of direction, and she refused to have a GPS system installed in that new vehicle of hers. She thinks I'd use it to keep track of her, which I would."

"That's good to hear. Where is she now?"

Mark heard paper rustling. "According to them, she's heading southwest in the direction of Brennan Avenue. Are you anywhere near there?"

Mark smiled. Brennan Avenue was the next street over. She was heading this way. "Thank you, sir. I'll look out for her and I'll make sure that she contacts you soon."

"Thank you. Good night."

Mark hung up the phone. As he did so, he saw a female figure coming toward him. She took a step into the misty halogen light and Mark recognized her. It was Julie, approaching the area on foot. A black bag hung from her left side. Her head was bent down and she scrutinized a piece of paper that, like her clothes, was quickly getting soaked. He closed his eyes and said a silent prayer of thanks. Then he wiped the rainwater from his face and headed toward her. She must've heard his footsteps on the wet pavement, because she looked up and stopped her approach. Her eyes opened wide.

Then she hastily made to hide the piece of paper she carried. "Mark! What are you doing here?" she greeted him in a whisper.

He raised an eyebrow. After everything that had happened, she was still going to pretend that he didn't know? "I was about to ask that of you."

Mark grabbed her left. She stumbled and almost fell as he dragged her away from the townhouse and the gathering crowds. When he felt that they were safely away, he stared into her face, watching the raindrops begin to cloud her glasses. Julie couldn't tell whether he was shocked, furious, or relieved to see her. "What the *hell* are you doing here?" he hissed.

Julie winced at the grip of his hand on her arm. Her face took on a look of panic. "I was on my way downtown, and I thought that I should at least try to get to know the area a bit. Also, there was this art store I thought I'd find. Unfortunately, I got lost, so I . . ."

"And your 'getting lost' just happened to bring you to this side of town?"

Julie shrugged. She gazed about and saw the brick structure aglow in red, white and blue lights. She looked at Mark quizzically and pointed to the building. "Mark, what's going on? Who lives there?"

Mark's eyes narrowed. "Don't pull that bullshit with me, Julie. I know that you know who lives there, because I know who you really are now."

"What?" She took a step backwards, and her face took on a look of shock. "You know?"

"That you're the daughter of the CEO? That *you're* the heir's whose life is in danger? Yes."

"But . . . how did you . . . I didn't tell . . ." She paused. Then her face began to scrunch up. "Oh, great. Not you, too."

She jerked her arm from his grasp and stepped away from him. Mark watched her wipe the rain and fallen tears from her face. Finally, he saw her shoulders sag and she turned back and re-approached him. "All right, Mark, I'll admit it. I know who lives there. A couple of weeks ago, one of our company's attorneys told me there were some weird things happening with that particular piece of land. I started looking into it behind my guardian's back. After you left, I went back over my notes. That's when I figured out who it was after it. I wanted to find out why he was. I managed to get my computer up and running, so I looked up his address, and . . ."

Mark had heard enough. He grasped the strap of her messenger bag and jerked it off her arm. She took a step backwards. "Mark!"

Mark ignored her and popped open the bag's latches. He rummaged through it, but all he found was a blank notebook, a pen, an eighteen-inch piece of silver-colored aluminum pipe that looked like a runner's baton, her music player, and her cell phone, which was off. He gave an outward sigh. Then he glared at her, his gaze unrelenting. "Where is it, Julie?" he asked, his deep voice dropping an octave.

Julie crossed her arms. "Where's what?"

"Your gun? The one that you probably left in your car or stashed in the alley just before you claim you spotted me?" He shoved her bag into her chest. "Admit it, Julie. You were going to confront him yourself, and perhaps kill him, weren't you?"

Julie stared at him. Her lips moved, but no words came out. After a bit, her gaze dropped to the ground. She began to kick the wet pavement with her left shoe. "Well . . ." she replied in a small voice.

Mark grasped her shoulders. Her actions were not something that he would've seen or expected of her. He reached out to cup her chin and bring her eyes back to meet his. "Julie, for God's sakes, why didn't you tell me? What did you expect to gain by coming here?"

"I don't know! I just thought that . . . maybe if he listened to reason . . ."

"Julie, he never would've listened. He would've killed you!"

"But he's a judge, Mark!"

"It wouldn't have mattered. You were the only thing standing between him and the land and money he sought. If you would've walked in there, you wouldn't have walked out." Mark sighed and let go of her. "You're incredibly lucky I got here before you did."

"You knew that I would come here?"

"Yes."

"But how?"

A whimsical smile came to his face. "Deductive reasoning. Also, I had a little help."

"Help?"

Mark paused. He wasn't sure if he should reveal her guardian's lack of confidence in her ability to stay safe. The stunt she had just tried to pull only went to prove his point. "When I couldn't get a hold of you, I called your guardian. I'm afraid you've got quite a tail."

Julie's expression became more confused. "A . . . tale?"

"Your guardian's security team? The one that he has following you right now?"

"His security team?" Julie looked at him in disbelief, and then shook her head. She smiled. "Funny, Mark. I'm glad to know that you have a sense of humor, too."

"I'm not kidding, Julie."

Mark could tell Julie still didn't believe him, as her smile only grew broader. "No, he wouldn't. He promised me that he wouldn't. I know that he's having a hard time with the thought of me moving out, and yes, he can be a little overprotective, but . . ."

Julie's voice trailed off. She stared off into the darkness. She turned to look behind her, and her brow furrowed. She looked back at Mark, confused about something. Then she looked behind her again. Finally, she looked over his shoulder. As her eyes came back to his face, Mark saw the proverbial light bulb click on above her head. Her mouth opened wide. Then she threw her bag to the ground and suddenly let out a string of profanities, all aimed at her guardian. Mark startled. This demure-looking woman had quite a vocabulary when she was mad. A bemused smile came to his face, as Julie grabbed at her wet hair. "How could I have been so stupid? No wonder I kept seeing that car!"

Now Mark was confused. "Car?"

"That blue sedan!" she screamed, pointing to a spot over his right shoulder. "I knew my guardian had one car following me today. I managed to ditch it. However, I was so focused on the move and coming here, I just realized that one's been following me, too!"

Mark turned to look at where she pointed. A dark, four-door sedan sat across the street, away from the growing crowd, but in perfect view of everything going on around them. He caught a glimpse of its occupants. The driver nodded to Mark, reached down for the gearshift, and drove away. Mark chuckled. Her guardian hadn't been kidding, he realized. "You should be grateful," he told Julie, turning back to her. "It's clear he cares about you deeply."

"Oh, you haven't seen the worst of it!" Julie retorted. "You have no idea what it's like to go through kindergarten with your own personal babysitter! Oh, and then there was college! I had a bodyguard escorting me around the first week, sitting in all of my classes. I was the laughingstock of the campus my entire first year!" She turned and stormed away. "I don't believe it!" Mark heard her fume. "*Every* time I show *one* little bit of independence . . ."

She grabbed her messenger bag, pulled her cell phone out, and turned it back on. Mark took that to be his cue to leave. He could hear Julie's voice raging at her guardian from half a block away and couldn't help but laugh. Cassie, who had just emerged from the judge's townhouse to look for him, approached. She heard a shrill voice and looked over his shoulder to see who was screaming. She recognized who it was. She too was relieved that Julie was unharmed. Then Cassie stopped to listen to Julie's conversation and found herself chuckling. "What's going on with her?" she asked, pushing a strand of damp hair out of her face.

"A family squabble. I suggest we don't get involved." He gestured to the townhouse steps. The uniformed officers had emerged with Judge Embry, his hands cuffed in front of him. "Did he have anything to say for himself?"

"Just the expected: 'I want my lawyer.' We just finished searching his study. There were a lot of papers dealing with the Foundation, along with another English translation of that agreement on his desk. There was also a vial of clear liquid in his desk drawer. Perhaps it's a sample of the poison that killed the Amendu children, and Madison. We also found a gun. It's still warm, as if it's been fired recently, but there are no bullet holes anywhere."

Mark thought he had detected the smell of spent gunpowder in the room. Mark looked at the judge, and then back at Julie, who still railed at her guardian, and his need to overprotect her. He remembered the Escape with the Washington tags he passed a few blocks back. He began to wonder whether she had made it here before him. He stared at the townhouse. If she had, how did she get in and out without anyone seeing her? Impossible, Mark realized. There was no way that she could, not with the bloodhounds that Simon had on her. He turned his gaze back to Cassie. In front of him stood the biggest reason he still stood there. He shrugged. "I must've had the Look on my face, didn't I?"

Cassie bristled. "Mark, I'm sorry," she babbled. "I know that maybe I shouldn't have, but you didn't seem to be acting right, and I didn't want to see you get hurt, and I . . ."

Mark put a finger to her lips. He looked deep into her eyes. "Cassie, I know what you did, and I understand." His gaze went back to the crowd. A swarm of media trucks had just arrived on the scene, just in time to watch Mason City's finest place Judge J. Jacob Embry into the back of a squad car. Lieutenant Michaels was on the judge's front stoop, fielding the barrage of questions being thrown at her. As she did so, she turned her attention toward him and nodded. He nodded back in reply, and then returned his focus to Cassie. "You did what I should've done," he continued. "I should've warned you that I can become a bit obsessive about things, and that I sometimes forget about the big picture. Forgive me if I snapped at you, or if you felt left out. I was only trying to protect you in case I was wrong." He gave her a broad smile. "And thank you for looking out for me."

"You're welcome. After all, that's what partners are for, aren't they?" She thought back to the comments that she had made at the beginning of the investigation and grinned. "See? I told you that it was about the land."

Mark shook his head and the two of them turned to look at Julie again. Julie had finished her ranting. She placed the phone back into her bag and fastened the clasps. Then she gave Mark a small smile and a shrug. "I'll . . . just head home, if that's all right?"

The detectives watched her take a few uncertain paces backwards, before turning and walking away from the scene, her hands stuffed in her pockets. After a beat, Mark motioned to one of the uniformed officers standing nearby. "Follow her," he instructed him. "Bring her to the precinct. I'm sure the lieutenant will want to talk to her, too."

The officer nodded, smiled, and headed off to follow the departing Julie. Mark looked at Cassie. She gave him a knowing stare. "Being a little obsessive about her safety, aren't we?"

"Maybe, but she's the one who chose to live with a cop. Besides, she's used to it." He gave her a pat on the back. "Now, if it's all right with you partner, I think that it's high time we get back to work."

XVII

Julie followed the squad car down the dark streets, silently congratulating herself for a job well done. Her act had been so convincing that the police escorted her to the station. She received a lecture from Lieutenant Michaels who, in her motherly way, warned her to never try a stunt like that again. Lieutenant Michaels called Simon to assure him that she was indeed all right, and had Officer Peterman escort Julie to her vehicle, and back home. When she left, she reached out to touch the thoughts of Judge Embry one last time. A mischievous smile came to her lips. Every part of him wanted to tell the world about what he had seen and witnessed in his study, but he couldn't. Although she was no closer to finding his accomplices, she felt certain that they wouldn't try to attack her or the Illani again for some time.

Twenty minutes later, she swung her vehicle back in Mark's driveway. The moving truck was gone, but all the lights in her apartment were on. She sat back in her seat. She sensed who was inside. The grilling she received from Lieutenant Michaels was nothing compared to the one going on inside her head, or the one that waited for her within that place. She sighed, grabbed her bag, climbed out her vehicle, and made the journey up the stairwell. She took a cleansing breath, and then opened the front door. An ice blue orb hovered in the middle of her living room. Within seconds, it changed shape and became the man who was with Elise a few hours prior. He wore black pants and a black turtleneck sweater. The color only emphasized the gray in his hair and the ice blue color of his eyes. He leaned forward on his cane, and gave her a look of solemn indignation and suppressed mirth. She made sure that there was no one around, and then quietly shut the door behind her. "Hi, Simon," she greeted him.

"I have watched over you all your life, Halbrina. However, I must admit that was one of your better deception ploys." Simon put a finger inside his left ear, as if trying to clear it out. "I'm glad that I wasn't there to actually hear it."

"Unfortunately, NIK was. During my so-called tirade, I accidentally sent a power surge through my link to her. Molin tells me I destroyed one of her secondary processors and caused three water lines to rupture in the Narcalonian capital. I won't be allowed to make contact with her for a day or two."

"Well, if that's the worst of it, I guess we should be grateful."

Julie set her bag down in one of the empty dining room chairs and gazed about her place. Then she turned her attention back to the being she had known all of her existence. She remembered what Mark had told her and what she had picked up from him. "You told Mark that you had me followed at all times?"

"You told him that I obsess about your safety. I thought I should be obliging."

Julie continued to stare at him. Then she shook her head. A whimsical smile crossed her face. "By the way, thanks for the assist. I wouldn't have thought to materialize the blue sedan."

"I wasn't worried. I know you well. As I told the others, I knew you'd be able to improvise."

His face immediately grew serious. The two of them instantly sensed that the jovial nature of what happened was over. He took an uncertain step toward her. "You realize the risk you took tonight," he murmured.

"He's a good detective, Simon. He would've found the man threatening to take that land, and sooner or later, he would've discovered that you and I are its sole owners. The question now is who outside of us knows about the Illani?"

"Perhaps they don't know. Maybe this is exactly what it appears to be."

"I'd believe that, if it wasn't for the *sorja* root the humans were poisoned with. No human could know about that, not without some help from off this planet."

"No, they wouldn't." He gave her a thoughtful look. "I take it you will not rest until you find them."

Julie's face took on the malevolent gaze Thomas had seen a few days prior. "No, Simon. In the meantime, I'll have to step up the security there. When my connection with NIK is re-established, I'll have her reconfigure all of their communications, and re-modulate my shielding." Her posture relaxed a bit and she smiled. "In light of what happened, I also think we should make some changes to the Foundation's leadership. I doubt that Jennifer would mind. It means she'll get to see me more often."

"And what about the human? When were you planning on telling him the truth?"

Julie sat down and stared at her hands. That question had been on her mind the moment she met Mark. She wasn't allowed to tell him, but inevitably, Mark would find out who—and what—lived in the space above his garage. When that happened, the others would force her to return to nether space. She wanted this life, this "human" life, and she would fight for it as long as she could, even if meant deceiving Mark at every opportunity. She breathed deep and clenched her hands into fists. "I don't want him to know, Simon, not yet, at least."

"The problem is you've already made him curious about you. I've reviewed the information the Illani have gathered. He's very astute and, from what they tell me, quite persistent. Eventually, he will discover what you are. Then what will you do?"

Julie stared out her dining room window toward Mark's dark house. Mark had not arrived home yet, as he and Cassie were still questioning Judge Embry. How long would it be before the questions that raced through his brain were asked aloud? How long after that until he stopped believing her answers? "I'll worry about that when the time comes," she told him in a firm tone. "It's all I can do for right now."

"The others won't find that satisfactory."

Julie didn't answer. She stood up and made her way to the kitchen. She had only taken a few steps when she stopped and rubbed her head. Simon approached her. "Halbrina? What is it?"

"It's the others. They're bombarding me with their thoughts again." She grimaced again and forced their chatter away. She sighed and looked at him, her expression a mixture of pain, frustration, and anger. "They haven't stopped since I told them. They're getting on my nerves! I understand their fear, but why can't they understand what *I* want? Why can't they just let me be my humanoid self for just a little bit?"

Simon thought carefully how to answer this. Then he stared deep into those brown eyes of hers and realized that the answer was right in front of him. He reached out to take her right hand. With a cold finger, he traced the fine lines and ridges of her palm; lines and ridges that didn't exist on his hands. "Because they've always had great difficulty understanding this part of you. They only see the power within it, what it's capable of, and the repercussions if emotions and not logic control its actions."

Julie gripped his hand and stared at him, afraid of the answer he may give to her next question: "And you, Simon? What do you see when you look at me?"

Simon smiled and reached out to stroke her cheek. "It varies. Some days, I see the little girl who liked to lie on wet grass at night and talk to the stars. On others, it's the child that chased the first snowflakes that fell from the skies and tried to catch them on her tongue. However, every day I see the infant who saved my life all those millennia ago, and who constantly gives of herself to help better the lives of others." He took another step closer and gazed into her tear-streaked face, and into the eyes he had fallen for the first time he saw her. "Today, I see a young woman who looks like the people who live on this planet, who wants to feel like she belongs here and to be like them, if just for a little while."

Julie's chin trembled. Simon wiped the tears away, gathered her into his arms, and stroked her head. "I'll talk to the others. I'll convince them to allow you the chance to experience this life. You've more than earned that right, and perhaps, maybe it's time that you do."

Julie buried her face in his chest. She listened to the rhythm of his powers as they tried to mimic her heartbeat. He wasn't quite successful, but she didn't care. Simon was the only one who made an effort to understand her humanoid side, even though he had never been one. "Thank you, Simon."

"You're welcome, Juliana." He paused, thinking about the name she had chosen for her return to this world. He pulled her away from him and gave her a rueful smile. "Your new name? I must admit, I like the sound of it."

"You do?"

"Yes."

"But you're the one who named me Halbrina."

"Yes, but while you walk amongst the humans, I will call you Juliana. Less suspicious, don't you think?"

"Much less," Julie said with a smile.

Simon winked at her. He stepped away and appraised the being in front of him with fatherly pride. Then he gazed about her place. "I should be going. If I'm not mistaken, you still have some unpacking to do."

"Not likely. I'll need to head back to the farm to start on the new security measures. Also, NIK told me the Selanian embassy contacted us. We're needed on Kelinar. They've elected a new queen, and her coronation is tomorrow night." She sighed. "Well, at least I'll get to spend one night here."

"And how will you deal with what you feel here? When you're alone, and you sense her presence, what will you do?"

Julie stared about her new home. Mark didn't know, but Julie had entered Jessie's studio before he arrived home from the bank. Julie sensed the remains of Jessie's spirit the moment she crossed the threshold. It had taken a great deal of willpower not to let it show the second time she entered. Jessie always would be here, Julie believed, and she had no intent of making her go away. She squared himself to Simon. "I'll enjoy it," she whispered.

Simon nodded. He had expected her to say nothing less. He bent down and kissed her forehead. "Take care, Halbrina. I'll see you at the coronation."

He took a few steps away from her. Julie watched as behind him, a door of light opened. He nodded at his young charge and stepped through it. Just as quickly, it disappeared. Julie waited until she knew that Simon was safe in nether space before she let out a sigh. She rubbed her head again. It was a few moments before the voices subsided. She waited for them to return. When they didn't, she paused to gaze about her surroundings. Now she could begin her new life, but first, she had one other pressing matter. She walked to the sofa and touched a spot on the bare wall. A small smile came to her lips. "Well Jessie, finally it's just you and me," she said aloud. "Let's get to know each other better, shall we?"

*   *   *

In a two-room apartment facing Puget Sound, the nurse who poisoned Madison Evans frowned at the television. The images there confirmed that the human failed in his mission. Although there was nothing to tie him to them, it didn't make her any happier. She looked at her accomplice. He had altered his appearance, but his now-smooth face was set in granite, like hers. She reached for a piece of silver metal that lay next to the remote control. The pressure of her thumb activated it and sent a signal to the recipient on the other side. She waited until she heard it beep. "We failed you, Master," she whispered into it. "I'm sorry."

Sorry? Sorry for what?

"We shouldn't have trusted this human to help us succeed. He has exposed us to danger. The immortal will soon know that we are here."

No, you have done well. We have more information now, and that's more important. The Illani may be out of our reach, but we have accomplished something more promising.

"Promising? There's no way we can touch the Illani, unless we find those who are on the outside. Even then, they will be well protected. We'll never defeat her."

Yes, we will. It will take time, but we will.

"And until then?"

We remain vigilant and patient. I've learned that she's decided to live on Earth for a time. In that time, she'll develop emotional connections to some of them, and like with the Illani, she'll risk everything to protect them. That's when she's weakest, and that's when we'll strike again. The Illani's precious miandi *will die, and then the universe and everything within it will be ours for the taking.*

* * *

Mark prepared himself for a long night with Judge J. Jacob Embry. He called District Attorney Natalie Bishop, who came to the precinct to sit with him and Cassie. Together, they readied themselves to question a respected member of the judiciary. Within the papers anonymously delivered to the precinct were details of Judge Embry's financial records for the past ten years. They contained all the evidence they needed to prove his involvement in the scheme. They also found the receipt for the cell phone Judge Embry sent to Terrance Carnegie—the one that Judge Embry had been certain was untraceable. Terrance Carnegie also verified that it was the judge's voice that he had heard. They also had his signature on the documents to the corporation and the payments to Leonard Bartman for his assault on Madison. However, the police discovered Leonard Bartman in an abandoned warehouse on the other side of town, dead. They were still performing the autopsy. Finally, the lab determined that the vial of liquid found in Judge Embry's study contained the same chemical makeup that had poisoned Madison Evans and the Amendu children, but they couldn't trace the source of the poison's base. Nothing like it existed.

For his part, Judge Embry only continued his request for counsel. Before the questioning began, Mark watched the judge from the other side of the mirror as he sat in the interrogation room. The judge hardly moved. His hands, minus his Harvard Law School ring, were folded in front of him. He had that same serene, peaceful, look on his face that Mark had seen when he first entered the study. When his counsel arrived, Mark, Cassie, and D.A. Bishop entered the room, and the questioning started. Mark doubted that the judge would repeat what he told Mark in his study. Judge Embry smiled at his attorney, and then to everyone's stunned amazement, began to give a descriptive account of everything he had done, including the poisoning of the Amendu tribe's children and the hiring of Leonard Bartman to assault Madison Evans. He even told them how he planned to assault and kill Julie. Time and time again, his attorney tried to warn him of his rights. He only smiled at her, and continued on in a dry, almost automatic voice. Eventually, she got up and left. Cassie and D.A. Bishop followed her, leaving Mark and the judge in the interrogation room. The two men stared at each other. Judge Embry still had that serene look on his face. Mark had yet to tell his dad what occurred, and he wondered if he should. Then Mark thought back to the offer Judge Embry had made him hours before he met Julie. If he had said "yes" then, if he had picked up that phone and dialed the number on that card, what would this moment be like?

"You seem disappointed in me, son," Judge Embry whispered, breaking the silence.

"It's . . . just hard to believe sir. You, of all people."

"What's so difficult to believe? That I would succumb to the urges of power and greed? That I would seek to better myself in ways that violate your sense of moral good?" Judge Embry gave Mark a wan smile. "Apparently, you didn't know me as well as you thought you did."

"I guess I didn't, sir." Mark leaned forward. The question hung on the tip of his tongue. He needed to know. Mark leveled his gaze with him. "Tell me something, Judge Embry, off the record: did you pay off my mortgage?"

Mark saw the familiar twitch of the moustache. Judge Embry stared at him for a moment. Then his gaze fell to his hands. "What do you think, son?"

Mark's face showed no reaction. Inside, Mark's stomach clenched. He continued to watch Judge Embry, unsure how to respond. Then he pushed himself away from the table, stood, and headed for the door. He had reached for the door handle when Judge Embry spoke again: "Now you tell me, Mark, that day at Scordalia's, when you and Ms. Warren had lunch? Is that when she told you who she was?"

Mark straightened. He stared at the door. "No, sir. Right before I came to arrest you was when I discovered that she's the daughter of the CEO." He stroked the handle with his right index finger. "She's also a brave young woman who was willing to put herself in harm's way to stop you."

"For a piece of land, Detective," Judge Embry countered. "She was willing to die for earth and shrubs and trees, dead limbs and dying fields of grass, a decrepit farmhouse, and a tattered barn?" Judge Embry's mustached lips twitched. "I would call that highly unusual behavior, wouldn't you?"

Mark paused. Yes, perhaps Julie's actions were immature and irresponsible. Then he remembered the look of conviction on her face outside the judge's townhouse. "I don't think so," he said aloud. "To me, she was seeking to protect the rights of the native tribe that own it, and preserve the agreement that her family's company entered into all those years ago." He turned to stare one last time at the judge he had once revered, who would spend the rest of his life behind bars. "It was something that you were supposed to do as well, Your Honor."

Mark exited and walked back out to the main precinct floor. Judge Embry waited until the door had closed behind him. Then he stood up and made his way to the two-way mirror. He pressed his head against the glass divider. He savored its cool texture and grimaced in pain that went beyond physical. The events of his encounter with Julie repeated in his head, an endless film loop that he couldn't shut off. He tried to tell anyone he could, but every time he did, gut-wrenching pain shot through him and his breathing suddenly cut to the point that he felt as if he was suffocating. He reached out to touch the glass. Jack had tried to tell him and now he understood. Judge Embry closed his eyes and trembled. "You may know who she is, Detective," he whispered, "but heaven help you when you find out *what* she is."

* * *

Mark and Cassie spent the next afternoon at their desks. Cassie leaned over his shoulder, calmly explaining to Mark for the fifth time how to complete his police reports on the computer. Lieutenant Michaels hoped that Cassie would succeed where Tyler and Charlie had failed. Instead, Cassie fought not to laugh as Mark struggled to type up his notes. He had enormous patience when it came to evidence and to people, but definitely not for machines. Mark stared at the blank boxes of information, ready to take his gun to the box of processors and microchips that gnawed at his patience. "This is time consuming, Cass," he muttered, slapping a key especially hard.

"This is the way of the future. Sooner or later, you're going to have to learn it." She stepped away from him and leaned against his desk to face the wall instead of the blinded windows. She frowned, remembering how he bested her at the shooting range that first day. She had challenged him again earlier today, and now she was out $100.00. "Of course, I could file the reports until you get the hang of it, although it's nice to be better at something than you."

Mark went to make a remark when he saw Lieutenant Michaels' head poke out of her office. She pointed to the two of them and gestured for them to come inside. Mark motioned to Cassie and they headed over to their boss's door. Lieutenant Michaels ushered them in. They made to sit down as she walked over to her desk. She handed each of them an envelope. "I just received these by courier," she told them. "They're addressed to the two of you."

Mark and Cassie took their envelopes. His curiosity piqued, Mark opened his. Inside was a handwritten note from Lord Simon Birmingham III, CEO of the Foundation, and Keanu, the leader of the Amendu, thanking him and Cassie for their work on the Madison Evans case, and discovering who poisoned their tribe. Also inside was a pendant necklace for each of them, made by artisans from the tribe. "Whoa!" Cassie exclaimed. She held it up by its chain and studied its craftsmanship. "This is real silver!"

Mark stared at the pendant. It was of an exquisite design. He glanced over at Cassie's. Hers was different from his. He reread the note, hoping that it would give some sort of translation. "They didn't have to do this,

Lieutenant," Mark said in a low tone. "We were just doing our job."

"Apparently, they disagree. I talked with Madison's mom. According to her, the Foundation paid for her daughter's hospital and funeral costs, and created a scholarship fund in her memory at the university. The Chief also tells me that this morning, he received a check from them for the policeman's benevolence fund in the amount of half a million dollars."

Mark looked up from his reading. "Half a million?"

"On top of that, I just got off the phone with Charlie. On April the first, someone paid off all of his medical costs that weren't covered by the department or his insurance, to the tune of almost a quarter million dollars. He asked me if I knew who did it, because he wants to make sure it wasn't some sort of practical joke and if not, to thank the benefactor and find some way to make arrangements to pay them back." She shook her head and stared at Mark. "Did you have something to do with this?"

"No, but I bet the daughter of the CEO did." He caught the lieutenant's inquisitive stare. A corner of his mouth lifted up. "Julie's my new tenant. I rented Jessie's studio to her."

"You're kidding. The girl that I ripped to shreds last night is living in Jessie's studio?"

"Yes."

The two women looked at him. "Well, if you see her anytime soon, tell her that Charlie and the Mason City police force thank her and her family's corporation for their generosity," Lieutenant Michaels instructed him.

"Yeah," Cassie added, stroking the pendant in her hand, "and so do I."

Mark kept staring at the note, rereading it while he and Cassie left the lieutenant's office and back to his desk. He had been commended for his actions before, but this time it was different. A surge of pride swelled within him. He looked at the pendant again, and then at Cassie. She had already slipped hers around her neck. It caught the light and glowed against her fair skin. She stared down at it and smiled. "I wonder what these symbols mean," she whispered, as she toyed with the chain it was on.

"Your note didn't say, either?"

Cassie shook her head. "Oh, well. We'll just have to surf the 'Net and find out."

Mark went slightly pale. "Maybe later, huh?"

Cassie thought back to when she met Julie that day outside or Scordalia's. She wondered if she had a thing for Mark and this was her subtle way of showing it. She gave him a wry smile. "I have to admit Mark, despite her actions last night, she's not bad."

"I take it this is my partner's way of giving me permission to date my tenant."

"Well, only if she isn't involved with any more of our cases." She directed Mark's attention back to the computer screen. "Now, let's see if we can at least get you comfortable with sending out an e-mail, huh?"

*   *   *

That evening Mark sat in his living room, sipping a glass of juice, and once again staring at the check Julie gave him almost a week prior. The events of these last several days and Judge Embry's question repeated in his head. How many times had he asked these same questions to himself? How many more secrets was Julie keeping from him? What would he have to do to find them out, and did he really want to know?

The doorbell rang. He set the glass down and slid the check back into the coffee table drawer. "Just a minute," he called, as he made his way to the front door.

He opened it. Julie waited on the porch, dressed in the navy business suit he saw her wearing a few days ago. She smiled. "Hi, Mark."

"Julie! Come in, please."

"Thanks, but I only have a minute. I'm late for the airport. I just wanted to see how you were, to thank you again for everything you and Cassie did, and to ask a favor."

Mark smiled. "I'm fine, and you're welcome. What's your request?"

She pointed to her place, its windows now dark. Her eyes took on that pleading look he ad seen in them the first day he had met her. "I was wondering if you could install a ceiling fan in the dining room while I'm gone. I'm willing to cover the cost of it. If it's too much of a bother, I can . . ."

Mark held up a hand. "I'd be happy to, Julie and I think the check you gave me more than covers it," he told her. "Is there a particular style you're looking for?"

"Nope. Whatever you choose will be fine, thanks." She glanced at her watch. "I need to be going or I'll miss my flight. I'll see you later."

She made to leave and Mark reached out to touch her shoulder. "Julie, wait."

She turned back to face him. "Yes?"

He stared into those clear and focused eyes hidden behind her glasses. He wanted to thank her for everything that her company had done. There was so much he wanted to ask her too; about the investigation she had indirectly become involved in, the land that had become the subject of it, the company she worked for, and why she had not told him that she was the daughter of the CEO. Mark moved his mouth, but nothing came out. She tilted her head, a puzzled expression on her face. "Yes, Mark?"

He stared blankly at her for a moment, then shrugged and rubbed his scalp. The questions still rang in his head, but he decided that now wasn't the time to ask them. She had her reasons. When she was ready, she would tell him. "So, where are you off to?" he finally asked.

"Oh, who knows? They like to keep me busy."

"I'm certain that they do, but what if I need to get a hold of you for any reason?"

"Well, if it's an emergency, you can call the main office, and they'll get my guardian to track me down. He's worse than a bloodhound when it comes to finding me."

"Yes, I've noticed."

He looked out toward the street. He spotted the sedan he saw the night before, now parked in front of Mrs. Johnson's. Its driver watched them with a thoughtful look on his face. Mark half-suspected that the man had a microphone pointed their direction, and had no doubt Simon would get a full report on their conversation on the porch. Julie followed his gaze and chuckled. "This is the last time they'll be following me here in Mason City. He promised. Anyway, I don't think that you'll need to contact me, or at least I hope not."

"Well, I hope so too. Let me walk you to your car."

He grabbed his keys hanging next to the door. They took the short walk toward her vehicle, saying nothing for a few moments. He opened her door, and she thanked him and climbed in. Mark went to shut it, but then another thought hit him. "One more thing, Julie?"

She fumbled in her purse for her keys. "Yes?"

He leaned against her open car door. "The pendants the Amendu gave us and the symbols on them? Cassie's was different from mine. There was no translation for them in our thank-you notes. We went on the Internet to try and find one, but we couldn't. Do you know what they mean?"

"I asked Keanu the same thing when I first saw them. Cassie's means courage, I think."

"And mine?"

Julie paused for a moment. Then she answered him: "Hope."

"Hope? Why hope?"

"I have no idea. They must've had a reason. Maybe time will reveal the answer to you." She started the engine and snapped on her seatbelt. "I'll see you later."

"Yeah. 'Bye."

Mark shut her door and watched her back out the driveway. She gave him a wave before she drove down the street, the sedan following closely behind. Then he pulled out his keys. He wasn't big on wearing necklaces, so he had gone to a jeweler. He fashioned the pendant into a keychain charm. Mark stroked it, and then turned to look at the dark space above the garage. A funny feeling came over him. Hope—Mark hoped and believed that Jessie would survive, right up until the moment she died. When she did, Mark believed Jessie took all of his hope with her. He clutched his keys and stared at the disappearing taillights that marked Julie's vehicle. Maybe he had lost hope, but somehow, Jessie had returned it to him—in the form of a woman named Julie Warren.

About The Author

Detectives and aliens are two of my favorite subjects in fiction, but rarely seen together in a modern-day format. It's taken some time to get my imaginary friend from my head to paper. I believe this combination of characters makes for intriguing and entertaining reading. This series focuses on the relationship between featuring Mark Daniels, a police detective seeking to reclaim his life after a series of tragedies, and Julie Warren, his mysterious new tenant. She's an immoral with the ability to kill with a thought, and an addiction to chocolate, coming to Earth in the hopes of reclaiming her humanity before the planet learns of her true nature.

A graduate of Penn State University and Thomas M. Cooley Law School, A.P. Lynn resides in Michigan.